My Body-His

Blakely Bennett

fannypress

Seattle, WA

fannypress

Fanny Press
PO Box 70515
Seattle, WA 98127

For more information go to: www.fannypress.com
blakelybennett.fannypress.com

Cover design by Sabrina Sun

My Body-His

ISBN: 978-1-60381-523-9 (Trade Paper)
ISBN: 978-1-60381-522-2 (eBook)

Printed in the United States of America

For Dana
My husband, lover, and best friend.
Thank you for your encouragement
and for being my biggest fan.

Acknowledgments

This novel would never have been written had it not been for my husband's support of my dream to be a writer. Not only did he implore me to try again to get *My Body-His* published, but he offered me suggestions and advice all along the way.

A huge thank you to Catherine Treadgold and Fanny Press for believing in my writing and bringing her editing expertise to *My Body-His*.

Thanks to the people who read parts of the story and provided invaluable feedback, including the Seattle Writers' Group and R., who inadvertently gave me, "Get Lost Creep."

Thank you to T., who was the first person other than my husband to read the story all the way through. His enthusiasm motivated me to keep at it.

Fellow author S. Twigg and I were editing buddies for a while and I owe him a shout-out for his support.

Thank you David D. and Shana R. for reading and encouraging me.

A big hug and kiss to Mauricio P. for his brilliant suggestion to lose "Luke" in the title of the first book. I knew the second he said it that he was right.

To all people who were willing to talk to me about living the BDSM lifestyle, thank you for your openness and your help in ultimately crafting MBH.

A final and huge thanks to you, my reader.

CHAPTER ONE

As on any other hot, sunny day in Florida, I returned from work to my apartment, which was located a mile from the beach and served as both my refuge and my cage. A lonely weekend stretched out before me. My two best friends had other things to do. Sandy had recently moved in with her boyfriend, Jason, so I hadn't seen much of her lately, and Parker had flown out of town to visit her sister.

If something didn't awaken me soon, I would surely die of apathy. I craved excitement, anything to get my adrenaline pumping so I would know I still existed inside this trapped, mundane life of mine. One of my outlets, other than running, was reading. However, whenever I returned from the other world of predestined love to my prosaic existence, I was even more aware of the stark contrast between those stories and my life. I had given up reading romance novels a few months earlier, knowing such bliss would never be mine. No man had ever swept me off my feet or made my pulse race like those in the stories I had read. My mother worried I would end up alone and, honestly, so did I. Sandy had found "the one" for her but for me love didn't seem to be in the cards.

I don't mean to imply I'd remained a virgin; I'd had boyfriends and lovers. Scott, my running buddy, occasionally offered his services, but for me earth-shattering orgasms existed exclusively in the realm of fiction. Maybe I lived too much in my head to experience heart palpitating attraction to another.

I had my dream wedding all planned out in my mind

and my dream man as well, although I couldn't easily identify him in a magazine. Sandy felt I was way too picky and Parker thought I should be more selective. In my fantasies, I wore an ivory wedding dress with a long train and matching veil and carried a daisy and baby's breath bouquet. I walked through a lush garden toward my man, who was dressed in a black tux.

Definitely too many romance novels for me, I thought.

Every now and again I would pick up a bridal magazine. It was like my own personal porn. I would hide the magazines from my friends, covertly looking through their pages until I grew depressed and threw all the copies away. Bridal magazines were as bad as romance novels, so I decided to shun them both.

Shaking my head to rid myself of dismal thoughts, I grabbed my running clothes. I needed the physical experience of running so fast I could barely catch my breath. I needed the release.

I jogged over to Hollywood beach, working up to my usual pace. After my legs finally warmed up, I felt someone approach me from behind.

"How would you feel about going to a party with me tonight?" Scott asked as he fell in beside me.

"Uh … I don't know," I said, briefly glancing in his direction. Normally we'd just hang out at his place if we were both in the mood.

"Come on … it'll be fun," he said, huffing to match my stride. "They don't let single men in alone, so I sort of need you to go."

"Oh … ummm. Are you sure you want to go down this road?" I raised my eyebrows. "I mean …."

"We can just hang out there, have a few drinks." He touched my shoulder so I would slow down. "Look, it's cool if you don't want to go or if you have something else to do."

"Why no single guys?" I said, slowing my pace to a slight jog.

"I figure they want a good balance between men and women," he said, averting his eyes and shifting his body in a way that indicated he was hiding something.

I brushed off my concern as I thought it over for a moment longer. I couldn't stomach another Friday night alone in my apartment. "Sure, why not," I said. "I need to run home—"

"Cool," he said, coming to a complete stop. "Meet me at my place around 9:30." He smiled, revealing his sexy dimples, and then headed in the opposite direction.

I picked up the pace again, more excited than I'd been in a long time.

ભ

By 9:15 p.m. that evening, I stood ready in front of the mirror. The beige, fitted spaghetti-strap top complemented the brown skirt. Tan sandals completed the outfit. I lined my bright, yellow-green eyes with brown eyeliner to make their color stand out. My wavy brown hair hung loosely, flowing over my shoulders and down to the middle of my back.

I avoided looking directly into my eyes because sometimes I could see my own desperation too close to the surface. I also wished my nose were a bit straighter. It didn't look large or disfigured, just slightly crooked. Parker always said I had a warped sense of my looks. Taking one last quick peek, I felt satisfied and grabbed my purse to head out the front door.

On my way back to Scott's place I remembered the first time he had run up beside me and struck up a conversation. He wasn't at all hard to look at. He had a runner's body— strong cut legs and a nice round butt—short-cropped curly black hair and bright green eyes. I wished I had his thick black eyelashes. He dimpled when he smiled and tilted his head in a way I found irresistible. Even though he didn't have my number and I didn't have his, our arrangement worked out fine.

3

As I parked in a guest spot, I could see Scott waiting by his car near the front of the building in a light blue Izod shirt and dark jeans. We drove in silence and in less than twenty minutes, we were parking on the lawn of a towering house surrounded by large banyan trees. Vines climbed the lattice on the front of the house, darkly and ominously cloaking the home. The windows were barely visible. The large wooden door might have adorned a castle on a set for a horror movie.

As I got out of the car, I had a feeling of foreboding but passed it off as nervousness. After all, I knew no one there other than Scott and hadn't been to a party in a while.

As we entered the dimly lit house, I noticed candles burning from wall sconces and candelabras. A chill ran up my spine that I should also have heeded as a second warning but again ignored. I noticed a staircase on the right, just past the foyer. On the left there was a sitting area with mismatched couches and chairs that reminded me of a frat house. The front of the house seemed devoid of human life other than Scott and me, but I could hear voices and music coming from deeper inside. The smell of candle wax combined with a faint sweetness reminded me of pie baking in the oven.

We walked along a tiled hallway that led to the back of the house. On my right was the kitchen, lined by a long counter bar. Across from the entrance to the kitchen was a large sectional couch crowded with people cozily talking and drinking. I looked around at the huge back room, where several couches and chairs surrounded a pool table off to the left. A wall of sliding glass doors covered with thick brown drapes lined the back wall, with one section pulled back to reveal an opening. "Use Somebody," by Kings of Leon, blared from speakers surrounding the room.

I could see people milling about outside. The three who emerged wore all black and reminded me of Marilyn Manson fans because of their androgyny. On the couches were people I guessed to be about my age of thirty-five or slightly younger.

They were dressed more sedately than their Goth counterparts. I turned to seek the comfort of Scott's presence but he had disappeared. Suddenly I felt very alone.

I walked over to the bar and filled a glass with the ladle from a clear punch bowl. I took a sip but quickly spit it back into the cup. I tried to find a garbage can to throw it away but couldn't locate one in the kitchen.

"Stay away from the punch," Scott said as he sidled up beside me, wrapping his arms around my waist.

"Yeah," I began, "figured that out for myself." I leaned into him, glad not to be alone. "Where's the garbage can?"

"Outside," he called over his shoulder as he strode away.

Abandoned again, I slipped through the hole in the wall of curtains and stepped onto a wooden multi-layered deck. The music followed me outside and switched to a song that escapes me now. An L-shaped pool wrapped around the side of the house and as I stepped forward a few steps, I could see that it ended in a whirlpool. I found the garbage can and, while disposing of the cup of punch, caught a glimpse of a naked woman slipping into the swirling water.

What the hell am I doing here? I thought.

I quickly turned around and claimed the closest lounge chair. The wooden deck started at the sliding doors and surrounded the pool. People milled about, talking and laughing. To the left of the open door stood two kegs. Several people circled the large aluminum barrels and drank beer out of red plastic cups with Japanese characters on the side. That made me wonder about who might own the place.

I couldn't tell the exact number of people because the crowd seemed to be in constant motion, but there must have been at least fifty or sixty. Two men and a woman sat on the lounge chair next to mine. The woman had the same dress as the rest of her Goth clan but the men both wore long shorts with button-down shirts.

Frat boys meet dangerous, dark-clad girl, I thought.

Moments later, I smelled the distinct odor of cannabis. There was no mistaking it, even if it had been years. Taking in the scene around the pool, I felt a soft touch on my shoulder. I turned to find one of the guys—rather cute—leaning over and offering me a joint.

"No thanks," I said, shaking my head.

"Don't drink, don't smoke … what do you do?" he said, cleverly mimicking Adam Ant's accent.

"I drink occasionally, but the punch tasted like hell so I threw it out."

"Bad stuff. It usually leaves a handful of people hugging the toilet by the end of the night. Would you like me to get you a beer?" he offered.

"Sure. Thanks."

"My name is Hank," he said, extending his hand across the gap between the chairs.

"Jane," I said, shaking his hand. "Have you been to one of these parties before? Do you know who owns this place?"

"Hang on a sec and let me get us a couple of beers. I'll be right back."

I watched his long, strong legs walk him adroitly over to the kegs. He had a bright smile that he shared with the other people around the barrels. His wavy brown hair, striking blue eyes and cherub-shaped face convinced me of his youth.

I scanned the other partiers, trying to locate Scott.

"Here ya go," Hank said, bringing my attention back to him. He handed me a red plastic cup filled to the brim, with foam spilling over the side. "Mind if I sit with you?"

I leaned over to take a sip from the overfilled cup and shifted my legs around to give him room. "Sure, have a seat." Although I found him cute, I had no designs on him. Mostly I just didn't want to be alone and I thought he might be able to satisfy some of my curiosity. "So the house … the Japanese letters—"

"Yeah. No one seems to know who owns it. There's a

party here once a month or so. I've asked a lot of the people who attend these events, but I've always gotten the same response." He shrugged his shoulders. "Don't know what the letters mean."

"I see." I noticed that several guests had shed pieces of clothing. I saw the naked girl from the hot tub strolling past with a towel wrapped around her waist. Her breasts sashayed freely from side to side as she walked. A group of men to the left of us wore only boxers.

While Hank sat watching me, he asked, "Are you here with someone?"

"Sort of, but I think I'm on my own," I said, trying not to make eye contact.

"You look surprised," he said.

"What kind of party is this?"

"A 'house' party," he said.

"And that means ... *what* exactly?" I leaned forward to whisper, "Is this like a huge orgy ready to happen?"

"No, not really. Some group sex, probably, but mostly it's just couples hooking up for the night or swapping partners. Most of the guests just watch the more adventurous."

"Oh," I said, completely distracted. "Where the hell is he," I said abruptly.

"Who? The guy you came with? We can just talk if you'd like."

I pulled out my cellphone to call Sandy. No signal.

"Can I borrow your cell?" I asked Hank.

"Never have been able to a get signal at this place, inside or out," he said.

"Look, you seem like a nice enough guy but this isn't my scene." I jumped up. "Have a good time and thanks for the beer," I said. Without looking back, I walked through the hole in the wall of sliding glass, searching for Scott.

In my absence, many people inside had disrobed and were already in varying states of copulating. I cast a quick

glance around but didn't spot Scott. Just past the kitchen, I noticed a bowl of condoms. *Had that been there before?* I hurried toward the front door, wondering what to do.

Why hadn't I driven my own car? Stupid ... stupid ... stupid! Breathe. Okay, relax. Go upstairs and find a phone. Call Sandy and ask her to come get you. You can apologize profusely for taking her away from her boyfriend while she's driving you safely home.

I hurriedly walked toward the foyer and mounted the first step, noticing the eerie quiet that pervaded that end of the house. *Did using a bedroom not occur to these people?* At the top of the stairs, I opened the first door on the right, which ended up being a bathroom. I knocked lightly on the next door, thinking maybe someone had snuck upstairs. Wanting to avoid more naked bodies being intimate, I listened carefully. Hearing nothing, I cautiously opened the door.

A canopy king-size bed occupied the left wall of a very large bedroom. The masculine space had thick, dark wood furniture that looked aged. Light emanating from the far right dimly illuminated the area. I focused my attention on the candle sitting in the large window at the back of the room. Next to it, I noticed an easel and canvas. The paint glistened and the smell of turpentine faintly filled the air. My curiosity became overwhelming and I felt compelled to move closer to the picture. A chill ran up my back and I immediately turned around. Out of the shadows near the door, a figure stepped forward.

"Oh," I said, bringing my right hand to my chest. "I didn't realize someone would be in here. I'm sorry."

He stared back at me. I felt my body blush as the warmth spread out to my limbs.

"I'm sorry ... I'll leave," I said, but I didn't move from where I stood next to the painting.

Still he said nothing. He looked like a statue—except for

his eyes. His eyes held the intensity of an animal about to pounce on his prey. I felt anxious and embarrassed at my intrusion into his bedroom but also intrigued by his powerful demeanor. I trembled, somewhat frightened by his male presence, but also aroused.

"Ah ... um ... is there a phone I could use?" I said, meekly. "Is there another room I could hang out in? This party's not my scene and ... I don't ... have my car."

Still he didn't speak. He stepped forward out of the shadows and took three long strides to stand in front of me.

"Go downstairs," he said, "and bring us back two Coronas."

"Oh but ..." I said, but the look on his face stopped me.

Then he spoke but I wished he would stop. "So alone you are ... it radiates from you. You're bored. You had hoped tonight would offer some excitement ... some diversion." The stranger spoke in a deep but quiet voice. "But mindless, meaningless sex," he continued, "does not interest you. You're disappointed with life and sad. You think if your life continues in this way you'll die of dissatisfaction."

"Stop it!" I said. "You don't know me. You don't know anything about me. Whose house is this? Where's the phone?" But I didn't move. I felt pinned by his penetrating stare.

He went on as if I hadn't spoken. "You are so beautiful, but you don't know it. You want something ... *need* something desperately and you don't know what it is. I know what it is and I can give it to you ... if I decide it's you."

I needed to get past him to the door and run out of that crazy house. Nevertheless, I didn't move. I just stood there riveted as though nailed to the floor. I couldn't breathe. I knew I needed to get out, that he was dangerous. *MOVE,* I yelled in my head, *MOVE!*

"You're scaring me," I said. I couldn't move. I wanted to cover myself because I felt so exposed ... naked in front of

him, but I just stared at him with my arms hanging at my sides. He seemed infused, empowered by my silence.

Finally he spoke again. "Take off your panties and bring them to me ... or you can leave," he said, holding out his hand for my underwear.

I shuddered when I realized I wasn't leaving. The intrigue clouded my sense of reason. I could see clearly on his face that he knew I wasn't going anywhere. In an attempt to regain my composure, I moved toward the door and then stopped. I looked back and diverted my attention to the painting to escape his gaze. The artful garden scene was colorful but felt subdued. Deeper inside the picture stood a white gazebo with ivy growing on it that reminded me of the front of the house.

"Do you own this house?" I asked, turning back to face him. He continued to hold out his hand, offering no response.

I studied the painting more carefully and noticed a girl in the gazebo. I couldn't make out her features, because the flicker of the candles made it difficult to see, but I thought she might be naked. The painting gave me an eerie feeling. Although the gazebo stood surrounded by what looked like a field of flowers, I felt sad for the girl.

The man brought my attention back to him with his deep voice. "Take off your panties and bring them to me ... or you can leave," he repeated, moving toward the door.

I struggled between my rational mind and my arousal. I could feel my panties moisten just being in his presence. I had never experienced such a strong reaction to a man. Desire won out as I slipped off my underwear from beneath my skirt and around my sandals. I walked toward him and placed them in his outstretched palm. As I blushed, wondering if he could smell my desire, his masculine scent overwhelmed my senses. I could smell lust mixed with sandalwood as he deliberately and confidently stepped up to me and neatly rolled the waist of my brown skirt, raising the hem so that it just covered my butt.

His touch sent a pleasurable frisson through my body as I observed his face up close. His hair was straight and sandy brown, and his bangs were tousled over his wide forehead. Although his angular nose and deep-set eyes made him look more menacing than handsome, when he smiled as he did then, his gray eyes sparkled, giving him a boyish appeal. A curtain of darkness quickly came down over his features, his forehead furrowed and his smile vanished.

"Go downstairs and get us two Coronas and grab one of the packs of smokes lying around. Lights … no menthol."

I turned to leave and as I walked by, he slapped my butt with his open hand. It startled me but also set my juices flowing. *What the hell am I doing?* I thought.

I went downstairs, frightened that someone would come up in the opposite direction and see my exposed buttocks. I passed the large couch opposite the kitchen and snaked around the corner. The idea that everyone could tell I was practically naked caused the wetness between my legs to increase. I avoided making eye contact as I entered the kitchen. Pulling the refrigerator open, I finger-locked two Corona longnecks and opened them with the church key hanging from a hook magnet on the door. I spotted lime wedges on a plate and chose two.

Cigarettes presented more of a problem. I spotted a pack on the counter next to the stove but they were menthol. I didn't want to go into the main room where the naked and the clothed voyeurs filled the couches and the floor around them. I checked the long coffee table just outside the kitchen. Nothing. I moved farther into the backroom and spotted a pack of Marlboro Lights on the opposite side. *Shit!* I thought.

I tiptoed over two men and a woman who were in the throes of a ménage à trois. One of the men reached up my thigh, almost touching my wetness, which sent me bouncing like a gazelle to the corner table. Carefully balancing the beer bottles and lime in one hand, I leaned forward to grab the

cigarettes. A guy grasped my wrist and I yelped, sure he had caught me stealing his smokes.

"Where'd you get the Coronas?" he said, pulling me down.

"The refrigerator," I barked, "let go of me!" Regaining my balance, I somehow managed to escape spilling any of the beer. I danced my way back through the contortions of people on the floor. "Oh my god," I mumbled under my breath. I breathed a sigh of relief as I made my way to the front of the house and began to ascend the stairs.

A man behind me grabbed my arm. "You're not allowed up there," he said.

"Let me go," I growled, trying to wrench my arm from his grip. "Do you own this house?" I snatched my wrist away from him.

"No," he said, standing his ground. "Them's the rules and you need to follow them like the rest of us."

"Oh buzz off," I said, turning back around and running up the stairs. I shoved the smokes under my chin and twisted the handle quickly to rejoin my new acquaintance before the man by the stairs could attempt to enforce the house rules.

"That took longer than I expected," the artist said in a stern voice as I entered.

I shut the door. "Don't make me do that again," I said. I laughed, shaking my head to rid myself of the thought.

"Let me see what you brought," he said, turning on the stool in front of the easel to face me.

"I got what you asked for. I even brought you lime for the beer," I said, smiling.

"Here's your first lesson, so listen closely—when I give you an order, you must follow it to the letter … nothing more … nothing less. Understood?"

"Huh?" I said but I knew what he meant.

"I'll let it slide this one time," he said, taking both the beers and the lime from my right hand. He squeezed the lime

into the neck of the bottles. I handed him the cigarettes and he handed me one of the beers.

"Thank you," I said, taking a sip.

He took a swig and placed his beer on the windowsill. Then he reached for my beer and placed it alongside his. Without warning, he spun me around, pulling me back onto his lap. Roughly spreading my thighs, he gently touched the wetness there. "I was right about you. You need this …. You need me."

I didn't know what to say. I was shaking, scared out of my wits, but his actions turned me on so much I couldn't say anything to stop him. I just sat there and allowed him to explore my labia. My heightened arousal from my jaunt downstairs and his expert fingers had me at the edge of release for several minutes. He sensed that I was close to exploding and stopped rubbing my clit to prolong the climb. He circled around my lips, dipping ever closer to my anus, and then brought his expert fingers back to my swollen bud.

I could hear my moans with no idea how to stop them. I felt outside of myself and so wholly turned on. I couldn't recall ever before feeling so desperate to cum. I had to cum. I mumbled, "Please, please, please," over and over again. He finally allowed my downhill run by grabbing my hard erect nipple tightly in his fingers while manipulating my clit. I grunted in a way that didn't even sound like me and cried out my release. After the waves of orgasm subsided, I moved to stand up, but he held me tight against him. He spread my legs even farther apart and, using more intense pressure, resumed playing with my clit. I have always hated it when men masturbated me hard and fast, and yet he had me climaxing again in less than a minute. The intensity of my cumming astounded me and I was stunned as I lolled, wholly spent, in his lap.

Leaning my head back against his chest, I closed my eyes. Feeling his heartbeat on my shoulders and his breath near my

ear, I melted into him. Having never behaved in this manner, I was at a loss as to what to do next.

I didn't have long to wait because he removed the arm he had around my waist and pushed me off his lap.

"Go sit on the bed," he said.

Still in a daze, I lumbered over to the footboard and sat down on the bottom edge, facing him. He watched me settle on the bed as I crossed my legs.

"Uncross your legs and keep them open," he ordered, leaning back farther in his chair.

"Excuse me?"

"Second rule, now pay attention—in my presence, your legs will always be open to me."

"In your presence?" I said. "I plan to never see you again. Never come to this house again. I'm still debating if I'll ever speak to Scott after he put me in this situation."

He cleared his throat and I realized I hadn't complied. I spread my legs, which felt awkward so I leaned back on my elbows trying to get comfortable. He couldn't see much with my skirt lying on top of my legs.

I put aside my qualms and focused on his body. He wasn't big but he exuded strength. His forearms were sinewy and I imagined the rest of him was as well. I looked at the bulge in his pants and could feel him staring at me. His eyes burrowed under my skin, as if stripping it away, opening me up so he could look straight into me.

I gazed up and as we made eye contact, I started. "I should probably leave—"

"Soon," he said, standing. He walked over to the bed and took my hand, pulling me to my feet. He led me back to the chair beside the easel and he sat down again. "Lay across my lap," he commanded.

"Excuse me?" I said.

He said nothing but continued to watch me. After a few moments, he pointed to his lap and then the door. I knew

what he meant. I should have run out of there and never looked back. I, however, lay down across his lap. My arms hung to the ground and my long hair touched the floor as well. My legs felt awkward, sticking out straight behind me.

"Move back so your knees are on the rug," he said. "I will give you a small taste of what will happen if you disobey me." He lifted my skirt, folding it against my back, and smacked my butt with his open left hand.

It hurt, but not badly. My nipples hardened against his leg and I could feel his erection grow against my stomach.

He spanked me again, harder this time, and warmth spread across my butt cheeks. He struck me at a steady pace six more times and then massaged my ass gently. As if in apology, he leaned over and kissed each cheek. A chill ran up my spine and I convulsed noticeably. He reached between my legs and touched the ever-growing wetness there. He smacked my ass one more time, much harder than before.

"I knew you would be into this when I saw you waltzing into this house."

I pushed myself off his lap in a huff and he guffawed.

I stomped to the other door in the room, assuming it led to a bathroom, which it did. After slamming the door behind me, I looked at myself in the mirror.

"What in the hell were you thinking?" I said quietly, not quite recognizing myself.

After peeing, I wiped myself several times trying to rid my vagina of its excess wetness. I thought of leaving by the other door and running down the stairs, but couldn't make myself open the door that led to the hallway. I closed the lid and flushed the toilet. I rolled my skirt back down to its normal length. Washing my hands, I avoided the sight of myself in the mirror, and sat down on the toilet. Leaning forward and burying my face in my hands, I tried to force the arousal out of me. My mind wanted me to leave but my body wanted the controlling artist to fuck me hard, to slam himself inside of me.

I jumped up when I heard his voice close to the door.

"I've called you a cab," he said.

I opened the door and said, "I don't have the cash on me to pay—"

"Here," he said, handing me forty dollars.

"I'll pay you back," I said. "Where should I send it?"

He laughed again to my utter vexation and said, "I'll see you after work on Monday. You can pay me then."

"What? I can't see you after work on Monday. I need to find Scott and tell him I'm leaving."

"I'll tell him," he said.

"Oh, you know Scott? I'll give him the money to give to you."

"That won't be necessary. So that I have something to call you, what is your name," he said almost kindly. He still looked like he could break out laughing again without much provocation.

"I thought you were clairvoyant," I said, sounding like a petulant brat.

Again, the laughter flowed out of him. When he smiled, he looked ten years younger and even more handsome.

"So?" he asked.

"So—" I said.

"You're going to be a stubborn one I see."

"I'm nothing of the kind. You bring it out in me!"

He chuckled again, infuriating me even more.

"Gladys," I said, crossing my arms in front of me.

"Try again. The beautiful woman in front of me could never be named Gladys."

Blushing at the compliment, I turned away so he couldn't see my face. "Jane," I answered. "Plain Jane, as my mother always called me."

"Well Jane, there's nothing plain about you now."

He confused me with his compliments. I felt as though he was trying to make sure I'd agree to see him again.

"What's your name?" I asked, trying hard to keep the edge out of my voice.

"That, my pretty lady, you will find out on Monday."

"Where on Monday?" I asked, wishing I could kick myself in the shin to awaken my rational self.

"I thought you couldn't meet me," he said.

He looked proud of himself. *I should kick him in the shin,* I thought.

"I'll meet you outside your office at five."

"You don't know where I work and I can't get away until at least 5:30."

"I'll find you," he said with confidence. "Be out front at 5:00."

"Scott doesn't know where I work," I said over my shoulder as I walked through the threshold of the bedroom. I scurried down the stairs and fled through the front door without looking back.

The cab pulled forward as I walked down the steps to the pavement. I gave the driver my address and relaxed against the backseat, breathing a sigh of relief.

I'll never see him again, I thought. *God, I'm going to kill Scott. What a shit! He knows the artist .... Are they friends?*

From the window, I watched the lights reflecting in the puddles from the rain that had fallen earlier in the evening. *I can't believe I just left my underwear,* I thought to myself. My mind flitted from one subject to another until it landed on him again. It seemed like a dream ... that he didn't really exist. *Did he? Did I really do all those things? Let him do all those things to me?*

As angry as I was at Scott—and I was steaming mad—curiosity about the artist took precedence. *Tomorrow's only Saturday so I could just show up at Scott's place and ring him from downstairs ....*

CHAPTER TWO

The night after the party, I slept fitfully, waking up from strange dreams that eluded my grasp. I ran in the evening at my usual time, planning to swing by Scott's apartment on my way back to pick up my car. To my surprise, Scott, who usually doesn't run on Saturdays, fell in beside me.

"What are you doing here?" I asked. I considered tripping him as payback for the night before but it wouldn't have served my purpose. "You're a real shit, you know," I said before he could respond.

"I knew you wouldn't come if I told you and I thought you might get into it."

"You're a jerk, plain and simple. I should've known better." I continued to run for a while faster than my usual pace. Scott struggled to keep up.

"So you know the artist guy?" I asked.

"Huh?"

"Did someone tell you I left?"

"Oh, yes. Him? He's an artist? A bit scary if you ask me."

"Do you know him? Do you know his name?"

"Know … wouldn't be the right word. I've seen him around. Don't think I ever got his name." Scott stopped running and leaned over with his hands on his knees. "Still recovering from a hangover," he said.

I shuffled back and forth beside him, not wanting to lose my momentum.

"Don't tell me you're interested in him?" Scott asked incredulously. "He gives me the willies. There's something

not right about that guy. You should stay away, Jane. He's bad news."

"I can take care of myself and I'm not stupid," I said. "I'll see you around." When I turned to run in the opposite direction I thought, *that proved fruitless.*

"Oh hell," I said. I turned around and ran back to Scott. "Do you know who owns the house from the party?" I asked, panting.

"I know that a couple of guys live there, although they change from time to time. Your 'artist' friend seems to come and go. I haven't seen him around for a while though, until last night that is. Really Jane, stay away from him."

∞

I spent Sunday reading the rest of *Servant of the Bones* and filing away in my mind every detail that had happened Friday night. *Did I really go downstairs practically naked?* I ran over everything several times, trying to make sense of it all. Some things he had said confused me but I couldn't be sure if I recalled the conversation completely or correctly. He must have been watching me because I am almost certain he said "he knew" the first time he saw me walking into the house.

Something else he'd said bothered me—that I was "more stubborn than the others." *Others? Is that what he said?*

The novel helped to distract me but by six o'clock my nervous energy overflowed so I went down to the community pool and swam laps. I swam until I couldn't lift my arms over my head for another stroke.

I struggled up the stairs and headed straight for the shower. The workout helped a lot and after stretching, I cozied up for a while and fell fast asleep.

In the morning, startled by a dream, I awoke before my alarm went off. In the dream I ran down an alley near a canal. I could smell the brackish water mixing with the gasoline

from the cars on the street. I kept looking over my shoulder, knowing someone was chasing me, but unable to snag a glimpse of him. In true horror film fashion, when I turned back around, my chaser stood straight in front of me. It was the artist from Friday night.

I gasped and sat up in bed. My heart pounded in my chest and I knew the dream carried an ominous message. I made up my mind. As intrigued and aroused as my experience at the party had made me, I still had no intention of seeing him again. *Why was I worried?*

I picked a blue fitted business suit—skirt and jacket—with a white blouse out of my mundane business attire. All my work outfits looked pretty much the same except for the color. I considered them my work uniforms. I added earrings and slipped on my favorite pair of black shoes. A fashion diva I wasn't, but the clothes served their purpose. I gathered my hair up into a twist, secured it with a clip and applied a pale shade of lipstick.

The company I worked for occupied the top three floors of the Bank of America building in downtown Fort Lauderdale. I arrived at my desk and checked my "in" basket, losing myself in the routine of the day. Mondays were especially hectic at the office and that day proved no different.

03

"Hey," Allison said, poking her head into my office around noon. She had bangs that skimmed her brows, giving her an almost school-girl look that translated into sexy. "Have you eaten anything?" she said, flashing a bright smile that lifted the corners of her clear blue eyes.

"How do you manage to look so good even on a Monday?" I asked.

She smiled, and I got the impression she heard compliments all the time and didn't mind hearing one more. I glanced at the clock and said, "No I haven't and I'm famished.

Let's go down to the pub for a quick bite."

"Great," she said, sashaying through my office door.

જી

I stayed relaxed through most of lunch until Allison asked me about my weekend. By the time I walked back into my office a knot had begun to form in the pit of my stomach. *What if he's out there? What if he waits for me until I leave?*

I buzzed Brian—my boss—on the intercom and told him I would be leaving a few minutes before five. I planned to tell … what's-his–name … that I was not interested and that Friday night was a fluke—if he showed up, which I hoped he wouldn't.

જી

"Didn't you say you needed to leave before five?" Brian said as he passed my office at 5:05 p.m.

"Oh crap," I said. Gathering my purse and jacket, I jogged to the elevator. *Slow down*, I told myself. *You're being ridiculous. He won't even be there.*

I pushed through the double glass doors and scanned the parade of business-clad people hurrying to their cars to go home, shop, or head for happy hour. He wasn't among them. I lowered my shoulders and breathed a sigh of relief. Turning toward the parking lot, I stopped. I felt him. I know that sounds crazy, but I felt him watching me.

I turned back and scoured the faces around me. I made a wide sweeping search of the area, finally looking across the roadway. *Shit!* There he stood, leaning against the brick wall on the other side of the street.

The breath stuck in my throat. He was eying me like his prey. His expression was stern and arrogant as he leaned on his left shoulder with his arms behind his back. He wore jeans, worker boots and a long-sleeved blue shirt with buttons

21

and no collar. He looked striking, strong and menacing.

He waited.

What the hell is he waiting for? Let's get this over with, I thought. I took a deep breath, noticing that I was shaking again—terrified yet aroused. *I'm not interested,* I told him silently, hoping that I would have the courage to say the words out loud, *please don't come around again.*

I waited for a car to pass and then hurried across the street. He pushed away from the wall, dropping a large bouquet of flowers, and moved quickly up the sidewalk, away from me.

"Flowers ... you brought me flowers?" I called out to him as I swooped to pick them up. I rushed, shuffling after him, trying to catch up. "Listen," I said to his back, "Friday night was a fluke. That wasn't me. This was a mistake. I mean ..." I was panting. "Hey," I yelled, "stop for a minute, will you?"

He continued to stroll briskly down the street. Why I followed him, I don't know, but I had to jog on my toes to catch up. "Are you going to slow down?"

"You're late," he said over his shoulder and continued to stride away from me.

"Well I just wanted to tell you that I think this is a bad idea," I hollered to him. "Are you going to slow down or what?" I stopped.

He slowed down, and then walked back to me. "Give me your shoes," he said.

"Give you my shoes? Why would I give you my shoes?"

"Take them off, put them in my hand," he said, holding out his palm.

I removed my shoes and handed them to him. He turned and strode down the street, dropping my shoes in the nearest garbage bin hanging on the light post.

"What the hell!" I said. "What'd you do that for?"

"So you can keep up," he said, pausing long enough to answer me.

"Those are my favorite shoes," I said, shaking my head—more at myself than him.

"Well, if you want them, then get them."

"Really?" I said and carefully reached for my shoes, attempting to avoid touching the food byproducts that filled the can. "Why are you treating me this way?" I said, not caring if he could hear me anymore. I pulled the shoes out and held them away from my skirt.

"I'm sorry," he said. He stopped, tilted his head slightly and said, "I made us reservations at a Japanese restaurant and I don't want to be late. I am never late. That's another thing you need to know if I decide to spend time with you."

"*You* decide?" My brain felt like it had imploded. "*You* decide? What the hell am I doing here?" I said, heading in the opposite direction.

"Here," he said. He grabbed my upper arm and turned me back around. He took the shoes from my hand and stepped into the restaurant to the right of us. "Wait here."

Returning a few moments later, he bent down and placed my shoes—fresh and sparkling—on my feet.

"Listen—" I said.

"I know what you're going to say, but wait until after tonight to decide."

"You promise to leave me alone if I say—"

"Of course, after tonight all you have to say is 'Get lost, creep!' and I will be a thing of the past."

That elicited a laugh from me. "Get lost, creep," I repeated. "I'll have to remember that."

His stride was longer than mine and even though he slowed down a bit, I had to jog to keep up. When he swerved onto a back street, I immediately thought of my dream. Despite my anxiety, I continued to followed him.

After several more turns we walked up to a door that looked like the emergency exit. My mystery man opened the door and I stepped right through into a kitchen. It wasn't

large by restaurant standards but it was busy, and the staff had to hustle. The delicious smells made my stomach grumble and the stir-fry sizzling in the wok commanded my attention.

My artist greeted an Asian man with a bow. He began speaking in Japanese as if he had spoken the language his entire life. I was stunned. *Where had he learned Japanese? College? Living abroad?*

He led me out of the kitchen, into the restaurant. Several employees greeted him in their native language as we followed our host to our table. Japanese flute music filled the air and ornate Japanese screens separated tables from one another. We were seated at a booth by a lush atrium. He sat facing the waterfall and indicated with a nod that I should join him on the same side. I placed the flowers he brought for me in the chair across from us.

"I don't know what to make of you," I said, pondering the man beside me.

"There's not much to get. I'm a simple guy," he said, smiling. "I like things the way I like them. For instance, you owe me for being late."

"Ah ..." I began but the waiter interrupted me.

He only addressed the artist and then moved away.

"What was that?" I asked.

"Oh, I ordered for us," he said.

"How would you know what I like?"

"Let's wait and see."

Again I veered between frustration and titillation. I wanted to hit him and yet my body wanted him to fuck me right there on our table in the middle of the restaurant. His hand clutched my thigh and roughly spread my legs.

"I can see you'll need a little reminding tonight," he whispered in my ear.

The waiter brought saké to our table. As he poured it into tiny ceramic cups, my artist worked his finger under the

elastic between my legs. I squirmed at his touch.

"Relax," he whispered.

The waiter moved away and he removed his finger.

"Go to the bathroom and take off your underwear," he ordered, gripping the top of my thigh.

"Oh ... um—"

"Now," he said. "I'll tell you something about me when you get back." He ushered me out of the booth and I stumbled to my feet, smoothing my skirt over my thighs. I snatched my purse from the seat and stomped off to the bathroom. He laughed at my ungraceful departure, making the hairs prickle on the back of my neck.

My need to flee the restaurant battled with my overwhelming desire for excitement. I went into the first stall, closed the toilet seat and sat down, trying to collect my thoughts. A mess of confusion swirled around in my head. I had never experienced such arousal combined with such utter annoyance.

I stood and removed my underwear, shoving them into my overstuffed purse. Leaving the stall, I approached the mirror, heaved a heavy sigh and looked at myself. I looked severe with my hair pulled back. I removed the clip that held my hair in place and ran my fingers through it to fluff it out. I can't explain why I cared what he thought, but I did. The strength he exuded made me want to please him, even though I hated him for it. The contradiction of emotions kept me off balance.

I opened my purse again and shoved my panties out of the way, rummaging for my lipstick. I chose a dark red, painting it on my lips and pinching my cheeks to summon the blood to the surface. My eyes had a wild look.

"Who are you?" I said to the reflection in the mirror.

I strolled back to the table with more confidence than when I left, feeling as though someone else inhabited my body.

"What took you so long?" he demanded, clearly irritated.

I sat down in front of the hot soup waiting for me.

"Following orders, sir," I said like a private to his commander. I spread my thighs to illustrate the point.

"I can see an attitude adjustment is in order, but we'll deal with that later."

I burst into laughter at that. I hadn't expected his reaction. I thought he would be angered by my insolence, but instead he laughed with me.

"Information," I said, furrowing my brow.

"Taste the soup first," he ordered.

I blew across the spoon to cool the miso soup. "Wow ... this is delicious," I said. "Really good. Now tell me—"

"Luke, forty-five, artist-slash-photographer. I sell most of my work abroad. I travel a lot. If this progresses I need to get a place with more privacy."

"That's it?"

"What else is there to know?"

"Family, friends, where you grew up ... hopes, dreams ... like that."

"I thought you had no plans to see me after tonight."

"Yeah, well," I said, stalling for a reasonable response, "just call it curiosity."

"Well, as the saying goes, 'curiosity killed the cat.' "

"What's that supposed to mean?" I said. The fear from the dream resurfaced.

"Always wear your hair down, but no makeup."

My anger flared at another order but the waiter circumvented my indignation by retrieving our soup bowls.

Luke distracted me with his hand between my knees, working his way to my wetness. Leaning closer, he whispered in my ear, "I will bring you to heights of ecstasy like you've never known, but you'll have to trust me." He slowly circled his finger around my clit.

"Ooohhh ...." I groaned, forgetting for the moment where I was.

"I know you want me and that I frighten you. You needn't be scared of me," he said, continuing his exploration of my labia. "My only concern is pushing you to greater heights and depths of pleasure." He increased the pressure. "We'll go to your place after this. I'll show you."

"Oh ... no!" I yelped, pushing his hand away as the waiter returned.

The waiter placed before us a small square plate with a variety of sashimi.

"I don't eat raw fish," I stated, crossing my arms in front of my chest and closing my legs.

"Try it," he said. "If you eat cooked fish, you'll love this. Open your mouth."

"I don't eat wasa—" I tried to say but he shoved an orange piece of fish with wasabi and ginger into my mouth.

"Hey," I sputtered, lifting the water glass in both hands and drinking the lot of it, "that burned my mouth. I don't eat wasabi and I don't eat sashimi and if you won't listen to me, I'm out of here." Putting my purse strap over my arm I scooted to get out of the booth.

He grasped my arm and said, "You're right. Don't go. I just wanted you to try it because I know you'll love it."

"You don't know anything about me," I said, sitting on the edge of the cushion, poised to stand.

"When did your father leave you?"

"What?"

"When did he leave you?"

"He didn't leave *me* ... he left my mother."

"Oh, so he's kept in touch with you?"

"Well ... he did at first but then ... it got too hard for him to ...." I looked away as my words trailed off. "Why am I talking to you about this stuff? How did you know my parents are divorced?"

"I know you. Don't you see? You were lost and now I've found you. You have trust issues because of your father

27

leaving you. Just try it," he said, holding out another piece of fish. "No wasabi this time."

I opened my mouth, accepted a piece of white fish lightly dipped in soy sauce, and said, "Hmm ... that's really good. What kind of fish is it?"

He gave me an I-told-you-so look and answered, "White Tuna." He shifted in his seat to face me. "I know your father's abandonment has left you with trust issues, which is to be expected, but just remember that my patience comes with a price."

"Well ... you will be rid of me tonight," I said, wondering if I completely meant it.

"No," he said, looking at me intently. "No, we'll be seeing a lot of each other."

"What makes you so sure?" I said. "How do you know I won't blow you off just to show you I can? Say the magic words that will make you gone?"

"Maybe down the road, but not tonight. You're not certain why, but you want to see what will happen next. You need me, Jane. You'll see."

I removed my purse from my shoulder and scooted closer to him. He fed me a few more pieces of sashimi and refilled my saké cup.

The waiter approached the table cautiously, giving me the impression that he'd seen Luke's earlier activities between my legs. Lifting away the appetizer plate, he placed two steaming dishes in front of us.

"I don't usually eat this much," I said, fixing the napkin over my lap.

"That's apparent. Your overall build is fantastic but you'll look better once you've put on some weight. It'll fill out your breast and hips."

"You can be so flattering and so insulting at the same time," I said.

"I was being neither. I was stating what I see. Why do you give value to anything I say?"

I've always considered myself a strong woman, but with Luke I felt like an insecure mess. Yet, there I sat, actually enjoying the craziness of spending time with him. I knew my choices, even if I deluded myself enough to believe I could stop at any time.

I watched the other women in the restaurant stare at him. They would walk the long way to the bathroom so they could pass by our table. He acknowledged them with a smile, raising a blush on their cheeks. Each time Luke brought his attention immediately back to me.

I felt confused over my attraction to him. He wasn't drop-dead gorgeous or even particularly handsome but some quality definitely attracted us all. I started to think, *Why me?* He sat there watching me eat and listening to me talk. I felt pinned ... no, more like *encompassed* by his attention. Clearly he could have had the pick of the lot, married or single. "So, why me?" I let slip out before I could stop myself.

"Why not you?"

"What do you want from me?"

"Everything."

"Everything? What does that mean, everything?"

"I want you completely and totally. I want to merge our lives and bodies. Your body—mine, and my body—yours."

"But you just met me," I said as I shifted to face him.

"Tell me .... How long should it take?"

"Until you get to know me better."

"I know everything I need to know," he said, leaning over to kiss me on my cheek. He lingered there for a moment and then said, "Let's have them wrap up the rest of dinner. We can eat it for a midnight snack."

"I have work tomorrow."

"Worry about tomorrow when it gets here. Let's enjoy ourselves."

Against my better judgment—hell, *all* of my judgment— we started walking slowly back to my car. He held my hand

and I could feel his energy entering my palm, permeating my body. In contrast to the hurried march on the way to the restaurant, he kept a relaxed pace and whistled softly.

"I think you must be the strangest person I've ever met," I said, as my arms swung slowly with his.

"Well, you must have limited exposure to people because I meet people far stranger than I all the time. I think up until now you've lived a sheltered existence. To please your mother maybe?" He wasn't looking for a response. "No matter," he continued, swatting his free hand in the air as if to push the thought away. "That will all change soon enough."

I started to believe everything he said. *Did I actually keep on the straight and narrow because of my mother? I've always felt rebellious of her ways but have I really strayed that much?*

We crossed the parking lot to my red Honda Accord and he held out his hand for the keys. He unlocked the car and opened the passenger side door for me.

"Where to?" he said as he settled himself into the driver's seat, moving it back to accommodate his legs.

"Don't you already know?" I asked. "You managed to find my workplace easily enough."

"Actually I do."

"How the hell do you know where I live and work?" I said, shifting in my seat to face him. The fear in me again raised its ugly head.

"The cabby was a friend of mine," he said, shrugging.

"Should I be worried for my life? Are you a deranged serial killer? Do you stalk women with wavy brown hair?" I was only half kidding but at the same time my head felt like it was splitting open. *What the hell am I doing?* I thought.

He laughed heartily and said, "Not to worry. I will never hurt you unless you want me to."

My heart beat rapidly in my chest. I didn't know how to respond. He turned over the engine and pulled out of the parking lot. I watched the familiar streets pass as he made his way to my condominium.

"Where should I park?" he asked as he drove my car into my complex.

Relief swept over me when I realized he didn't know my apartment number. "Park in the spot over there," I said and pointed.

He maneuvered into my space and quickly got out of the car. I began to get out as well but he caught the door in time to open it himself. "Thank you," I said. "I'm not used to having men open doors for me."

He held out his hand. I swung my legs around and he pulled me to my feet, embracing me around my back and lifting me onto my toes. He lowered his mouth to mine and kissed me for the first time. My body caught fire, making me feel like it had been asleep all of my life up until that very moment. He kissed me deeply, exploring my mouth with his tongue. As he sucked my lower lip into his kiss, I could smell his warm spicy breath on my face. His kiss took me on a journey of sensation. He encouraged me with his lips to explore his mouth with my tongue. I kissed deeper than ever before, lost in another plane of existence. The kiss took away any possible resolve I had left. When he finally pulled away I felt light-headed, the way I did after an orgasm.

"Wow," I whispered.

"Let's go," he said, lifting the leftovers and handing me my purse and flowers.

He strode over to the elevators, leaving me behind to catch up.

"Hey," I called.

"We definitely need to get you more practical shoes." He walked back and handed me the bag of food.

Swooping me up in his arms like a bride, he carried me to the elevator. My weight didn't slow him down.

"What floor?" he asked, waiting to push the call button on the elevator.

"Third," I said, smiling.

"What's taking so long?" he asked after a minute.

"Elevator's slow," I said, laughing.

He headed for the steps with me in his arms and climbed the two flights of stairs to the third floor.

"Three-o-nine," I said, pointing down the hallway with a chuckle in my voice.

"Of course it's the farthest one away from the stairs," he said, grinning.

Finally he put me down gently in front of the door. "Which key?"

"Here," I said, reaching to take the keys from him.

"Which one?" he said, holding firmly onto the keys.

"This one," I said, pointing to the bronze-colored one. He opened the door and closed it behind us.

I stood by the door not knowing what to do. I felt young and inexperienced all over again. He found the kitchen and placed the brown bag in the fridge. Then he glided back over to me, removed the purse hanging from my shoulder and placed both the purse and the flowers on the counter.

"Come here," he said gently, pulling me close. "Where's the bedroom?"

"There." I pointed behind him.

He took my hand and led me in. I started to unbutton my shirt but he stopped me.

"No. Let me," he said in a serious tone.

I stood there with my arms at my sides, being undressed for the first time since childhood. The act seemed more fatherly than sexual as he carefully unbuttoned my blouse and slid it off my shoulders. I'm not sure why, but I wanted to cry. I held back the tears by watching him neatly fold my shirt and place it on the dresser. Reaching behind me, he unzipped my skirt, holding the waistband as it slid down my legs. Leaning on his shoulder I stepped out of the skirt, which he laid neatly on top of the blouse. Kneeling down in front of me he removed my shoes.

Something about the way he moved stayed with me. I thought of him rushing down the street in front of me earlier that night. He didn't just walk, he flowed—without wasted effort, with an absolute precision that exuded strength and sexuality. As he stepped back my eyes fixated on his body. He moved with such confidence, as if the dance of life came easily to him, a dance I hoped he would soon teach me.

There I stood, wanting to be free of my bra, incredibly aroused and yet feeling like my heart could break if he turned his eyes away from me just once.

As he rose to his feet I saw in his expression a look of such compassion and love, it frightened me. I shook my head to clear the confusion from my thoughts, but with little success.

"Are you okay?" Luke asked.

"Yes," I said, a bit tremulous.

"You're very beautiful," he said as he circled around me to unfasten my bra. "You look much better without clothes." He faced me again as he folded my bra and added it to the pile. I noticed my shoes were lined up next to the dresser.

"Shall I undress you?" I asked nervously.

"No," he said, sweeping me up in his arms and lowering me down onto the bed.

He undressed quickly, taking the same care with his clothes as he had with mine. My pile lay next to his. His workman boots were neatly lined up beside my black heels.

When he turned to face me, I was struck by two things. The first was a scar running down his stomach from just under his chest on the right to his hip bone. I wondered what might have happened to him. My eyes trailed up his body to his lean chest. He had to spend considerable time in the gym to get his body so muscular and sinewy. The strength he displayed carrying me up the stairs was evident. The second thing I noticed was his sizable girth, easily visible as his cock stood immensely aroused. I wondered how much pleasure

and pain I would feel once he entered me. The thought shocked me; I'd never considered the possibility of pain in sex, but I couldn't help it. Memories of his hard touch that first night at the party house and how it had heightened my senses brought those feelings back to me, and my juices began to run down my thighs.

Lying down on the bed, he pulled me on top of him. His energy so encompassed me I couldn't feel myself apart from him. Slowly, passionately, he kissed me. His lips lingered, devouring my mouth, sucking my lips, wrapping his tongue around mine. I was lost in the moment, the whole of my body consumed by his deft tongue as his lips stoked the desire within me. I had forgotten time and space and was floating in absolute contentment when he finally pulled his lips from mine.

With strong hands he gently rolled me onto my back and held my arms above my head. Instead of feeling confined by him, I felt released. He lay beside me, using his free hand to brush his fingers down my body. In my heightened state of excitement I could barely stand his touch, knowing that if he tried he could make me cum with just one more caress.

Then he turned his attention lower, trailing his lips to my breast. He breathed my nipple into his mouth, making me gasp. He sucked softly and slowly at first but as he added more pressure to his manipulations of my hard tip, he caused me to cry out. I writhed about as he moved his attentions to my other breast. He already knew how to read me, because as I felt myself coming closer and closer to release, he instinctively pulled back, causing my bliss to slip just enough.

"Oh you smell so good," he said, kissing his way up to my neck, taking in my scent and suckling and nibbling there as if I were dessert.

Then, in a frighteningly quick movement, he swung himself on top of me, widening my legs apart with his own as he propped himself above me. I could feel his cock brushing

against my inner thigh as he eased his hips forward ever so slowly. I shuddered, anticipating his girth and the sensation of him filling me, but instead he ran the full length of his phallus over my clit. My pelvis arched upward, wanting him inside of me, but he only grinned as he slid the thick head of his cock back down until it hovered over my longing lips. He held it there for a second, teasing me, as I tried to move my hips onto him.

Having brought me to the desired state of frenzy, Luke finally eased his cock inside of me as I arched my back to receive him into my wetness. Involuntarily I shifted my body to accommodate his size as his length entered me, inch by filling inch. I had expected him to fuck me hard; instead, he moved slowly in and out of me, looking into my eyes the whole time, sealing our connection. He had me hooked. I could have cum a dozen times in those first strokes, but the look in his eyes told me to restrain my body.

As he continued to leisurely slide in and out of my wet pussy, I could see a new look in his eyes giving me permission to release the absolute joy building within me, and for the first time in my life, I had an orgasm solely from intercourse. That orgasm seemed to last forever as he continued to slide his full length into me with a confident, controlled rhythm. I entered another realm that shook me to the core. Though he said nothing, his eyes spoke volumes as he claimed my heart with every penetrating stroke.

Frightened by what his look said to me, I closed my eyes. His stare felt too intimate, too potent. *Love could not happen that fast,* I thought. But as my exhilaration rose to an even higher sphere I opened my eyes to a blur of blending colors. He touched my clit, releasing a second and third orgasm that wiped out all my cares and concerns. Then, one last time, he pulled his cock all the way out and thrust back into me. When he came it reminded me of a roar of a lion. He looked fierce and powerful and his gaze matched his physical penetration.

"This is just the beginning," he whispered, as he lowered himself beside me, his sweat glistening in the soft light.

As he spooned me to him, I felt as if my childhood dream—every girl's dream—had finally been fulfilled. Floating in complete relaxation I dozed off, thinking, *This doesn't really happen to people, certainly not to me.*

The shift of the bed as he sat down brought me back to the real world as the smell of stir-fry filled the room.

"We need to fatten you up," Luke said, holding a bowl of steaming food.

As I sat up in bed I giggled as he temptingly fed me leftovers, teasing each bite in and out of my mouth until I'd lunge for it with my teeth. When he laughed at my antics, I knew I was a goner. It was by far the most romantic moment I had ever experienced.

He scooted me over to the center of the bed and got in on my side. When he embraced me, I knew we would make love again. He kissed my eyes and then my forehead, but he must have noticed my desire to please him. He must have enjoyed knowing he had inspired such uncontrolled passion and fulfilled a longing that rendered me young and vulnerable. So, after asking his permission, I kissed the craggy line of his scar, which stood out on his otherwise smooth, taut body. I found it sensual, twisted and poignant. I wanted to know what had happened, who had hurt him. I wanted to kiss away his pain as he had relieved me of mine.

He allowed me to explore him. As my lips gently glided over his brawny body, I breathed him in as though he were an elixir that would cure all my ills. I committed his aroma to memory, never wanting to lose that moment.

Working my lips over his body, I felt his growing response against my breast. In a surprising move, he grabbed my arms just below my shoulders and drew me upright. He positioned me above him just before allowing me to lower

myself onto his rigid phallus. Then he gripped my hips and pulled me down onto him as he lifted his hips to meet mine in a single deep orgasmic thrust.

"Oh god!" I said. He filled me, wholly and completely, holding still for a minute before using his hands to move my body rhythmically back and forth. I matched his pace while clutching his chest for support. Then he skillfully reached his right hand between us so I could rub my clitoris against his index finger.

I churned my pubis down on him, crying out in pleasure and pain as he filled me past comfort. I was so engrossed that I slammed my pelvis into his again and again as he twirled my clit with his fingers, bringing me closer and closer to orgasm.

"Cum only when I say you can," he commanded.

I looked straight into his eyes, my hips rising and falling in a fury as my pussy burned with a fire all of its own. My orgasm hovered close, the need to cum intense, but the brazen look in his eyes forced me to hold back against everything my body demanded. As he twirled my clit once more, I forced myself to contain my orgasm. It could've been five seconds or five minutes but it felt like an eternity. I didn't want to disappoint Luke as I bit my lower lip, holding myself at the edge of ecstasy until I saw him nod once.

Like a tidal wave crashing against the shore, my orgasm sent the force of my energy into him as the contractions of my pussy squeezed his hard cock. "Oh yes Luke, I'm cumming for you! Ohhhh, yes," I groaned as I clawed at his chest, my senses screaming. I finally collapsed forward onto his chest, gasping for breath.

I could feel his cock still pulsating inside me. I resumed wriggling my hips back and forth, loving the way he filled me, only to have him grab my buttocks and propel them in a circular motion. We ground our bodies together until the lion growl ripped through him. Fascinated, I watched his ferocious release as he impaled me with his cock. His features

twisted in agonized pleasure as his load burst against my uterus, causing my own muscles to clamp on as if milking every drop of him.

A moment later his body went from rigid to relaxed, his lips curving into a warm smile. Eyes still closed, he reached up and pulled me to his chest, wrapping his arms around me. In that moment, I felt so cared for, so loved. He held me like that until we both fell back to sleep.

ॐ

Luke left sometime during the night. I slept so deeply, I had no awareness of his departure. When I awoke in the morning, I had a slight headache from the saké and felt soreness between my legs. Smiling at the sensation, I touched my inner folds, thinking of him. He had completely controlled every aspect of the night before and for the first time in a long while, there had been no need for me to think. It had been a relief to be out of my head, only conscious of the sensations coursing throughout my body. I really did believe at the time that those kinds of experiences only happened in fairy tales. Luke had aided me in becoming a fully sexual being.

I will always be grateful to him for that but ....

As I lay on the bed resisting getting into the shower, I recall already being confounded by Luke. He frightened, even terrified me at times, and yet I felt possessed by him, filled by him, freed by him. How can you feel freed and captured at the same time? I started to get anxious.

Would I see him again today? Would he call me?

I dragged myself to the bathroom for a hot shower. On the counter, laid out neatly, I found my underwear from Friday night.

For some reason this made me laugh.

CHAPTER THREE

By the end of the first hour of work I had averted several crises, finding temps to fill in where needed. On the plus side, I was too occupied to think about Luke.

At two o'clock a knock at the door startled me. Pierce, an executive assistant from the twelfth floor, brought a large bouquet of burnt orange and yellow spotted lilies into my office. The aging college preppy wore khaki pants and a button–down, long-sleeved Polo shirt. His loafers were shiny brown and I wondered if he used the same shine from his shoes on his slicked back hair. The grapevine had previously informed me of his interest as had his meek overtures, so I immediately assumed the flowers were from him.

"Flowers for me? Why are you buying me flowers?" I asked.

"When you didn't respond to me, I just figured you for a lesbian," he said. "They're not from me. It says, 'from Luke.' "

"You opened the card?" I said as I made room on my desk for the vase.

"No, it's written on the envelope," he said, placing them in front of me. "So you're not gay after all?"

"Get out," I said as I pushed him through the door and closed it quickly behind him.

I plucked the envelope off the plastic stick and held it for a moment. I admired the bouquet of large yellow lilies.

Did I tell him I liked lilies?

Shaking, I slid my nail along the edge of the envelope, pulled out the card and saw his handwriting for the first time.

The distinctive slant indicated that he was left-handed. "Last night was everything I'd hoped for," the card said. "I will be away for a couple of days. Think of me. P.S. You still owe me for being late. I have not forgotten."

He had me twisted in knots. My arousal confounded me. I couldn't be sure if my nipples hardened because he said he'd enjoyed last night or because of what I suspected would happen when he got back. I didn't like the way his card made me feel. I tore it up and threw it in the trash. I thought of throwing away the flowers as well, but I've always adored lilies. I left them on the desk and crossed the hall to attend a meeting.

∞

After work I met up with Sandy to go for a walk. She had a scrunched expression on her freckly face as she approached me as if she was trying to sum me up. Although barely five feet tall, she swung her arms and carried her back so straight that she gave the illusion of more height. No one would call her beautiful but she was the epitome of cute, with her button nose and bouncy red pageboy cut. Her deep brown eyes fringed by thick light lashes gave her away every time. She couldn't hide her true feelings if she tried.

"Look at you! What's happened?" she said.

"What do you mean?"

"Have you looked at yourself? You look like the cat that swallowed the canary."

I feigned complete ignorance.

" 'Fess up, Jane. Who is he?" Sandy said, turning to face me with her hands on her hips.

"I have no idea what you're talking about," I said with a sheepish grin.

"It's fine if you don't want to talk about it, but I thought—"

"Okay, okay," I said. Sandy's shoulders dropped as I interrupted her. "I went to a party with Scott and—"

"You don't look like that because of Scott. There's no way! You said he wasn't even—" Sandy threw up her arms.

"It wasn't Scott," I cut in to explain, "someone I met there."

Sandy and I had been roommates in college. Assigned the same dorm room in our freshman year, by our third year we moved off campus to share an apartment. She knew me pretty well, probably better than anyone. I felt happy for her and Jason. She seemed to be doing well but in all honesty, I felt a little jealous. Okay, maybe what I felt wasn't so much jealousy as envy. I wanted happiness for her but wanted it for myself as well.

"Well, what's his name? What does he look like? Is he nice? What does he do? When do we get to meet him? Why didn't you come right out and tell me? Or call me on the phone?!" she said in rapid succession.

"Take a breath, will you?" I tried to figure out how much I wanted to tell her. Usually I would tell her everything, including the size of his cock, but I wasn't sure how I felt about Luke. I didn't want to hear, "Run toward the light, Carol Ann" or essentially "What the hell were you thinking?"

What the hell was I thinking?

So there I stood, trying to figure out what to say. I'd never lied to Sandy before. I didn't want to start now. I broke into a confession. "Scott brought me to a sex party."

"You went to a sex party?! You met a guy at a sex par—"

"Let me finish for god's sake."

"Okay, okay," Sandy said, lowering her arms to her hips.

"When I figured out what kind of party it was, I went upstairs looking for a phone. I couldn't get a signal on my cell. He was … Luke was up there. He loaned me money to take a cab home."

"Why didn't you call me? I would have picked you up. A sex party?" Sandy said, shrugging her shoulders and shaking her head.

"I didn't want to bother you. I did think of calling you." I wasn't sure what else to say.

"Well, do you think this will turn into something? You met him at a sex party?" She giggled. "Do you know where he lives? I feel like you're leaving something out." Sandy stopped walking and turned back to face me.

"I'm not sure how I feel about him," I said.

"So …. What does he look like and what does he do?"

"I'm not sure how to describe him, other than he is very fit." I laughed. "He says he sells his photographs and paintings abroad but I don't have any idea if that's a hobby or how he pays the bills."

"It's still early," she said.

"I think you're more enthusiastic about this than I am," I said.

"Well, you know, I want the best for you and you have been single for a while now."

"I get it, you want to double date," I said, laughing.

"That would be great, wouldn't it? Jason gets along with everyone."

"That is true. You found a great man; I hope I get as lucky."

"Well, if you don't know for sure, then I'm right, it's still early," she said, patting me on the back.

Was it? I wasn't so sure. I really didn't know what to feel. Luke confused me and I didn't want anyone to point out what I already suspected.

"So have you set a date for us or what?" I said playfully.

"Yes, Jane and Luke will be married on June seventh of next year in her beautiful ivory dress. Is he a black tux sort of man?" Sandy asked.

"Oh, bite your tongue, girl. I'm still not sure I'm the marrying kind."

"Oh, but of course you are. You're exactly the marrying kind. You just haven't found the right one yet."

For the rest of the walk I filled her in on the mundane details I felt comfortable sharing. I told her about Luke waiting for me outside of work with flowers, but not that he had dropped them. I told her about the wonderful sex and the lilies the next day but not about the note. *Who was I kidding?*

Sandy and I shared a dinner and I went home feeling more confused than ever. Sitting on the edge of my bed, I replayed what had happened the night before with Luke. His presence had filled the place. I could see him standing in the kitchen, putting our food in the old style refrigerator with the freezer on the bottom. I pictured him looking in the white cabinets, trying to locate a glass to bring me water. Maybe next time we'd watch movies together on the beige leather love seat I'd never shared with another. I envisioned him in every room. I went to bed early to avoid dealing with my thoughts and emotions.

That night I had another disturbing dream. I walked down the same ally as in my previous dream but this time it rained heavily and the water spun quickly into the grates in the middle of the road. The water dragged and pulled against me like the outgoing tide at the beach. I struggled to get past the grate and fell sliding backward.

I woke up sweating and gasping. I took a couple of deep breaths to calm myself down.

As the water from the shower rained down on my face, I couldn't help but wonder what my psyche was trying to tell me. Was I drowning? I've always thought that falling in love was like drowning, but in a good way. This felt different. This felt like I couldn't swim to the surface if I wanted to. I decided there and then that I would end things when Luke got back.

When I got out of the shower and dried off, I found that my feelings were under control again. I didn't know when I would hear from Luke but I was convinced I knew how to end it.

When I stepped foot in my office I immediately got into the flow of work. I moved the flowers to the table on the side of the room so they no longer sat straight in front of me. Parker called early in the day to see if I wanted to go to a movie after my run.

"Yes," I practically yelled into the phone. My strategy of keeping busy fell into place. I actually considered returning my mother's plethora of calls and finally making plans with her, but I wasn't yet that desperate to occupy my time.

At the pub downstairs I got a salad to go. When I returned to my desk an unaddressed envelope waited for me. Placing the salad to the side, I sat down. It had to be from Luke. I knew I'd find his slanted writing staring back at me. I couldn't open it. I didn't open it. Comprehending the extent of my overreaction, I felt sick to my stomach. Throwing away the salad I no longer planned to eat, I noticed that although the garbage had been removed, the pieces of the card I had torn up were still there. *How is that possible?* I knew I had thrown them out on top of an already filled garbage can.

I gulped a huge uptake of air and held it in for a moment. *Stop it, Jane ... get a grip on yourself.* I threw the card in the trash along with the to-go box that held my salad. I grabbed my purse and walked by Brian's office to tell him I planned to call it a day. Women's issues worked in a pinch. He waved me off and said he'd see me tomorrow.

I drove straight home, changed into running gear and ran to the beach. Running could clear my head better, faster than anything else. Picking up my pace I turned into the paid parking lot for beachgoers. I jumped over the parking stumps and headed out onto the boardwalk. On any normal day I'd run between three to five miles. Occasionally I'd push myself and run up to seven or eight miles. I usually did that on a Saturday so I could take it easy for the rest of the weekend. Today I ran until I could no longer run. Having boiled out my thoughts with my sweat, I stopped, exhausted. I'm not sure

how far I'd gone but I had to walk the whole way back from the beach.

When I arrived back at the apartment I took off my shoes and socks and dove into the pool to rinse off the heat. On the stairs leading to my apartment I left a dripping trail of water. At the half-bathroom by the front door I pulled off the decorative hand towel and began drying myself off.

I checked my messages. *Maybe my mother's finally given up on me.* Again I considered calling her but opted instead for the oblivion of a nap. I stripped off my wet clothes, hung them on the rack that had contained the towel, dried my hair as well as I could and plodded to the bedroom.

I awoke to a pounding on the door. I instantly popped up out of bed, catching a glimpse of myself in the mirror. *Could it be Luke?* I grabbed the wet towel off the corner of the footboard, wrapped it around my nakedness and ran toward the door. As I got closer, I could hear Parker yelling my name.

"I'm coming, I'm coming!" I yelled back.

"I thought we were going out," Parker said as she entered the apartment, eyeing my lack of attire.

Long and sleek, Parker always reminded me of a gazelle. She towered over me even when she stood back as she did then. She looked formal and regal in her royal blue business attire, a source of intimidation for her coworkers, no doubt. She wore her hair cropped close to her head and curly, which took nothing away from her striking, high cheek-boned face.

"Sorry, I left work early and went for a long run and then apparently took a longer nap than I intended," I said as I walked back to the bedroom. "Do I have time for a quick shower?" I asked over my shoulder.

"Very quick," Parker said and followed me into the full bathroom. "You left work early? That's odd for you. What's up?"

Again I was at a loss as to what to say, what to share, but then that seemed ridiculous. After all, I'd be ending it as soon as I saw him again.

"Well?" she said, getting impatient.

"I met this guy, but I've decided I want to end it. It's a long story ... well, actually a short story, but not really worth mentioning other than I've decided that it won't go any further."

"Then why did you leave work early?" Parker asked.

"I felt like I needed to get in a good run and try to gain some perspective. What's new with you?" I said, hoping to change the subject.

"They are considering me for a promotion at work so I'm excited about that."

"That's great. I'll keep my fingers crossed for you. Any chance we can eat first and catch the later film? I skipped lunch."

"I'll go check the times," she said.

∞

I enjoyed the evening with Parker but kept finding my thoughts drifting back to Luke. I can't recall the details of the movie, because it didn't hold my attention. I obsessively repeated in my mind what I would say to Luke the next time I saw him, how I would explain that we had to be done. I tossed and turned all night, hardly sleeping at all, anxious to resolve the conflict within myself.

CHAPTER FOUR

When I awoke Thursday morning to the sound of the alarm, I happily didn't recall any of my dreams. That feeling of relief only lasted a moment. Somehow, I knew that Luke would be back that day and I'd have to end things. Part of me wanted to ditch work altogether, but he knew where I lived and that scared me. I couldn't hide. I truly believed he'd find me anywhere if he wanted to. Forcing myself out of bed, I reluctantly shuffled to the bathroom and readied myself for work.

By the time I arrived, the tension in my body felt like a vise clamped around my chest, making it difficult to breathe. I walked into my office, worried that Luke would be sitting there waiting, but to my utter relief my chair sat empty. When I looked down at my desk I almost screamed. The envelope I'd thrown away sat squarely centered on my blotter. I looked over the side and released the breath I'd been holding; at least the garbage can was completely empty.

I sat down and picked up the envelope. I was contemplating it, thumbing the edges, when a knock on my door startled me.

"Feeling better today?" Brian asked, leaning into the office while holding the door jamb.

"Right as rain," I said, forcing a smile.

Right as rain? What the hell does that mean?

"All right, then," he said, departing with a little wave.

Okay Jane, open or don't ... shit or get off the pot ... there's a fork in the road, pick a direction ... Fish or cut bait ... do something for god's sake!

I grabbed the letter opener out of the cup on the desk and sliced the top of the envelope. As I pulled out the card, I started laughing. The card turned out to be an invitation to Allison's wedding. In a rush of thoughts, I remembered her mentioning it over lunch on Monday. I had to ask, what was I doing to myself? Maybe he wasn't the crazy one. *Maybe it is me,* I thought. Maybe he should be worried about me. Taking a deep breath, I grabbed a Kleenex to blot my eyes. The release of tension I experienced should've been a sign, but I ignored it. Was I losing it? I put the invitation into my bag, cleared my mind, and got on with the day.

I kept expecting the phone to ring and to hear Luke on the other end or to receive a delivery from him, but by the end of the day I realized he wasn't going to contact me. My emotions were so raw by day's end that when Allison came by and lightly knocked on the door, I jumped like a spooked cat.

"Are you okay?" she asked with a look of concern.

"Oh ... yeah, just a lot on my mind. I'm a bit distracted," I said, holding my head in my hands for a moment.

"Are you ready to leave? I thought we could walk down together," she said, swinging her bag over her shoulder and flipping her shimmering blond hair.

"Okay ... sure," I said, dropping the application I had started to review. I took hold of my bag and we headed toward the elevators. "Love the invitation," I said to Allison.

"Will you be able to make it?"

"You can count on it," I said.

As soon as the elevator door opened, I knew that Luke waited for me across the street. I briefly thought of saying I'd left something upstairs but I knew I'd have to face him eventually. He didn't seem like the type to take a hint. So, I kept pace with Allison and told her I planned to meet up with someone. Looking across the street, certain I'd see him there, my heart dropped. No Luke. I was clearly losing it. The utter disappointment took me by surprise. I realized in that

moment that my reactions had betrayed me. I'd prepared myself to say goodbye, to turn off the emotions that swirled inside of me, but when I saw that he hadn't shown, I had to accept how I really felt.

I turned around to head to my car, and there he stood, leaning against the wall of my office building. Relief set in and I smiled, my resolution to end the relationship forgotten.

"Good to see you, too," he said, opening his arms to enfold me in his embrace.

With his scent already embedded in my consciousness, his hug felt like home. I felt so comforted that all thoughts of him being malevolent were gone.

"I have something to show you," he said, releasing me from his hold.

"Okay," I said, "where to?"

"We can walk from here," he said, taking my hand in his.

"I don't want to have to chase you down the street—" I started to say.

"No rush today," he broke in. "We have all the time in the world. By the way, you need to take tomorrow off from work."

"I don't take time off from work," I said. "I've been sent home because I was too ill, but I can't remember a time I called in sick. Especially not twice in one week. I left early yesterday, so there's no way. I can't take a full day off tomorrow as well."

Even as I said it, I knew what he'd say and I knew what I'd do. I would call in sick and I'd spend all day and night with him if he wanted.

We strolled at a leisurely pace two blocks up from my work, made a left down an alley, and then headed back up the next street over to a red brick building, where we paused and gawked.

"What are you looking at?" I asked as I followed his gaze to the second floor.

"Our new place," he said without taking his eyes from the building.

"What?!" I said, stepping away from him.

Living with him ... I don't think so.

"Let me show you around before you decide," he said, taking my hand, "Plus, you owe me something." He pulled me through the door that led to the stairwell.

How can I describe that moment? It felt surreal, dreamlike, and, although I was scared out of my wits, at the same time I was excited as never before. My stomach twisted and turned because I knew what I owed him. I just wasn't sure how he'd make me pay. I decided on the way to the apartment door to keep an open mind. He said I could end it anytime, I reassured myself. I held my breath as he steered me through the door.

I don't know what I expected, but an empty apartment wasn't on the list. Hardwood floors as far as the eye could see. Standing inside the door, I could gaze straight through the living room into the bedroom, where the sun cascaded through the back window, illuminating the dust particles floating in the air. To the left stood the kitchen and to my immediate right I could see through a door into what looked like a half-bath. Further into the apartment and to the right another door stood closed. I assumed it was a second bedroom.

Luke told me to wait by the door. He walked around the inside wall to the kitchen, and I heard the refrigerator door open and close, then cabinet doors. I leaned forward and saw a small ottoman in a space that should have held a dinner table. Luke came back to the front door holding two glasses of white wine.

"I thought you might like a glass of wine after your workday. We have a lot to discuss and I'd like you to be relaxed," he said, pausing to take a sip from his glass. "We won't be staying here much longer but I did want to take care

of the matter of payment." He took the wine glass from my hand and said, "Please undress."

I just stood, looking at him. Adrenaline coursed through my body. I felt hot all over as it spread from my rapidly beating heart to my limbs. A rush of wetness began in my folds as I kept my eyes fixed on him. He held out his hand in a familiar manner. I knew my choices. I took off my jacket and laid it in his outstretched palm. Self-consciously unbuttoning my blouse, I felt a chill run up my back as I slipped it off my shoulders and draped it over his arm. Next I stepped out of my shoes, postponing exposing more of myself right away. When I looked up, the intensity in his eyes made my heart skip a beat. How do I explain that in that moment two contrary thoughts—no, more like sensations—rushed through me?

Jane, run!

And ….

Jane, you've made it home, finally.

My arousal won out over my practical nature that day and the idea of running away seemed crazy. Quickly ridding myself of the rest of my clothing, I handed it over to Luke.

"Jane," he said, "this is how I expect you to be in this apartment at all times. You should step through the front door and disrobe immediately. If we are going out you will dress at the last minute in the bathroom to the right. The same goes for work in the mornings, although I'm not sure how much longer you'll be going to work. We can talk about that later."

Luke slowly and deliberately walked to the bathroom and placed my clothes on top of the toilet seat cover. I still hadn't moved. I felt another shiver convulse my body. He clasped my hand and directed me to the ottoman.

"You need this, Jane," he said, looking at the ottoman and then back at me. "You need to know what I expect so you can avoid this happening again. My guess is that you not only need this, but want it too."

He put pressure on my shoulder to make me drop to my knees; then he gently pushed my body forward so that I was draped over the ottoman. When he knelt down he placed something under my knees to cushion them and began tying my thighs to the back legs of the ottoman. He moved around in front of me and tied my wrists to the stunted front legs. The ottoman didn't shift or move.

If I had thought my adrenaline maxed out before, I now knew the difference. I was so turned on at that point that I panted. My heart beat loudly in my ears, a cacophony of fear and thrill. I had never been so confused.

I couldn't see Luke but I could hear his footsteps, and then, what sounded like a key unlocking a door. I tried to look behind me to identify his intensions but as much as I strained I couldn't twist far enough around. He found whatever he'd been searching for quickly and returned to my side.

"Try to relax, Jane," he whispered to me as he trailed his hand slowly down my back, over my butt, and down my thighs. Shivers cascaded down my body, leaving me even more aroused. The fear I'd felt earlier was gone. It seemed strange, given the circumstances, but I thought he was right: I needed this.

Close to my ear, he whispered, "I will start now. There will be ten. The next time I need to discipline you, expect twenty." I heard a whoosh through the air and a resounding smack as the belt made contact with my butt.

It stung. It burned, too, but then it felt almost pleasant. I thought that I might actually enjoy the experience until the second one fell ….

"God help me," I screamed and began squirming against the ropes.

"Jane," he said sternly. "You must stay still or I will start over. Are you going to settle down?" He spoke the last words louder, for emphasis.

Then I was really concerned. Where had the fear been when I needed it, before he'd tied me down?

Clearly I'm crazy.

"Are you ready Jane? Eight more to go if you keep still."

I stayed perfectly still and felt the wind pass by me, thwack!

"Oh my god, oh my god, oh my god, oh, oh, oh," I yelled as the pain burned through me. By this time, I realized that the stinging from the second crack of the strap still lingered, amplified by the third strike.

"I can see we are going to get a lot of the rules out of the way right now. You can moan, yell and scream all you want, but no words. So that was three, seven to go."

I wanted to yell, "Just get it over with, I can't take the waiting," but he must have sensed my frustration. He took a leisurely stroll around me to the other side before whipping me again.

"Ooof, oh, fuuuu—" I screamed, uttering a string of curse words in my head.

Then the lashes came at a steady pace. Having them closer together didn't help matters. I screamed and yelled, but somehow managed to stay still. I felt the belt crisscross my backside. The sting and pain from each hit remained as he applied more stripes. By the time he finished, a layer of sweat covered me. I felt as I did after a long run, with the addition of a burning, uncomfortable ass. I was exhausted and angry. Really, I flamed livid. I just lay there—not that I could have moved—trying to catch my breath and figure out what to do next. I expected him to untie me but instead he lightly touched my buttocks. And, even though my head was mired in confusion, my traitor of a body responded to his touch. He spread my folds and there found a copious amount of wetness. How could my body betray me that way? I was angry, helpless and excited all at the same time. As an experience, this was totally new.

He trailed one hand all along my body while the other explored my labia. He pulled on my nether lips, increasing my desire and wetness, causing me to arch my back. I could feel my anticipation growing, my heart pounding, my breathing quickening, and the moisture trailing down my thighs. By simply spreading my lips apart, he had brought me close to orgasm. A lust to be taken surged through me as his hands fondled my buttocks and then moved below, caressing my hips, running a lone finger through my wetness before stopping. I craved more and wondered why he left me unattended, but then I could hear him removing his pants. Soon he had sidled up behind me, causing my hips to move backward against my restraints.

Though my body betrayed me again, this time I didn't care. I only wanted him inside me, filling me. I gritted my teeth and heard a primal animal groan tear through me. Having brought me to a frenzy, he finally inserted his large erection, inspiring guttural sounds I hadn't known I was capable of. It didn't hurt the way I thought it would to have him pounding against my reddened, beaten ass. In fact, as I became even more aroused, he elicited groans from the depths of my being. He reached under me and concentrated once again on my clit. I began thrashing about as much as the ropes would allow, groaning and moaning in pleasure.

"I knew you would enjoy this," he whispered into my ear, his face pressed against my cheek. "I have so many plans to bring you to higher and higher realms of passion. All you have to do is trust me, give your body to me, and follow my lead." He pushed his body tightly against mine with unmistakable force and strength, letting me know in no uncertain terms that he was the master and I was there to serve him. I lay there, completely at his mercy.

Luke clearly meant to take over my body and make my body, his. My body-his? I wanted to resist, but the sheer pleasure of that moment made all my earlier doubts

disappear. I climaxed with such force I thought I would break through the ropes that bound me. As my body shook from my release, he continued to slam into me from behind with abandon, his balls slapping against my aroused clit in steady rhythm. I could hear my vagina sucking on his cock, along with his loud gasps of breath, as he drove in and out. Feeling him enlarge against my walls, I knew his release would fill me with more than just pleasure. A moment later he pounded more furiously as the lion's roar began to rumble in his chest and he shot his hot load into me, filling me until his cum flowed past my lips and down my sensitive thighs.

Fighting tears, I took a deep breath and sighed out slowly as he lowered his body to cover mine. His heart beat rapidly against my back.

We lay like that for a few minutes until he pushed himself up, slowly stroking my back and buttocks as he withdrew. He began untying each of the ropes that kept me secured to the ottoman. Helping me up onto my shaky legs, he turned me around into his embrace. At that moment I began to cry uncontrollably. The tears poured down my face, onto his shirt, and down my chest. The sobs wracked my body with such force that Luke had to physically hold me up. When they finally subsided, I looked up at him.

He kissed each of my eyelids, tasting my tears.

"We have much to talk about but I imagine you're hungry as well. Off to the bathroom," he said, shoving me on my way.

I understood him to mean that I should dress again. Shutting the door behind me, I gathered my clothes and placed them on the edge of the sink. I sat on the toilet, trying to collect myself. I expected my movements to cause me discomfort as I dressed, but there seemed to be no residual pain from the ordeal. Once dressed, I felt brave enough to look at myself in the mirror, but scared of what my eyes, looking back at me, would tell. To my surprise, they looked

soft and happy. I smiled at myself and left the bathroom.

Luke handed me my wine glass and I finished what remained. "Thanks," I said.

He took my glass, placed it on the floor by the door, pulled me into his arms and held me. I felt at peace—a sensation that in retrospect completely baffles me.

He led me onto the street and we walked to a restaurant on the opposite side. "I've heard this place is good," he said, leading me to a booth in the back. "Would you like me to choose?" he asked.

I shook my head and said, "No, thank you." I smiled, gazing into his eyes, and then I glanced at the menu placed in front of me. I felt encouraged that he'd asked about ordering for me that time. Perhaps I still had some say when it came to moving in with him.

After we placed our orders, Luke started laying out the plan.

"I am looking for a strong, independent woman. You'll make all decisions with regard to your life but one. When it comes to your body, everything pertaining to your pleasure and mine is entirely up to me. You'll have no say-so. You will essentially be giving your body over to me for my use."

I raised my hand but pulled it down quickly, feeling ridiculous. "What if I don't want you to do something you want me to do?"

"You always have the option of leaving. We will come up with a safe word or phrase that you can say when you want out."

" 'Out,' as in the relationship is over?" I said.

"Yes, exactly," he said, leaning back farther in his seat. "When you decide to give me your body it will be on my terms, not yours. I promise you that I will never do anything to hurt you permanently. The only exception would be a tattoo or piercing ... and those heal."

"So let me get this straight .... For us to have a

relationship it has to be on your terms? You aren't willing to consider anything else?"

"There aren't any other terms for you and me, Jane. You need this. You've needed this for a long time. We have finally found each other and we will have a great life together. This is how it has to be."

"I was barely able to make it through today," I said, indignantly.

"Please, Jane," he said, laughing. "Were you hurt so badly I wasn't able to fuck you from behind? I'm pretty sure you enjoyed yourself. You can take much more than that … and will. I have a question for you: have you ever cum as hard as you did tonight?" he said with a knowing smirk. "Well, tell me, have you?"

"No, but—"

"But nothing. This is just the beginning, Jane," he said. "Let's just finish dinner and you can go back to your place and think about it. If you decide to stay with me, you will show up at our apartment at nine a.m. sharp tomorrow morning. We will review the rules on the way back to your car."

"Rules?" I said, but really, I expected this.

"Yes, rules. Shall we do it now?"

"Let's get it over with," I said, shifting in my seat.

"Number One. Your body is mine. You will no longer have control over your own pleasure. I will use your body as I see fit for your pleasure and mine. Number Two. Follow my directions totally and completely and without question. You must follow them to the letter, nothing more, nothing less. Number Three. Always have your legs open for me. Number Four. When you are receiving discipline I expect you to be completely still. Number Five. No words during a discipline session unless you are asked a direct question. My favorite response is 'Yes, please.' The exception to this rule is speaking the safe word.

"You should know in advance that if you use the safe word, I will put up a wall between us."

"A wall?"

"You will be in charge of your destiny at all times. Use the safe word and we will be done."

"I don't understand. What are you talking about?"

"My emotions. I've learned over the years to have very good control over them. If you choose to leave, I will turn them off."

"You can just turn your feelings off? I can't do that," I said, shaking my head and getting more scared. "So you're saying that if we don't work out, you won't be hurt at all 'cause you'll just turn off the damn faucet? Great—"

"I didn't say I wouldn't be hurt. Let's just say we cope with our emotions differently. Shall we continue?"

"I guess."

"Six. You will be punished for questioning an order. If you don't understand, that's fine, but if you are trying to talk me out of it then you will be punished. This refers back to rule Two—follow my directions totally and completely and without question.

Number Seven—my personal favorite—you will be naked in our apartment always as I showed you earlier. Clothes off by the front door."

"Is that all of them?"

"Yes."

I didn't know what to say. Stunned, I just sat there looking out the window at the blur of the building next to us.

⌘

After dinner, Luke walked me back to my car. He held me tight in his arms and kissed me goodbye. "You have a lot to think about," he said, opening the car door for me.

"Yes I do," I said, looking into his eyes. My heart quickened and I had to look away.

"See you tomorrow," he said, a laugh rumbling in his chest.

I couldn't help but smile back at him. He turned and I watched him move away into the light that cascaded from the streetlamp then disappear into the darkness. I started the car and headed home.

I breathed a sigh of relief as I pulled into the parking spot in front of my building, but as soon as I made my way upstairs, the walls seemed to close in on me. I didn't want to spend the rest of my life alone. Maybe this was my last chance. I needed to talk, to share my experience with someone, anyone, but my mind was blank. I had already told Parker that I would end this craziness, and I had kept so much of the truth from Sandy. I didn't know how to talk this through with another person. I tried to imagine calling my mother and saying, 'Hi, Mom. Met a guy who wants control over my body and, well, I just might be considering it.' *Yeah that would fly really well.* But … I needed to speak to *someone*.

I picked up the phone and dialed my mother's number. My gut wrenched as I heard the first ring. I couldn't even hang up. My last hope was that the answering machine would pick up and save me from my own disgrace.

"Jane, is that you?" she said. The dreaded tone was already in her voice.

Ah crap, I thought. "Yes it's me, Mom." I already regretted my impulse.

"Well it's about time. I thought we were going for the all-time record, but I think you are shy a couple of days. Want to call back then?" I could hear her lighting a cigarette and inhaling.

"Have you ever considered, Mother, that I postpone calling you so I won't have to deal with crap like this?"

"Are you cursing at me Jane? I will hang up this phone!" she yelled.

"Look, can we start over? I called to find out how you are and talk to you about something."

"I'm fine, as always. I would like it much better if my only child would come and see me now and again."

"Did you check out the programs at the local center like you said you—?"

"What do you want to talk about, Jane?" she said, cutting me off.

"Well, I met a man and he wants us to move in together."

"Jane, that's truly wonderful. I had thought you were destined to be alone. I mean, all these years and no prospects."

"Mother you make it sound like I've never been in a relationship before."

"Have you ever lived with a boyfriend or preferably a husband? The answer is no. So forgive me if I'm a little surprised. Is he attractive? Does he make good money? Will you finally get your dream wedding?"

"How about, does he love me and make me happy? What about those questions?"

"Well, does he?"

"Oh well, yes, but ..." I hesitated. I figured saying he scares me but also fucks me superbly wouldn't go over well. I knew there was no way she could handle it.

"But ...."

"But I'm not sure if I'm ready to give up my apartment."

"Well, dear, then don't. Move in with him and keep your place. Then if things don't work out you can move back. It's good in this day and age for a woman to have her own security. Men can't always be the answer."

"Thanks for the words of encouragement. I'm going to go, Mom. I'll call you soon."

"I hope so, Jane, but I won't stay up at night waiting."

Just another useless knocking-my-head-against-the-wall conversation with my mother. I had missed my run and felt it. And so, emotionally exhausted, I went straight to bed.

Tomorrow ... I would decide tomorrow.

CHAPTER FIVE

I arrived on time at the new apartment to discover movers hauling boxes and furniture and a man attaching something to the ceiling. I didn't know what to do and just stood in the doorway until Luke noticed me at around 9:10 a.m.

"You're late," he said as strutted past me and then looked back.

"No, I'm not late, it's just I didn't know what—

He turned to face me. "Rule Number Seven. You will be naked in our apartment always. What part of 'always' don't you understand? Good to see you, by the way," he said, smiling. He came forward with a kiss and a hug. "Now strip and just know you owe me again. This time twenty but we can worry about that later."

"Where do I go when I've undressed," I said, shaking.

"I'll come to you. Just wait for me." He smiled warmly and touched my cheek as he moved away.

My emotions were all mixed up. Pleasure at his smile, deathly fear, and abject embarrassment flowed through me. I felt mortified to have to undress with all the traffic in the apartment—all male. The two burly men passed me again, carrying in a large armoire, and a carpenter anchored another eyebolt into the ceiling. One was already in place, centered over the door to the main bedroom. I had some ideas what they might be used for, and it scared me, but I felt my nipples get hard just the same. I knew if I delayed too much longer I would be in even more trouble. The movers playing follow-

the-leader left the apartment, allowing me to undress with a smaller audience. I hurriedly removed my clothes because being watched as I took off my clothes seemed worse than being seen naked. As soon as I looked up again, the guy on the ladder stared at me in shock. Clearly, Luke had not warned them.

My body blushed and modesty prompted me to hold my clothes in front of me. I didn't know if I should put my clothing in the bathroom or drop it on the floor. I needed Luke to tell me what to do and at the time, it should've dawned on me that I had already begun the transition into becoming Luke's property. I stood waiting as minutes passed until I heard loud laughter coming through the second bedroom door.

Someone else was laughing along with Luke.

Oh fuck, I thought. Energy surged through my body. I felt turned on but it made no sense to me. I had never done anything like this before and yet my body responded as if it was being given what it always wanted. I knew that I would be naked in front of one of Luke's friends with nowhere to hide. I couldn't make myself any smaller as they approached.

"Thank you so much for coming over," Luke said as he walked a handsome sixty-something-year-old man over to where I stood. He obviously took great care of his body and had an air of strength about him, but his presence also had an edge that reminded me of gangsters I'd seen in movies. I shivered when his gaze met mine.

"Nice one, is she here for pictures? She's awfully eager," he said, smiling down on me. "A real looker, I say. Should turn out well. Would love to see them when they're done."

They shook hands and Luke followed him out of the apartment. The movers were back and to say the men gawked would be an understatement. The guy walking backward stumbled as he carried his half of the couch into the living room. The guy carrying the other half moved quickly forward

so he wouldn't lose his end. The front door opened wider and Luke strolled back in. *Save me,* I entreated him silently, but that was like asking a hungry shark to pass on eating you for dinner. Save me, he would not.

"Who was that man, and what pictures?" I asked.

"I'll take those," he said. He took the pile of clothes that had offered me some protection. "We can talk about that later. Come sit on the couch and watch the movers work." He took hold of my upper arm, although my arms remained glued protectively around my breasts. He led me to the couch and made me lay down. Then he unlocked my arms and placed them at my sides.

"Jane," he said, putting pressure on my right thigh.

"Oh, right," I said, and parted my legs.

This brought a smile to his face. "Relax," he said, "I'm going to make us some breakfast."

Relax ... relax? How am I supposed to relax?

I felt breathless as I had the day before. I tried to watch the man screwing in the eyebolts along the ceiling but he kept looking back with a lecherous creepy smile that made my skin crawl. The movers distracted me when they brought in a coffee table and positioned it near where I lay. Then a second distraction took over. The smell of eggs and toast inspired me to take a deep breath, settling me down a bit.

How do I explain the war that raged inside of me? I stopped and looked around, understanding that this was all wrong, not how it was supposed to be. At the same time, it felt so right. Although I was beyond exposed—and I know it doesn't make sense—I also felt cared for, held, encompassed by love and passion. This push and pull inside of me had me on the verge of tears and yet so turned on, so energized, so alive. I could see that I had lived my life in a fog until then. The walking dead I had been, shuffling through the drone of my existence. Here Luke offered me a path I would have never, ever considered and yet, it had my soul reaching out

for his acceptance and approval. I had difficulty separating my rationalizations from reality. How could he fall in love with me so quickly?

"Here," he said, handing me a plate filled with an omelet, toast and sliced tomato while making room for himself at the other end of the couch.

Taking the plate, I sat up, making sure to keep my legs slightly open. "Thank you for making me breakfast. This is a first."

"You're welcome," he said taking a bite of his eggs. He ate quickly. "You look really good on my couch by the way. A first?"

I blushed at his compliment. "Someone making me breakfast. I could get used to this."

"Ahhh." He shook his head as if he found what I said impossible to believe. "There are many wonderful things for you to get used to," he said and reached over to gently touch my cheek. Then his face and demeanor shifted away from me both physically and emotionally. "I have work to do. Still need to set up my equipment and do some unpacking." He rose to his feet.

"Oh," I said, sighing and feeling my shoulders fall. "Do you have to?"

"Yes, unfortunately, I have to. I need to be up and running by Monday and there's still much to do."

"Can I at least keep you company?" I asked. I felt like a dog left home alone too long.

"That's not a bad idea, but I was going to send you home to pack up. How about this? You go home, get what you will need for the next few days. Come back later and you can sit next to me while I work. We still have much to discuss about your apartment, your work, and most importantly, payment due." Grinning, he leaned in to kiss me on the forehead. "Finish up and you can get dressed."

ॐ

When I made it back to my place, I felt so excited that I ran up the stairs and rushed through the door. Then I came to a sudden halt. I looked around, noticing how different the apartment seemed, how different I felt. The place was like an old shirt that no longer fit me. Even the smell seemed foreign. In such a short time Luke's masculine smell had come to represent home for me. I decided to go for a run before packing what I needed. My life was changing so rapidly that only my running was keeping me sane. Usually I would run to feel more like my old self, but on that day my new being held more power over me. *Today,* I thought, *I run as Jane of Luke and Jane.* I hurriedly changed my clothes, grabbed my iPod off the counter, and bounded out the door.

It felt good to be on the beach, running with my hard alternative songs blasting their driving beat into my headphones. I settled into a rhythm, following the beat of the music while the sunshine engulfed me in warmth that made my entire body relax into a steady pace as the waves of the Atlantic Ocean pounded the shore. Negotiating the crowded boardwalk during the second mile, I felt a decision finally overtake me: I wanted what Luke offered me. I couldn't be sure what he would ask of me, but the unknown stimulated me to such a high degree that even as I ran down the beach I experienced intense stimulation. When I thought of Luke my nipples became erect and tingles shot through my body. My panting breaths reminded me of his body on top of mine. I fantasized what he would do to me. He had found the trigger to my sexuality and I was prepared to explore it with abandon.

I slowed down, jogging lightly along as I changed the music to my cool-down playlist. After a time I slowed to a walk. "Sideways" by Santana and Citizen Cope began to blare through my headphones, perfectly illustrating my state of mind. That is how I felt … sideways. I looked back in

amazement on how much my life had shifted in such a short time. My relationship with Luke had left me completely off balance, and I had always avoided quick changes in my life. None of that deterred me then. I had dived into the deep end of a pool without my mask or snorkel, not at all concerned about breathing underwater.

 લ

I finished stretching, took a quick shower, and made a mad dash to pack. I pulled two suit sets out of the closet. I grabbed a handful of underwear, a couple of bras, a pair of jeans, three sets of workout clothes, shorts, and a few t-shirts. I chuckled to myself at the thought of taking clothing that I wasn't allowed to wear in the apartment. There would be less laundry for sure. Quickly I scooped up all my bathroom stuff and shoved it into my overnight cosmetic bag.

What am I forgetting? Oh shit, my pills, I thought, reaching into the medicine cabinet for my birth control pills. Grabbing my favorite black shoes and sneakers, I headed out the door.

After throwing all my stuff into the trunk, I climbed into the car. It dawned on me in that moment that I needed to call my friends and mother and give them my new number. I also needed to get the number from Luke.

"Crap," I said and slammed the steering wheel.

I ran back upstairs to grab the charger for my cellphone and realized I should clean out the refrigerator. For once in my life I rejoiced to see it mostly empty. I threw away everything except the condiments into a garbage bag. With bag in hand, I locked the door behind me and used the far set of stairs to flounce to the dumpster. I tossed the bag in and made a quick beeline back to my car.

Okay, I thought. *We're doing this.* I maneuvered the rearview mirror to look at myself, just wanting to make sure that it was still me looking back.

ର

Excitement rushed through me at the thought of seeing Luke again. I grabbed all the stuff from the car, including my purse, and hurtled up the stairs. I knocked on the apartment door. Luke answered it and laughed out loud.

"Why are you knocking?" he said.

"Oh," I said, laughing easily with him. "I don't know." I shrugged. "I don't know what I was thinking." I pulled my stuff through the door.

"Let me take those things," he said, taking the bags from my hands.

I stood by the door, leaning back against the wall and realizing that I would never walk into our apartment like a normal person. I felt relieved to find the place empty for my disrobing, but something told me not to get too used to it.

As I removed my clothes I looked across to the living room. Along with the brown couch I had laid on earlier sat a matching chair. The far right corner of the room held a bulbous oriental urn that I assumed had come from Japan. He had told me to wait by the door, so I leaned over as far as I could to see more of the apartment. I could see half of a round table and chairs made of wood. As Luke returned, I pulled upright.

"I put your bags in the bedroom; you can unpack later. I hung the suits in the closet, but I insist on taking you shopping and getting you something that will better do you justice." He reached for my clothes and clasped my hand in his. "You took longer than I expected and your hair's wet. Did you go for a run?"

"Yes," I said, "I needed it."

"A treadmill is being delivered so on the days you can't make it to the beach you can still run."

"Wow, that was very thoughtful," I said with a smile.

"Or resourceful … either way," he said.

" 'Resourceful,' what does that mean?" The comment

dashed the idea that he had acted out of consideration.

"Never mind, it's wonderful to have you back," he said, leading me into the bedroom.

I recognized the furniture from the party house. It filled the bedroom, not leaving much space to move.

"We have a lot to talk about, but we'll do that later. I have a conference call in about thirty minutes. You have a choice. We can get your punishment out of the way now or you can lie down on the bed and I will show you the true meaning of indulgence. I've wanted to taste you ever since that first night."

Call me a procrastinator, but I chose the second option. If I thought anything would be straight up with this man, I was mistaken.

"Lay on your back in the middle of the bed. Spread your arms and legs to the four corners," he said, reaching down for something I couldn't see alongside the bed.

When he straightened up I saw a black leather strap that appeared to have Velcro on it. He pulled the two touching parts away from each other, and I concluded that he held a cuff that attached under the bed. He placed my left wrist inside and securely fastened it. Prowling around me with the grace of a lion, he made quick work of his task, securing both my ankles and my right wrist.

Just the act of securing me to the bed started a groundswell of stimulation to move through my body. My movements limited, I felt terribly vulnerable, but the anticipation flared, becoming more intense. I began to rationalize that the restraints provided pleasure and all of that was okay as long as I wanted it. My breathing quickened as I felt more and more out of control. I looked at Luke in a panic.

"Jane, take a couple of deep breaths and relax. You will really enjoy this."

I obeyed him, taking a couple of long deep inhalations and pursing my lips as I slowly blew out the air. It did seem to

slow down the panting, but did nothing to contain my craving. He began running his hands softly down the underside of my right arm. It tickled me slightly, and as he continued to treat my whole body to his soft touch, the panting came back worse than before and the moistness between my legs began to trickle onto the bed. I gasped and moaned, trying to move my body away from the touch that had me crying out.

I felt tortured with desire. I was raw passion with no inhibitions. Anger and passion had found a new outlet. He teased his way down my lower body, gently gliding over my sweet spot but never actually touching it.

"Please," I begged. "Please, I need you to make me cum." I groaned. I'd never been so brazen. "Pleeeeasse," I repeated, pulling against my restraints.

"Not to worry, my love, your need will be fully satisfied," he said as he walked to the end of the bed. Reaching down, he released the strap on my left leg, allowing for more movement. He repeated the processes on the other side, lifting my legs so that my calves touched the back of my thighs, completely exposing my saturated flower. Then he slid his forearms under my butt and lifted me up. I felt his deft tongue flick across my now rock hard clit. I never knew I could feel this sensual.

Until that moment, I had never been a huge fan of cunnilingus. Every man always said the same thing, that the guys before "me" just didn't know what they were doing. Well let's just say that until that day, I had not known a single man who had any idea about pleasuring a woman with his tongue. Luke, on the other hand, had it mastered. He seemed to be able to gauge my growing intensity and withdraw just before I was about to trip the light fantastic. With each subsequent climb a cavalcade of new sensations pushed me to new heights. He had a way of using his tongue softly, with just the right amount of pressure.

He slowly, cleverly brought me to a plane of pleasure I had not yet experienced. I screamed, "OOOOhhhhh, let me cum, let me cum, please oh god, please, let me cum!" And, praise god, he did. My orgasm hit with such force, with such intensity that my throat grew raw from my screams of ecstasy. I lay there satisfied and blissful, melting into the bed.

Slowly my bliss began to fade, but I still basked in deep satisfaction. As my awareness came back to the room, I heard a clicking sound around me. I opened my eyes and Luke whispered, "I've never seen you look more beautiful. I will need to taste your sweet juices often. Close your eyes again for me, love."

He changed my position a couple of times, tilting my head to one side and moving my legs into a different position. He adjusted my arms.

I saw a flash.

At the time I made no connection between the pictures Luke was taking and the man who asked about viewing pictures of me. Floating on a cloud of love and fulfillment, I could think of nothing else. I lay submerged in a warm pool of lust and contentment. I could barely open my eyes. I really didn't care what was taking place as the flashes continued to illuminate my eyelids.

"Luke," I said, opening my eyes once again, "please make love to me."

"As much as I would like to, love, I have to go back to work," he said as he shuffled through the frames on the camera.

Looking away, I sighed deeply. I knew that if circumstances were different and Luke wanted to make love, I would have no choice in the matter. I felt a little edgy and sad but pushed the emotions away.

"It shouldn't take long," he said, removing the leather cuffs from my arms. "Are your wrists okay? You were pulling pretty hard against them." He massaged my wrists as he

revealed them from under the leather. "Take a nap, sweet one; you will need all of your strength for later." He kissed me on my forehead and left the bedroom.

I pulled a long pillow between my legs and curled up on my side. I drifted along in a haze of pleasure and light sleep until the rude interruption of a dream.

In the dream I stood naked with my wrists bound together. A rope attached to a D ring on the cuff lifted my arms above my head to the eyebolt centered in front of the doorway to the bedroom. Hoisted by those restraints, I had to stand on my toes. I wiggled around, trying to balance my weight on my feet but found it difficult. The strain on my shoulders as well as my calves had me shaking. Just then, I realized a party was taking place around me. People milled about drinking and partaking of hors d'oeuvres. They passed by, taking the time to look me up and down, but they didn't speak a word to me, as though looking at a slab of beef for purchase. Panic and dread gripped me as I hung there naked and helpless. A few people actually touched me, and a man who resembled the older man I'd met previously with Luke spun me around, causing me to lose my footing altogether. I helplessly fought to regain balance, to little effect. Then Luke came by, slapped me hard on the butt and announced that the bidding was about to begin.

"Aaahhhhhhhhh," I screamed as I sat straight up in bed startled by the dream.

"What is it?" Luke asked as he rushed into room. He cradled me in his arms as I struggled to catch my breath. I retold the dream in gasps, slowly regaining my composure.

"This is really amazing," he said, holding me tightly and smiling.

Though confused, I felt safe and cared for in his arms.

"You see, after the call was over, I started thinking about your punishment. How you described yourself tied up is exactly what I had planned. Not the party part, at least not

yet," he said, chuckling.

I slugged his shoulder with the side of my fist and said, "Hey!"

"I was only joking, trying to get you into a better mood. It was funny, admit it."

"I will admit no such thing," I said but couldn't suppress a smile.

"Well, at least admit that we're already very connected and that you are picking up my thoughts."

"Hmmmm. Maybe," I said.

"Are you sassing me?" he said, touching his nose to mine.

"Moi? Sassing you?" I laughed. "Maybe," I said with a big smile.

"Well I like it but it won't keep me from giving you what you deserve."

"And what is that?"

"Your penalty for being a bad girl."

"I thought you liked bad girls."

"Let's just say I like disciplining bad girls," he said, leaning me forward and smacking my butt.

"Hey," I said, but giggled.

"So it seems we need a different discipline for tonight, but expect that at least the tying up part of your dream will happen at some point. This changes our plans a bit. Okay, so let's get dressed and get something to eat. We can talk later."

CHAPTER SIX

After we arrived at the restaurant and were seated, Luke said, "So, how attached are you to your job?"

"As it pays for my bills and home and car, very attached."

"Money is of no issue. I have plenty of it."

"Luke, that's *your* money. What happens if this doesn't work out? I need my job."

"Well let's just say I'm much more optimistic about us than you are. This will work out. Think about it, okay? There are far better ways for us to spend our time. I travel a lot and if you're working, we will be apart more than I'd like."

"Do you go to Japan? Is that how you speak Japanese?"

"You're a curious girl. How about this? I will answer up to five questions. You can ask anything. It will cost you an extra lash for each question."

"An extra lash? You mean adding more to my discipline?"

"Yes."

"How is that fair?"

"Fair or not, it's your choice."

"Fine, five. Let's see. I have to make them good .... Okay, where were your born and raised?"

"That's two questions."

"Wait, that's not fair. I take it back—"

"Seattle, Washington. Raised in Tacoma. Three more, and you better make them good," he said with a smirk.

"That's just bullshit. You're incorrigible! That was one question."

"Two: where was I born *and* where was I raised. They're two separate questions."

"But I didn't mean it that way."

"Again, choose wisely."

"I'm going to the bathroom," I said in a huff and marched off.

What an asshole. I mean, really! How can he be so nice and compassionate one minute and then piss me off so badly the next? Okay, get a grip on yourself, Jane. What do you really want to know? Cause this is your chance to find some things out.

While using the toilet I decided on my questions. I needed to be careful about the wording. I knew what I wanted and needed to know.

"Took you awhile in there. Pondering the weight of the world?"

"Something like that." I sat back down in my seat. "Here goes nothing."

"Wait," Luke said.

"What?"

"We need a safe word or phrase for later tonight and for the duration of the relationship. Have anything in mind?"

"In reference to what? To your discipline or correction, as you call it?"

"Yes, in reference to your 'Get Out of Jail Free Card' for when you are done. When you're ready to end your disciplining because you don't think you can handle it or just because you are done with me. You say the words ... and out you go. So do you have any ideas?"

"Yes as a matter of fact. 'Get lost, creep,' " I said and leaned back causally in my chair.

Luke laughed so hard that I thought he might fall off his seat. "Oh, that is good. Never heard that one used before."

"So how many others have there been?" I asked.

"That's question Number Three," he said, chuckling.

"Oh come on, Luke, that's not what I wanted to ask you. This is so pissing me off."

Still laughing, he said, "Okay, babe. I'll give you this one. There have been others, of course, as I am a man with needs. I didn't get to forty-five behaving like a monk. But I will also say that I have been waiting a long time for 'the one' and I have finally found her."

"You think I could be 'the one'?" This made my head spin. "What do you know of me, sense of me, that would make you think that?"

"It just fits. You are asking for an intellectual response to something intuitive. It's the way we feel together."

"Does your body react the way mine does? How could we be in love so fast?"

"Jane, how about asking fewer questions and just listening to what your body is telling you? I will say one thing and then back to your questions: this doesn't need to make sense. It just has to feel right, and it does. We are meant to be together. That's why you feel alive and brand new and no longer alone. I'm right about that, am I not?"

"Yes but ...." I couldn't think of a *but*. It made no sense and really, when did love ever make sense? There was much I wanted to ask and yet I only had three lousy questions left.

"So, Jane, what do you want to know?" he said, smiling with his eyes as well as his mouth.

His eyes did something to me. They infused me with such intensity that it was as if they held my soul. Even without his touching me, I felt cradled in his arms.

"Ahem," I said, clearing the haze of my desire. "Okay, here's an easy one and probably a waste of a question but my curiosity is driving me nuts. Do you own the house where we first met?"

"Yes."

"Just yes? Care to elaborate, like are you the one throwing the parties?"

"You may use that as your next question. I answered the third one already."

"No, then. I don't want to waste my remaining questions on that."

"Next?"

"What exactly do you do in your business, which I have deduced is photographing nudes?"

"Pick another, my love. I will show you when we get home."

"Home?" I said. "Are we really living together? How is it that my life has changed so much in less than a week?"

"Jane, are you okay?" he asked, leaning forward to take my hand into his.

"I'm scared," I said. "This seems so fast and so intense."

"When it's right, it just is, babe," he said. "And we are right. Want to save the questions for later?"

"Oh, no. It's just that I need to come up with another one. Ummm, okay, how did you get your scar?"

"The wrong place at the wrong time, with a sword. Let's leave it at that."

"That's not an answer, Luke. Tell me the whole story."

"I'm not a fan of talking about the past, and that's all I'm willing to say."

"But—"

"I'll allow you another question," he said. He gazed out the front window of the restaurant as if trying to will the past away.

"Could I save one for the future?"

"Sure, I'm feeling generous," he said with a grin.

"Okay, then here's my last question: do I need to be worried for my life?"

"That was good." Luke laughed, bringing his attention back to me.

"I'm completely serious, and how the hell did you know where I work?" I asked.

"Oh ... really, that's what you want to ask?" He looked astonished. "Of course I would never really hurt you. Plus you have the 'Get Lost Creep' card. It's in your power to end this whenever you want. Just because our relationship is alternative doesn't mean I'm dangerous. Not in the life and death sense anyway. I love you, Jane, and given time, you will come to trust that and me. "

I felt better. His words rang true on a deep level, allowing me to let my guard down.

"Okay, but I've got to tell you it's all a bit overwhelming at this point," I said. I paused and then continued, "Can I ask you something about us? It's nothing about you personally. I really like the idea of saving a question for later. Plus, twenty-four 'thwacks' are way more than enough." I wondered if he would use the belt again for my discipline.

"Oh, I forgot to mention it costs two licks to save a question for the future." Laughter spilled out of him before he had finished speaking.

"I don't think so," I said with a stubborn pout, and laughed all the same.

"So ask," Luke said. "Question is stored for later use."

"Have you felt this way before? Have you thought you met 'the one' before?"

"I have been in love before and have thought I'd met my match, the one I would spend my life with; so yes. In some ways this is the same but in other ways it's different and new."

"How is it different? I don't want to be like everyone else to you, or why even do it?"

"There is a deeper connection between us, as is evident in the dream you just had. There's an energy between us that is undeniable and stronger than any I've felt. I'm not just talking about chemistry, although that is very strong too."

"So you do feel it. That's good to know."

"Of course I do. Let's ask for the check and get out of here. You need to be disciplined, because you have been a

very naughty girl, and I'm all done answering questions for a while. I want to show you my studio and make plans for the rest of our lives together. A tall order for one evening, but let's see what we can accomplish."

"Oh, before I forget," I said, "I need to get the phone number for our place to give to my mother and friends."

"I like the sound of that, 'our place.' Very much, in fact. You have a cellphone, right?"

"Well, yes—"

"I will be using the land line for business calls and would prefer if you use your cell."

I hesitated. "Okay, I guess."

❧

The ritual of undressing at the door had already started to become a routine. As I had never entered farther than just inside the door with clothes on, it had been ingrained in me from the start.

"A choice, yet again," he said, taking my clothes and leading me deeper into our apartment.

"Hmmm." I had a hunch what might be coming.

"Discipline, which will of course end in your orgasms, or learning more about my business. In what order would you like to indulge?"

At that moment the idea of avoiding the inevitable seemed worse than getting it over with. Plus, my body continued to betray me because even the thought of what he might do to me had my nipples almost painfully erect and my nether lips wet. "Let's get it out of the way," I said. I remember being scared and so turned on, my body sizzling with anticipation.

"So how many do we have … twenty-six, by my count."

"NO! That's twenty-four, not twenty-six," I said, getting pissed off again.

"Okay, okay," he laughed. "Twenty-four. You sure are

sexy when you're mad." He smiled and pulled me into his embrace for several long seconds. Then he took me by my shoulders and moved me back away from him, looking me up and down like a bird of prey. "It's a shame I won't be stringing you up to the eyebolt tonight," he said wistfully. "Another day."

Taking me by the hand, he led me over to the couch. He tugged the coffee table and then the couch away from the wall and pulled out what I had thought to be decorative artwork. He attached it to a base that had been hidden underneath the couch. I stood there in amazement, wondering what other little surprises he had in store for me.

He set the wood structure at an angle. "Turn around," he said.

He had me step up on the wooden platform and face it. Grabbing a leather strap out of the end table, he attached my right arm to the high right corner, securing me to the slat of wood. He did the same to my other arm on the left side. It was awkward to be facing the platform; I had to pick a side to place my face. Once he lifted my right leg, I realized that my arms would be bearing a large portion of my weight. He attached my right leg to the far right corner, leaving me balancing on my left leg. My body trembled as he strapped my other leg to the corner.

Oh, this does not seem so bad, I thought at first. The angle seemed to help distribute my weight so I didn't feel the strain.

"I have a different hoippu for you to experience tonight," he said.

"Huh?" I mumbled into the wood planks.

He struck me with something I couldn't see.

"Ouch!" I screamed.

"Not another word, young lady, or I'm adding more to your punishment. So let's start, shall we?"

I shook my head frantically no as best I could from my position. He ignored me. I didn't know what he had chosen to

use but now knew the whip to be an unfriendly sort. I tried to look over my shoulder to see it, but that proved impossible.

"You want to see it, do you?" he asked.

Call me a slow learner, but I said, "Yes."

"Ohhhhhh!" I screamed as he wacked me much harder. I wanted to yell "motherfucker" but thought it best to shut up.

He leaned close to the side of my face and whispered through his hot breath, "You sure must like this, Jane, because you keep adding on, and we haven't even begun. Here is your new friend," he said as he put an odd-looking whip in front of my face. It had a long wooden handle. My new friend, a paddle, not a whip, scared me. It reminded me of a very large paint stirrer—a foot and a half long and stained dark brown. The hole in the bottom of the handle I assumed made for easy hanging.

My body, my new enemy of betrayal, responded. I could feel moisture collecting and falling on the wooden base below me. I felt so exposed, so stretched, so embarrassed by my arousal.

"Okay, Jane, we're starting now. No talking, but feel free to scream to your heart's content."

That scared me. Really scared me. "Wait, wait," I said. "I don't think I can stand twenty-two more hits from that."

"Twenty-four and you have two choices," he said. He roughly grabbed my hair in his fist, jerked my head back and talked right into my face. "Say the words and get the fuck out of my life or shut the fuck up. Which is it going to be?"

Frightened beyond belief, but also crazy in love, I knew I didn't want it to be over.

"I choose to shut the fuck up," I said, tears streaming from my eyes.

"Good," Luke said.

The discipline turned into a beating. Luke slowed down his approach, making me lose all sense of time. I learned a valuable lesson that night. Do not piss off the one giving the

punishment just before he starts. His hits on my thighs hurt far worse than on my buttocks. Certainty stole over me that it would take days before I would be able to sit down again. It was a relief to realize I wouldn't have to call in sick again, given that tomorrow was Saturday. I knew I couldn't come up with a good enough story to explain having to stand the entire day.

Before half the punishment was complete, I wailed like a new-born baby. But by the time there were only five strikes left, a calmness overtook me. The pain subsided and a raw, burning desire to be fucked hard took its place. I alternated between breathing out and holding my breath in anticipation of the next strokes. The pain reached a plateau and I could feel the rush of endorphins anesthetizing my entire body. It felt exhilarating. I wanted to yell out, "Oh god, Oh my god, Oh god," but instead what came out sounded like ugh, oopf, ahhhh, ugh.

"Now that wasn't so bad," he said. He breathed heavily as he leaned his body against mine.

"Owww," I said.

He moved his body over to the side and I thought he would lower me from the X position that held me. Instead he did something no man had ever done. He began spreading my ass checks with one hand and moving his finger tauntingly around my asshole. He teased it gently and I was shocked to find that his slow circling of my bud became more and more enjoyable. He wet another finger with my juices that now coated my inner thighs, brought it back to my anus, and worked it in and around my hole.

"Oh … yes oh … yes oh … my god," I kept groaning.

"Yes, babe…the things I plan to do with you, to you. This is only the beginning," he said as he deftly took command of my body. "You will find you want more and more, and I promise, you have found the man who will give it to you."

He stepped off the platform and I heard him quickly undress. When his body pressed against mine again, he began running his very hard cock up against my wet fleshy labia. I responded by widening my thighs against the restraints. He glided his cock in and out a few times before pulling out completely, eliciting my plea not to stop. Luke ignored me as he tried to force his engorged cock into my ass, but it didn't work.

"Relax," he said.

"Relax?" I asked. "I think we are dealing with physics here. Large cock, small hole."

He laughed at me. "Relax," he said as he once again used his little finger and thumb to spread my butt cheeks, while his index finger circled my anus. Again my body responded with pleasure at that strange touch as he worked one finger back into my ass before adding a second. My tight bud resisted his two fingers, but within seconds the pain subsided, and as it loosened, I craved more. Then his fingers withdrew and he sidled up behind me.

I knew what was next.

"Luke, Luke … wait," I pleaded.

"Jane, here we go."

As he began to work his cock inside of me, I thought it might tear me in half. He took wetness from my sopping vagina and spread it around my hole and on the remainder of his exposed cock. As soon as he had fully penetrated me, he began massaging my clit. I felt so spread and exposed.

The orgasm ripped through my body, a rollercoaster of convulsions that lasted until the next orgasm struck. In time for my third explosion, he spent his load inside of me, and I could feel the warmth invade my bowels.

When he pulled out of me, I hung, expended, on the wooden structure. I could no longer feel my wrists and my thighs shook uncontrollably. First he unstrapped my legs, which were tight and sore as he eased me toward the ground.

When he released my left arm, intense pain soared through my shoulder. He helped me lower my arm and rubbed my shoulder and upper arm as I cried out in distress. He released my right arm and I had to use my other hand to get it to lower.

"You might want to stretch your body out," he said.

I bent over and immediately comprehended the fallout from the thrashing I had just taken.

"Ah, I don't think so. Bed ... I need to go to bed."

He helped me under the covers and kissed me on the forehead. I lay on my side, which was all my body would tolerate. He left the room and came back seconds later with my toothbrush and a glass of water. I quickly brushed my teeth, took a mouthful of water and spit it back into the same cup.

"Tomorrow is soon enough for you to see my workshop. I will come to bed in a while." He sat on the side of the bed and tucked my hair behind my ear. "I love you, Jane. I knew you were the right one." He rolled me onto my stomach, pulled the covers down and applied a cream that smelt of coconut and lavender to my buttocks and thighs. The coolness soothed the burning sensations on my backside.

As I dosed off I wondered what else he had in store for me and if I would survive it.

CHAPTER SEVEN

$\mathbf{M}$y first thought upon waking that morning did not concern my paddling. I was recalling his words.

He loved me.

As I moved to sit up, my body ached with reminders of every last stripe he had inflicted, leaving me with second thoughts about what his love might ultimately mean for me. Wincing, I carefully sat on the edge of the bed. I had begun to stand when Luke entered the bedroom, carrying a tray of bagels and all the fixings. At that very moment I realized my body craved nourishment and since exercising was out of the question, I packed my belly full.

"Yum," I said between bites.

"You were brilliant last night."

"What an odd thing to say. I was simply tied up. There's not much brilliance in that."

"Quite the contrary. You easily found your way to what I refer to as subspace. You crossed over from pain into ecstasy. I could have gone on far longer and you would have continued to enjoy the experience."

"Enjoy? I beg to differ, Luke. *Tolerate* is more like it."

"Say what you will but I saw your face, I heard your moans. How are you feeling, by the way? You seem to be moving okay."

"Tight and sore. Very sore," I said, gently touching my buttocks.

"I'll take care of that as soon as we're finished with breakfast. You'll be fine by tomorrow."

After we had eaten our fill, he moved the tray off the bed. "Lie on your stomach," he said.

I did as I was told. He scooped out a large amount of the coconut cream and worked it into my shoulders and upper arms. "Ahhhhh," I said. "That feels so good. I can't believe how stiff I am from being tied up."

"Oh, wait until I tie your arms behind your back. That's another tricky position. You don't really feel it while it's happening but when you are untied …."

"Mmmmmm." I barely heard what he said. I remember that massage clearly, as it marked the first of many. He worked his way down my back and across my butt. His gentle touch took extra care on my thighs where it hurt the most. His massage not only soothed my body but also aroused my libido.

"Oh, Luke," I said, breathing deeply and heavily.

Shedding his robe, he climbed onto the bed with me. He gingerly turned me onto my back and pulled me up into a sitting position.

"Let me know if this hurts too much, Jane," he said. His voice sounded different, causing me to wonder why his tone seemed so loving right then.

He pulled me onto his lap and we faced each other in the middle of the bed. He looked straight into my eyes and deep into my soul. Everything about him tugged at my heart, reassuring me it was safe to come out, safe to be me. In his eyes I saw such love and devotion that tears began to slide down my cheeks. Those tears spoke of the extent of my desires being fulfilled by Luke.

He lifted me onto his rigid penis and moved my hips up and down on his lap. We made eye contact continuously as we kissed and moved our bodies as one. He rocked me back and forth in a rhythm that brought me closer and closer to orgasm. I buried my hands in his hair, and we increased the speed of our journey into a deeper realm of connection.

Never had I held eye contact this way. Never had I wanted to feel so close to another person. I wanted to crawl deep inside of him and have him wrap himself around me. The tears continued to stream down my face. He took my heart in his hands, looked through me clear to my soul and said, "This is who we are." I knew exactly what he meant. How could it be that the man who frightened me so could also be the man who made me feel safer than ever before?

When I reached orgasm, I cried out from a deep place as I grappled with his body, wrapping my arms around him and pulling him in close as he joined me with his deafening roar. The love I felt shining from his eyes and heart captured me and freed me at the same time. I started crying in earnest then. He held and rocked me as I released the tears accumulated in years of loneliness, now replaced with joy.

℘

I had to come out to my friends. As soon as he walked out the front door, I called both Sandy and Parker and postponed my confession by leaving messages on their phones. I meant to sit and write about all I felt but instead decided to explore the apartment. I found the second bedroom door locked. I couldn't understand why Luke kept it inaccessible if he'd planned to show it to me in the first place. Then I went to the kitchen and explored every cabinet without discovering anything but utensils, dishes, and the usual supplies.

A cautious search through the drawers in the bedroom yielded only clothing. He had a minimalist fashion sense. All of his clothes were similar to what I had seen him in already. The biggest surprise I found was in the bedroom closet, where a garment bag hung, filled with three very expensive-looking suits. I couldn't even imagine Luke in a suit. The idea of it made me laugh.

By the time he got back, I had searched the bathroom

drawers as well. I had learned nothing, for all my snooping.

"Ready to see my office?" he said.

"Sure," I said, jumping off the couch and sauntering over to him.

He unlocked the door with a copper key and said, "Woolah … mystery solved, my lady, if you please." He bowed, bidding me to enter.

Mystery solved? For some reason Luke saying that made my heart skip. Did he somehow know I had been looking around the apartment? I quickly lost my apprehension upon seeing so many of his possessions to explore. The second bedroom was far larger than the one we occupied. A counter extended all the way along the right wall, with cabinets above and below. A sink occupying the center of the counter reminded me of the chemistry class in high school.

"What's in all these cabinets?" I asked.

"Photography stuff … paper, chemicals, old film, old pictures, cameras and other supplies. I don't do much self developing anymore but occasionally I want a particular effect. Digital is an amazing platform but it still has some limitations."

I wanted to search every cabinet but instead turned my attention to the rest of the room. Several different types of lights stood in the farthest corner. On the left wall hung a white tarp that covered a portion of the floor as well. A simple metal chair sat in the middle. Against the wall next to the door leaned a handful of wooden structures that reminded me of the one behind the couch. Farther down the wall I saw what looked like a Pommel Horse from gymnastics, only lower to the ground and not as wide. Above it on the wall hung a framed photograph. The angle from where I stood made it difficult to see the person in the photo.

Against the far wall were two five-drawer filing cabinets. "What are in those?" I asked, pointing to them.

"Files, of course," he said with a smirk.

"Hmmm." I continued my scan of the room.

To the left of the cabinets he had hung a rack with all types of whips and paddles. I moved in to get a closer look and removed a nicely carved wooden device that reminded me of a spatula. It had holes throughout the paddle.

"Don't think I want to experience this one," I said, laughing.

"Then don't disappoint me," he said. He narrowed his eyes and I knew he meant it.

"No problem," I said, but my gut twisted. I hung the spatula thing back in its place.

On a spindle attached to the wall dangled a set of whips that looked similar but had varying lengths and widths of leather strips. I saw the paddle he had used on me the night before and several other varieties of wooden paddles. I noticed a riding crop and wondered how that might feel.

"Why do you store the paddles and whips in here?"

"I like to keep them under lock and key, and they are quickly accessible when I need to use them in my pictures."

"I'm confused," I said. "What does one have to do with the other?"

"You will see soon enough."

"Explain, please." I started to get annoyed, which felt much better than scared. "Those pictures you took of me after sex …." I put my hands on my hips and pivoted to face him. "The guy who was here that first day …. Do you plan to use me for your pictures? And other girls? Will you be having sex with other girls? Disciplining them?"

He didn't respond right away. We just stood there looking at each other. I realized in that moment if I ever did leave him it would be anger that propelled me out the door, not fear.

I walked over to the picture on the wall and said, "Who is this?" I could now see that it held a photo of a voluptuous woman dressed in a leather corset bound by rope. The angle

of the model as well as the lighting made the scene erotic. The woman looked suspended in the throes of an orgasm.

"Boy Jane, you have a pretty good jealousy thing going on there. A little bit of jealousy is sexy but too much is a real turn-off."

"You haven't answered my question—"

"I would have thought that the love and connection we just shared would be answer enough, but apparently not for you. I will whip other women for photographs. A great many of the photographs that I sell include bondage and whip marks—like the one you are looking at—but I will not sleep with anyone but you."

"And orgasms?"

"Jane, you are trying my patience."

"I believe you told me you would answer all my questions regarding your work, did you not?"

"Well, get them out of the way, because after today I'm done with them."

"Fine …. Will you be photographing any previous girlfriends?"

"No, and I will not be providing orgasms either. If they happen to cum just from the whip alone, that I cannot help. Are we done here?"

He was bristling. My interrogation had clearly annoyed him but I didn't understand why. How could I be finished? I could've gone on asking questions all day. Instead, I said, "One more question. Where is the Japanese connection?"

"I sell my work in Japan."

"Do you sell it anywhere else? Do you sell your paintings, too? Is that how you've learned to speak the language?"

"You said 'one more question,' and I'm all questioned out. Please get out so I can get some work done. Go out with your friends if you want. I'll be busy for a while."

He practically shoved me out the door and locked it behind me.

I felt dismissed, like a child leaving the principal's office after being punished for bad behavior. His mood shifts left me dizzy.

The idea of seeing my friends had seemed appealing after our wonderful lovemaking, but now it felt dreadful. I grabbed clothes from the bedroom, dressed in the bathroom, and quickly left the apartment.

CR

I went back to my place, climbed into bed, and lay there feeling sorry for myself. I was realizing more and more how isolated I had let myself become. I had no one to talk to. No one who would understand what I had chosen to do. Hell, I didn't even understand it. Why did Luke's control over my body turn me on so much? Why did I feel so safe and yet so afraid? His moods bothered me the most. He could be so cold, so mean, even, but then hold me with such care and gentleness. I sat up in bed and rummaged through my bag for my cellphone.

"Parker?" I said, holding the phone out and pressing the speaker button.

"Hi, Jane, I was just about to call you back," she said. "Do you have time for dinner tonight?"

"Dinner would be great. Where would you like to meet?" I sat up in the bed.

"There's a new Thai place on Hollywood Boulevard. Know where it is?"

"Sure. I'm pretty hungry right now so can we do it a bit early?"

"Five o'clock work?"

"Perfect."

CR

I drove to Try My Thai still uncertain what to tell her. I

just knew I had to speak to someone. I had thought of calling Sandy but she had been so busy with life that I didn't want to bother her.

Parker and I hugged our hellos and took a booth in the mostly empty restaurant. As always she stood impeccably dressed and statuesque.

"I've called you a few times and left messages. I even called you at work yesterday. They said you were out. Twice in one week. What gives?" Parker said.

"I've met someone and it's moving fast."

"The guy that you barely mentioned the other night?"

"Yes, him."

"Well, fill me in, girl. You must have had a change of heart because you said you weren't interested or something to that effect." She moved her chopsticks to the side and placed her napkin on her lap.

"It was more like I was confused. Nothing like this has ever happened and it was just moving so fast. *Is* moving so fast. But—"

"Are you in love with him?"

"Yes," I said, finally acknowledging that fact to myself.

"And does he love you?"

"Yes, he says he does."

"But what? You don't believe him?"

"It's just that at times it feels so right ... so *there*, and at other times I get scared." I shifted in my seat, unable to meet her penetrating stare.

"We've been on our own for a long time, Jane. I think it's perfectly normal to be scared. What's he like? When do I get to meet him?"

"Well, he looks a bit dangerous, but when he smiles his gray eyes light up his face." I looked at her and smiled. "He's really fit, too. I haven't quite figured out what he does to stay in shape but his body is amazing. We're living together. Did I say that yet?"

"What?" Parker said, slapping both hands on the table top. "How long have you known him?"

"A week."

"A *week*? I thought you didn't believe in love at first sight? You fell in love with him in a week? Have you lost your mind?"

"It's all your fault, anyway," I said, pointing at her. "Had you been in town last week, we would've gone to a movie and I would've never met him. I planned from the start to blow him off but he was persistent and—"

"And ...."

"And I guess sometimes these things just happen. I mean, not usually to me, but there are all kinds of stories of people falling madly in love with each other quickly."

"Are you madly in love with him?" She shook her head in amazement.

"*Madly* would be a good word for it," I said under my breath.

"What does that mean? This is so out of character for you. You are the pickiest person I know when it comes to men."

"The word's 'selective'—your word for it, I might add— and that's true. That should make you confident I've made a good choice. Let's order, shall we? I'm starved."

"Promise me I'll get to meet him soon and I'll drop this," Parker said. Her look of concern unnerved me.

"I promise," I said but wasn't sure I meant it. I saw her shoulders relax and I sighed in relief.

ℭℛ

The drive back to Luke's apartment—our apartment— had me brimming with anxiety. I parked by the building and sat in the car stoking my courage. I had just decided to get it over with, when a knock on the window scared the hell out of me. Looking out the passenger side, I saw Luke standing

there. I got out of the car and walked toward him. My stomach was twisted in knots and I felt close to tears.

"Hi, babe," he said. "I was starting to worry about you." He pulled me in and engulfed me in a warm hug.

"I thought you were mad at me," I said. My voice sounded young and scared.

"Something you should know about me: I never stay mad for long. Anyway, you were right that I said I would answer your questions about my work and I was right that you need to let go of the jealousy thing and trust in us. We are an 'us,' you know, and I like 'us' very much. So trust in the safety you feel in my arms and everything will be fine."

I wanted to believe what he told me. I needed to trust the way I felt in his arms. I wanted to know that I was truly *the one* to him and not just one of many. He walked me upstairs into our place. I knew that only time would reveal the truth. Time would be the judge and executioner. I decided to give time a fighting chance.

CHAPTER EIGHT

A week passed and we settled into a routine. He granted me permission to wear my running clothes in the apartment when I used the treadmill. That felt like a minor victory. I would get up early in the morning and run before work. Luke slept in. While I showered, Luke would wake up and make breakfast, including strong coffee I soon came to appreciate. We would eat silently while he read the paper and I devoured my newest novel. Every day I would head off to work with a smile on my face.

Luke filled my every thought. How I managed to get anything done in my haze, I do not know.

Our daily ritual included sex. He consistently found new ways to tie me down and get me off. His imagination seemed limitless. I managed to avoid any more discipline during that first week of cohabitation and almost believed we were in a normal relationship. Almost.

∞

"I'm going to Japan on Monday and will be home on Sunday," Luke said.

"What?" I said. I threw my hands up in the air. "Why didn't you tell me sooner?"

"What would be the point?"

"To help me prepare myself, I guess. How long have you known?"

"I've known since before we met."

"What the hell?"

"Jane ..." His voice was stern.

"I don't understand this. You think it's a normal thing for a boyfriend to tell a girlfriend just two days before he leaves? Why did you keep this from me?" I felt so infuriated and his apparent lack of awareness of my anger left me even more incensed.

"Quit your job and come with me," he said.

"No chance. First, I don't plan on leaving my job, which I've already told you, and second, even if I did, I would give two weeks' notice. So have fun." I sat down on the couch, naked as the day I was born, and crossed my arms over my chest.

"Oh, I will. No doubt about it." He grabbed my thighs roughly to spread them.

I just looked at him and watched him walk away.

We didn't have sex that night for the first time since we had moved in together. I acted angry but felt more scared than anything. How would I manage a week without him? He had become my obsession, my fulfillment, my freedom from the lonely days and boring nights.

By Sunday I had let go of my fear and anger and looked forward to the first entire day Luke would spend with me since we had met.

"Put on your running clothes," he said as he rummaged through his drawers. He dressed in running shorts and a tank top.

"Where are we going?" I asked.

"You shall see," he said, taking my hand and leading me out the door.

We got into his black Honda S2000 two-seater that looked a lot like a Porsche.

"Wow, nice car," I said. He kept it impeccably clean on the inside as well as on the outside.

"I've told you that money is of no consequence. I do hope you'll think about leaving your job while I'm away."

"I'll think about it," I said.

I tried desperately to forget that I would be driving him to the airport before work the next day.

"How do you know where I usually run on the beach?" I said as we pulled into the parking lot.

"Oh, is this the place?" he said.

My stomach churned as he walked over to the area I typically stretched. I couldn't be sure if my stomach responded to the fact that Luke knew exactly where I ran without me telling him or the fact that we might cross paths with Scott. But as soon as we starting running and found that our strides suited each others', I had completely let go of any anxiety.

Somehow running with Luke made me love him even more. It flashed a beacon of commonality that I so desperately needed. After the run, we enjoyed breakfast at Coral Rose Café. He made it so easy to be with him. The world fell away when he looked at me. There were no tables or waitresses, no customers around, only Luke bringing me into his world, his sphere of existence. Nothing else mattered. Life felt wonderful and whole. I stopped and stared a moment at Luke, taking him in. I could see the energy that animated him, as if the energy itself provided a force field that pulsated around him. His sandy brown hair hung across his broad forehead, framing the gray eyes that had conquered me. I breathed a sigh of relief that he had chosen *me*, plain Jane.

Later that night I felt inspired to write. I hadn't been much into using the computer, except at work. Friends had given up emailing me after a while because it would take days, sometimes weeks before I'd respond. I found all the forwards one had to wade through annoying and really hadn't gotten into all the IM-ing everyone else seemed to enjoy. I wasn't technology-challenged, just less interested than most to use my computer apart from work.

On Sunday all of that changed. I felt inspired to describe

our lovemaking experience. I'd had such an amazing orgasm I felt that, if I didn't chronicle it in some real way, I'd forget all the details and it would be as if it never happened. I snuck out of bed and went into the living room. I planned to search for a pad I'd previously seen in the kitchen and select a pen from the cup on the counter; however, Luke had conveniently left his computer out and still logged on. I loaded up Word and began to write:

> After breakfast we spent the rest of that day shopping and later dined out again before returning home. The outfits Luke picked out and bought for me were far more stylish and sexy than any I'd ever owned. He also purchased three pairs of what he referred to as 'practical' shoes. I liked the brown sandals the best.
>
> When we finished unloading the groceries and clothes Luke said, "Let's shower and fuck."
>
> I smiled broadly. We had established a shower routine. As the shower couldn't accommodate both of us, I'd shower first and he'd get in after me.
>
> We dried off, combed through our hair and walked into the bedroom. There we lay naked in bed, gazing at each other and touching. He ran his hands over my body slowly and thoroughly.
>
> "You have sexy legs, very soft and smooth," Luke said.
>
> "And may I say you know exactly how to touch me."
>
> "We were made for each other, Jane. And once you come to fully trust me you will see how well I know your body."
>
> Luke moved me onto my side facing him and we wrapped our legs around each other. Cupping my head in his hand, he lowered his lips to mine. During

a long and passionate kiss, our tongues danced around as we explored each other's mouths. He had a way of breathing in my lower lip and taking it gently between his teeth that caused me to gasp. In the early throes of our lovemaking, he planted kisses down my neck, sucking and biting his way to the hard, protruding nipple that craved his mouth. He did not disappoint. He had a way of drawing in my nipple that combined suckling with intense pressure that made me arch my back and cry out. He pushed my upper shoulder away so he could reach my other breast. Cupping it in his large hand, he brought my deep red nipple up to meet his lowered mouth.

"I love your big nipples, my Janey," he whispered in a husky voice.

"They love you, too," I cooed.

For a time, we lay in each other's embrace and listened to the sound of our blended breathing. Finally he moved my top leg so that it lay over his side, spreading my legs wider, and began to play with my swollen clit. He then guided my hand and I awkwardly resisted the direction, mistaking his intentions. I thought he wanted me to take over stimulating my clitoris but he had other plans. He moved my hand between my buttocks, guided my finger into my ass, and pushed it in as deep as I could manage in that position. I felt self-conscious about touching myself in that way.

He roughly grabbed my hair and pulled my head back. "Jane?" he said. "Baby, insert another finger in your ass for me," he said softly, but I realized the request was a demand. He played with my clit while he sucked and nibbled my neck. He took control of my hand and pushed it in deeper, in and out of my ass. "Another finger," he said. The combined

stimulation of the pressure on my clit and Luke using my own fingers to fuck me made me scream out my pleasure, "Oh god, oh that's good, oh, oh my … Luke!"

His physical strength engulfed me.

"Yes, babe, I know what you need," he said as he tightened his grip. "Remember that while I'm gone."

"Ohhhhh my god!" I screamed, as the forceful contractions took over my body.

After I recovered, he lay back and maneuvered me so that I knelt over his lap. As I rode his cock, he directed my hips downward, rubbing my clit against his pubis on every stroke.

"Tell me when you are ready to cum again," he said, looking directly into my eyes.

"Ummmm," I said. Our eyes locked and I knew I'd never truly connected with another person before Luke. His look held me, opened me.

The wetness between us made it easy to increase the pace.

I muttered primal, guttural sounds as I got closer and closer to orgasm. "Luke, oh Luke, I am so going to cum, LUKE, NOW!"

"Oh yes, babe, cum for …." He roared into me, through me. He pulled me in, held me tightly, only relaxing with each wave that he released into me.

I lay on his chest, my frantic breathing finally beginning to slow down. I never wanted to move from that spot. I couldn't stand the thought of him flying off the next day. I didn't want to have a week to think of all that had happened so quickly. I knew I'd see my friends and probably suffer through a meal with my mother, but all I wanted to do was to stay right there.

I closed the computer, still feeling the energy from writing my journal entry, and returned to bed with Luke. I curled up next to him, keeping my hands to myself with some difficulty. I knew he needed rest.

In the morning I felt less anxious about his departure and looked forward to sharing my writing with him. "Last night," I said, "after we made love, I borrowed your computer and wrote about it. You had left it open, I hope that's okay."

"Did I say it was okay for you to touch my things?" he said, grabbing his computer off the coffee table and moving it to the counter.

He spent several frantic minutes searching through applications before his shoulders relaxed and a sigh came through his parted lips.

"Well, no," I finally replied, "but I didn't think you'd mind. I only opened Word, wrote my story, and then saved it to a folder I labeled 'Jane.' I'm sorry if I upset you."

"You owe me for this. I thought I'd been clear. My things belong to me and require my permission for your use. I don't let anyone use my computer. If you need money to get your own—"

"Well no, I mean, I don't use a computer all that much."

"Do you not have your own laptop?"

"No."

"Get one while I'm gone. I want to be able to email you from Japan. You owe me for this, Jane. Know that. When I come back you will see just how much. I had hoped we'd have a sweet morning goodbye, but I can see that's not happening. I'll call a car to come get me. You'll hear from me in a few days. Here's my email address," he said, handing me a business card. "Email me once you've gotten the new computer. Oh, and Jane? Leave my things alone while I'm gone and do not answer the phone." He took out his cellphone and made a quick call.

"Luke wait," I said when he'd finished with the call.

"Please don't leave like this. It's going to be hard enough without you here. Please don't leave mad at me. Maybe if you read the story you will see—"

"There is a certain amount of respect and common sense I expect from you. I will cool off, but right now, I need to leave for the airport. Have a good week," he said matter-of-factly. He walked over to me, kissed me on the head, and headed out the door.

I just stood there in shock. My throat felt constricted and I desperately needed to talk to someone. I flipped the business card in my hand, over and over again. I knew I had to get ready for work. I placed Luke's card on my end table.

I went through the motions of getting ready. For the first time I didn't need to be naked in the apartment, but it felt strange not to follow the rules. Luke and I never discussed having people over so I couldn't be sure if he'd allow it.

Just how brainwashed am I? I thought. *Allow?*

The thought angered me and motivated me to get going. I left for work determined to buy a laptop and send an email to Luke telling him how I felt.

CHAPTER NINE

I settled into the hectic activity of a typical Monday. When I looked up at the clock again both hands were straight up. I walked by Allison's office and said, "Hey there. How about some lunch?"

"Sounds great," she said, closing her computer and retrieving her purse. Her loose skirt swayed to and fro as she made her way around the desk.

"Do you mind if we go to the place across the street instead of the pub?" I asked, not making direct eye contact.

"All right. Are you okay, Jane? You seem stranger today than usual," Allison said with a laugh. "Seriously though, how are you doing?"

"Relationship problems," I said as I headed for the door. "Feeling confused and a little bit lost. How long have you been with your fiancé?"

"Oh, I didn't know you were seeing anyone …. We've been together two years," Allison said to my back as she followed me to the elevator.

"How long did it take for you to know he was the one for you?" We stepped in as the doors opened.

"Two years," she said with a wry smile. "Relationships aren't easy. You're constantly negotiating each other's needs and wants against your own. Deciding who gets to be right which time."

"That sounds pretty grim, Allison."

"Not really. You can call it anything you want but ultimately it's negotiating a shared life with another person.

Sometimes people get really lucky and find someone that's enough like them so that the negotiations are minimal. Too many times though, it's usually one person who gives in most of the time. Not much of a negotiation."

"What about the old adage, 'opposites attract'?" I asked. We had made our way across the street and down a block.

"My experience is that it makes for great sex but not so great relationships. Way too much negotiating," she said as we were seated. "Is that what you're dealing with? Opposites?"

"No, well, maybe. It's more his moods." I paused and said, "Thank you," to the waitress as she handed me the menu. As I looked it over, I told Alison, "One minute he's so there and warm and affectionate, but then something happens and a massive draft of cold air blows in, heralding the impending ice age."

"I know exactly what you mean. Men have a different way of dealing with their emotions and you just have to figure out a way of not letting their mood affect yours."

"How do you do that?" I said.

"You have to find a place in yourself where you can allow him to act out and it can still be okay. Not saying it's easy, but regardless of who you're involved with, you—and all women—need that skill."

"Really? Do you believe that?" I said, still staring at my menu but not really seeing it.

"Absolutely. I couldn't survive my relationship, let alone my impending marriage, without it."

We placed our orders and waited in silence until Allison said, "Want to tell me what happened with your guy?"

"It's silly, really. I used his computer without asking him. I thought it wouldn't be a big deal, but it was to him." I shrugged my shoulders and looked up at her.

"Did he tell you not to use his things?" she asked with her eyebrow raised.

"Well, not directly, but let's just say it was implicitly implied."

"Well, then, I would apologize and let it go. Don't use his stuff without asking and that problem is solved." She swiped her hands a few times to indicate that we had solved another mystery of the world and placed them in her lap. She looked up at me with a twinkle in her eyes.

I smiled. "Yeah, I get your point. I need to get my own laptop today. Any ideas?"

"Costco maybe?" she said as the waitress placed the steaming stir-fry between our place settings.

"Oh yeah, good idea," I said. "Thanks."

ରେ

When I returned to my office a large box sat atop my desk. The Dell logo gave its contents away. The fact that Luke negotiated getting me a computer just before leaving on a plane left me awed. He'd managed to have it delivered as well. It's good to be the king, as they say. After I moved the box to the extra chair in my office, I set about finishing my paperwork. I found it hard to focus, wondering repeatedly how Luke had turned a suggestion into reality so quickly. His money and influence had proved formidable and I began to enjoy the possibilities.

ରେ

I placed an order for a chicken Caesar salad prior to leaving work and picked it up on the way home. I set up the salad ceremoniously alongside the box, unpacked my new computer, and frenetically dove into both. I was eager to send Luke an email to thank him for the laptop. Would I hear from him right away, or would he make me wait?

In the past loading up a new computer for the first time had proved an arduous process, but when I turned on my new laptop, it loaded immediately. On the screen an electronic Post-it waited. It read:

I thought I would take care of this for you.
I'm sure you'll find the computer adequate.
—Luke

I looked at the business card Luke had given me previously. *Luke Hall.* I stared at his last name. Somehow it felt right.

I opened up the browser and Yahoo automatically loaded for me to sign in. I couldn't come up with a subject line. I typed in "I'm sorry" and erased it. Then "My Reaction" and erased that. Then I wrote "FUCK it!" I finally settled on "This morning …."

To: LukeBandDphotos@controlme.com
From: PlainJane368@yahoo.com
Subject: This morning ….

Luke,

Thank you very much for rescuing me from having to choose the right laptop. It was very thoughtful of you to do that.

I hope you're having a safe flight. I don't know what time you'll be arriving but I wanted you to know that I'm truly sorry that I used your computer without checking with you first. I hope you take the time to read what I wrote anyway.

Please email me the story I wrote on your computer when you get a chance.

Hope you're not still mad.

Love,
Jane

CR

Monday night and all day Tuesday he sent me nothing. I checked my email obsessively. I even checked it whenever I

woke up to pee in the middle of the night. Wednesday I checked it at least twenty-five times, even at work. Those three days crept by very slowly. During that same time the apartment phone rang incessantly. I finally figured out how to turn the ringer off in the living room but I could still hear it through the second bedroom door.

Wednesday night the email finally arrived. I didn't open it right away; I was too filled with apprehension. I just stared at it, as if it would open on its own. I took a deep breath and finally double clicked on the email.

> To: PlainJane368@yahoo.com
> From: LukeBandDphotos@controlme.com
> Subject: Re: This morning ….
>
> Apology accepted. I'm no longer mad and won't be the least bit disappointed after I discipline you. I have been thinking there is something you could do while I'm gone to make it up to me. Let me think about it a little more.
> Expect an email from me tomorrow.
> —Luke

I once again felt dismissed—the way I had after he evicted me from his work room. I figured he didn't expect me to email him back but I just couldn't hold it back anymore.

> To: LukeBandDphotos@controlme.com
> From: PlainJane368@yahoo.com
> Subject: re: re: This morning ….
>
> Luke,
> I find your mood swings incredibly hard to handle and you pissed me off with your immature behavior. You could have made this time apart much easier to bear but instead you made it as hard as

possible. And on top of it all, you made me wait two lousy days for that short meaningless email of yours. No 'I love you' in there ….

Of course I deleted that email and never sent it. It felt good to write it, though. I decided not to write him back and see what he sent tomorrow. Even though I knew he wouldn't write again that day, I still couldn't help checking my email another twenty times before I fell asleep.

◌

The moment I woke up Thursday morning I turned on the computer that I had left beside the bed. Sure enough, I found an email waiting for me.

To: PlainJane368@yahoo.com
From: LukeBandDphotos@controlme.com
Subject: Your task if you should so choose

Jane,
    I thought I would have heard back from you again. Hope you're busy seeing all of your friends and family while I'm gone. I'll want you all to myself when I'm home again. I miss having your body to please and play with. I will DEVOUR you when I get back. Count on it.
    So … some choices for you to make; you can wait until I get home at which time I will use the paddle you called the spatula on you to make my point, or you can give a hand job to the cretin who brought my flowers to your office. What did you tell me his name was …?

Pierce, I thought. He offered no real choice … worse and worst. He had drawn a line in the sand and if I crossed that line I truly would be handing my body over to him. Pierce

was an idiot and the idea that I could touch him in any way seemed impossible. Nevertheless, I knew I couldn't survive the paddle. He hadn't even said how many strikes. Ten and then twenty …. Were we up to thirty?

A wave of anxiety washed over me as the realization that today was Thursday. I had very little time to decide. If I waited until Sunday, my decision would be made by default. I continued to read:

> … Prince or something, as I recall. So, either have Prince's cum in a condom for me on Sunday or have yourself ready for discipline.
>
> Here's a third option, because I'm feeling generous. Go to Pandora's Box on Dania Beach Boulevard and US1 and buy an anal plug called the Tulip. Wear it to work on Friday under one of your new outfits—no underwear. Make sure you bring your laptop. You may close your office door but it must be unlocked. Use the webcam on your computer to record yourself masturbating. If someone comes into your office, do not stop. Your desk should provide ample coverage. I want to see you cum, babe, and make it good. If you choose this option, email me the video so I can watch it here.
>
> Decisions, decisions …. What will you decide?
>
> The trip is going really well and I have many new ideas I would like to try out with you. How would you feel about being my subject? I am hard just thinking about it.
>
> I would love to hear about your week. Write to me.
>
> Loving you,
> —Luke

Door #1, the spatula, was out of the question. I knew I wouldn't be able to survive the paddle with the holes in it. Not being an expert on all things painful, I could still tell that the much thicker wooden paddle would hurt more than the others and in my imagination the holes could only make it easier to swing harder and faster. Behind Door #2, Pierce. Oh god, no way was I going to subject myself to those images for the rest of my life.

Door #3 had to be the answer but what if someone walked into my office? Like my boss? I felt ambiguous, but only for a moment. I had one day to plan it all out. I had to figure out how to use the webcam; I'd never used one before. I decided to run at the beach after work and swing by Pandora's Box on the way back to pick up the Tulip plug.

I had to admit, Door #3 had its appeal. As I dressed for work, my body grew so stimulated by the idea of what I had to do the next day that I fell back onto the bed, lifted my skirt, and took care of myself.

❦

It was great to be at the beach running. It made me feel like my old self again. I pushed myself to run a bit faster than usual and reveled in the power of my strong body. My running had countered Luke's attempts to fatten me up. If I gave in, quit my job, and spent all my time with Luke, I'd no doubt fatten up in no time. The man liked to eat.

Eating, I thought. As I continued down the boardwalk, I fantasized about Luke tying me up and going down on me again. Oblivious to my surroundings, I was shocked when a voice woke me from my dream world.

"Jane?" It was Scott. Running in the other direction, he'd stopped and called out to me.

"Hi," I said. I walked over to him, not really wanting to talk but not wanting to be rude, either.

"I haven't seen you around in a while," he said. He had

his hands on his hips and leaned forward to catch his breath.

"I've been busy," I said. I bent over to stretch my hamstrings.

"Want to come by my place?" he asked. He gave me a onceover, scrunching his eyebrows, and said, "You look different."

"I do?" I said, bringing my stationary jog to a halt.

"Yes, you do. Happy. That's it, you look happy. I don't think I ever seen you happy before."

That made me laugh. "What are you talking about? I'm happy all the time."

"Really, I never got that impression from you. Anyway, it's good to see you."

"Well, it was good to see you, Scott. I have some errands to run after I'm done here. See you around." I didn't wait for a response. I took off running in the opposite direction and headed back to my car to stretch.

That was awkward, I thought. I wondered if everyone could see my unhappiness. I thought I had hidden it so well. I wondered if Luke had cured my sadness. It did seem so.

◌

When I arrived at Pandora's Box, I became incredibly self-conscious. I sat in the car for a few minutes, summoning the nerve to go into the store. I entered with as much nonchalance as I could muster, meandering about. Then I noticed an attractive, long-haired young guy sitting behind the counter.

"Oh," I said, smiling at him.

He smiled back. "Can I help you with anything?"

"Yes, actually … I need to buy …." I hesitated. Blushing, I stepped forward to whisper it to him.

"The store is empty other than us, so you don't have to worry," he said, coming around the counter to stand in front of me. "Besides, you won't get any judgments from me. This

is my store and I'm very fond of many of the toys myself." He picked up a large black vibrator. "I'm assuming you want to buy a toy for yourself?"

"Uh … well … yes," I said, giggling nervously.

He walked closer and I could see that his curly brown hair made it halfway down his back. His hazel eyes looked friendly and the scruffy growth on his chin reminded me of the skateboard guys in my high school, although I guessed him to be in his late twenties.

"Something in particular?" he asked, sweeping his hand around at all the objects on display.

"Do you have the Tulip Butt Plug?" I said, casting my eyes to the ground.

"Yes, and I highly recommend it," he said, walking between the stack of shelves lining the large store.

I followed behind him. "I never realized …." I said, taking in all the toys and vibrators that filled every available spot on the shelves.

I spotted a huge tan dildo that had to be fourteen inches long and wider than my forearm. I picked it up, turned toward the store owner, and said, "This is a joke, right? A gag gift?"

"You'd be surprised," he said, winking at me.

"No way," I said, putting the huge phallus back on the shelf and wrinkling my nose.

"Small or large?" he said as he stopped in front of the display of anal plugs.

"Oh, he didn't say." I shrugged.

"Small then, I would think."

"Right, okay."

"Pink, purple or black,"

I laughed nervously. "Purple, I guess."

"Do you know how to use it?" he asked. He pulled a box off the shelf in front of us and handed it to me.

"Is there a trick to it?" I said, chuckling, trying to hide my embarrassment.

"Lube makes a big difference."

"Oh, lube? Should I get some of that?" I scanned the different shelves for the section that held the lube.

"What do you usually use?" he asked to my back.

"Lube? I don't …. This is all new to me," I said, turning back around to face him.

"Oh, I see. I think I'm getting the picture. I personally prefer a light virgin olive oil or almond oil to anything else, but we have many different kinds of lube, some with fragrance and some without."

"Will it be hard to get in?" I asked, feeling very nervous and very much out of my league.

"It's fairly small, so I wouldn't think so. I do recommend you loosen the area first and lube it well. Also, make sure you clean the plug with soap and warm water before you use it and after. Will you be wearing it for a while?"

"Ah, I think so, yeah."

"Then you should clean yourself out first. I recommend the Fleet disposable for that."

"This has got to be the strangest conversation I've ever had." I laughed and breathed a big sigh. "Thanks for your help. I imagine it could've been a lot worse."

He laughed and extended his hand. "Christian, good to meet you."

"Jane," I said, shaking his hand.

"If you'd like I could help you try it out," he said as he walked back around the counter, making penetrating eye contact.

"Um … Oh … So it's like that here, is it?" I said. I laughed off his interest.

"Let's just say I'm getting the feeling you're my type of woman." He chuckled.

"Well, let's just say my boyfriend isn't much into sharing." I laughed at myself and the irony of what I'd just said. I did realize that putting the hand job of Pierce on the

list of payback implied otherwise but I figured Luke knew it to be an option I'd never take.

"If you were mine I'd feel the same way. Forty-four ninety-nine plus tax." I handed him my card and he bagged my purchase. "This lifestyle can be hard on relationships. If you ever need someone to talk to—"

"Thank you for the offer, Christian, and thank you for all your help." I smiled as I took my card and bag from him.

"The pleasure was mine," he said as I headed for the door.

☙

As soon as I walked into the apartment I put down my purse and bag and hung the hanger with my work suit on the door handle. I stripped naked and went straight to the shower. After drying off, I was anxious to email Luke.

To: LukeBandDphotos@controlme.com
From: PlainJane368@yahoo.com
Subject: My New Toy

Dear Luke,

What are you turning this girl into? Yes, I chose Option #3 as I imagine you knew I would. As soon as I finish writing to you I'll figure out how to use the webcam and open my new toy. I chose purple (as you didn't specify a color) and I chose small (as you didn't specify a size).

I miss you horribly and think about you all the time. I wish you hadn't left on bad terms because that part leaves me sad and lonely. I need to see your face and your eyes to know we're still very much connected.

I haven't seen anyone as of yet. I did make plans for lunch with my mother on Saturday, which I know

I'll regret, but at least I'll have gotten it out of the way for a while. I haven't touched base with Sandy yet and plan to see if Parker wants to go to the movies tomorrow night.

I ran at the beach this evening and crossed paths with Scott. That felt awkward. He did say that he thought I looked happy. I am happy, you know. I don't like you being away, though.

Have a couple of questions about the task at hand. Do I have to wear the plug all day at work? Or just wait until I finish masturbating? What if someone comes in and asks me to go with them? Can I stop then?

Please tell me about Japan and how the trip is going.

Did you read my story? Please send it so I have it on my computer.

Well I guess it's time for me to eat dinner and get ready for tomorrow.

I'm nervous and excited about tomorrow and hope to hear from you soon.

I love you,
—Jane

CHAPTER TEN

I awoke with a start Friday and immediately checked my email. Having received nothing new from Luke, I reread his previous email to make sure I hadn't missed any of his instructions. I found it more difficult to consider going to work without underwear than wearing the butt plug. I managed to use the Fleet on myself—much more difficult than I expected. In order to squeeze the contents of the bottle into me, I had to contort my body, but it took just a few minutes to work. The Tulip provided a much bigger challenge.

I should have taken Christian up on his offer to show me how to do it, I thought, laughing to myself.

At first I put too much oil on the plug, which kept slipping out of my hands. I decided to start over. I washed the Tulip again and made sure to apply the olive oil only to the top part of the plug. Then I lifted my right leg onto the toilet seat and used my fingers to oil my anus and spread my hole open. The butt plug slipped in, hurting slightly as I pushed it over the widest rim. I realized I needed to turn the handle to make it line up correctly. As I washed my hands again, I was newly aware of my body. The Tulip wasn't uncomfortable— just undeniably present. I felt naughty and excited.

I dressed in a form-fitting batik blouse that flared at the sleeves and waist. It buttoned down the front with the first button situated a bit lower than I was used to, leaving me positively abashed. The shirt extended over a flowing purple skirt that skimmed my calves, just above my ankles. Brown sandals completed the outfit. I wore my hair down; Luke

wouldn't want my hair any other way in the video. I'd never dressed in anything but my business suits for work—even on Fridays, when the dress code was more flexible. I knew the outfit in itself would attract attention.

I left for work fifteen minutes early. It felt strange to drive my car while the pressure of sitting pushed the plug deeper into my ass. My nectar started to flow and I hoped it would not show through my skirt. I planned to arrive at my office seen by as few people as possible and make the recording right away. As soon as I walked through the doors of the building, I knew my plan had failed. I rode up the elevator with two executives plus Allison and Pierce. Pierce wouldn't stop staring.

"Nice look," Pierce said. "Are you leaving work early?"

"Ah, no," I said.

"I really like this outfit, Jane, where did you get it?" Allison said as she followed me out onto the marble floor.

We left Pierce standing in the elevator with the two execs as we made a beeline toward my office.

"Oh, Luke took me shopping at the mall and we were in so many different stores ...." I said.

"Well, you look great. It really suits you. I don't think I've ever seen you with your hair down, have I?"

"Probably not. I'm not much for dressing for work. Made an exception today."

"So Luke is his name. Are things better?"

"Oh yes, and thank you for your advice on Monday. I did apologize and don't plan to touch his stuff anymore without asking. You were a big help."

"Good. How about lunch today?"

"I'm going to have to pass. I have a lot to get done and will probably eat at my desk. How about lunch on Monday?"

"Sounds great. Have a good weekend if I don't see you in the halls."

"You, too," I said as she left my office.

I got up and closed the door behind her. Although tempted to lock the door, I decided against it, realizing that if anyone had to knock on the door it would be recorded on the webcam. I unpacked my laptop and placed it on my desk. Checking my in-box to see if anything needed to be addressed immediately, I quickly ascertained that all of it could wait.

Methodically I went through the next steps. I placed a tissue on my chair and lifted the backside of my skirt. I settled myself behind the desk and turned on the computer. It was at that point that I literally prayed.

I looked toward the sky and spoke anxiously but quietly. "Dear goddess of orgasmic phenomena, may I reach my peak faster than I ever have before, amen." As the laptop booted up, I laughed at my silly antics.

It seemed like the computer took forever. I finally loaded the webcam. I had just lifted my skirt up onto my lap when the first interruption occurred. The sound of the doorknob turning caused my adrenaline to go into overdrive, making me feel like I could faint. I must have looked completely crazed but managed to keep my composure as Pierce burst in without knocking.

"So is this outfit for the famous Luke?" He walked right in front of my desk as I hurriedly pushed my skirt down. I could feel the veins in my neck throbbing.

"Get out of my office," I said, pointing at the door. "And knock next time you want to come in, Pierce."

"I brought this from Spence on fourteen and I was going to say you look nice, but …." He dropped a manila envelope on the desk and left the office with the door wide open.

"Shit," I said. I got up and closed the door again.

I sat back down and reluctantly opened the envelope. I needed to call the temp agency and get things settled for Spence. After Pierce's interruption, the day took off and I barely had time to breathe. I decided lunchtime would be the answer to my prayers.

Carefully setting up my laptop again, I situated myself behind the desk. I lifted my hem and wet my clit with my saliva. I ran my other hand up under my shirt and began to pinch my nipples over my bra. "Oh Fuck!" I said. I had forgotten to hit record. I straightened my shirt and began again. I made sure the cam was running and lifted my skirt once again. Looking straight into the computer, I could see on the screen what I recorded. I continued to rub and flick my clit and massage my breast. I found when I pushed my ass down into the seat it increased the sensations coursing through me. Getting closer and closer to cumming, my eyes automatically closed. I envisioned Luke under my desk sucking the juices off my wet lips. I grew closer and closer to the tip-off of a beautiful orgasm when a knock on the door startled me.

"Fuck, shit," I muttered to myself. Without thinking, I shoved my skirt down. What now? "Come in," I yelled. I almost laughed. It seemed so ludicrous.

"Sorry to bother you," said Brian as he walked into my office. "I was wondering if you might join me for lunch today."

"Oh … um …." I said, stalling. *Why the hell was my boss asking me to lunch?* I knew wearing these clothes had been a huge misstep. "Could we do it another time? I have some things I'd like to get done today so they're off my plate for Monday," I said, offering the first excuse that came to mind.

"Sure, sometime next week, then?"

"Sounds good," I said, forcing myself to smile. "Have a good weekend," I said to his back as he left my office, thankfully shutting the door behind him.

The moment he was gone and I turned back to the computer, realizing I had recorded the whole conversation with Brian. I hit the pause button and covered my face with my hands.

"Fuck, fuck, fuck," I groaned. I had screwed it up. I had

to start over. I would just delete what I had done and start fresh. But I couldn't bring myself to do it. I hit record again, lifted my skirt and squared myself to the camera. I managed to make myself cum but the intensity was nowhere near what it would have been without the interruption. I felt it would fall short of Luke's expectations. I had to do something. That's when the despicable idea of talking Pierce into a hand job reared its ugly head. I shuddered at the thought but knew if I didn't do something I'd end up getting the spatula. I also knew, without a shadow of a doubt, that it would be the end of our relationship. I wouldn't be able to bear it.

Before I could change my mind, I walked like a prisoner to the gallows out into the hall and onto the elevator. My body, my sick crazy body, continued its treachery as the friction of my stride and what I planned to do had me struggling to control my breathing. Alone in the elevator, I rode up to the 14th floor. I continued the walk of shame that inflamed my body. My nipples pressed against the material of my bra and I could feel my arousal between my legs. I knew if I went through with this, I was taking the chance of putting my job at risk. I also imagined a wildly difficult time trying to deal civilly with Pierce again.

I decided not to worry about it at that moment. I walked into his office without knocking, strode right up to the edge of his desk and leaned forward onto my hands. He sat behind his desk eating his lunch. When he looked up at me, he knew. It must have been written all over my face. Sick desire, none of which had to do with him. My crazy body had taken over this game.

"What?" he said. He looked confused and a bit scared.

I turned around and locked his door.

"Do you have a condom," I said, over my shoulder with my back to him.

"Yes, but …."

"Get it," I said, turning around and walking deliberately toward him.

"Okay," he said, standing. He straightened his tan slacks as he nervously fumbled with his wallet. He looked up at me questioningly as he pulled out the condom and showed it to me. I knew in that moment he was used to being turned down. I could imagine him in high school with his pocket protector and his hair slicked back.

"Pierce, are you listening to me?" I asked because of the glazed look in his eyes.

"Yes," he said, obedient as a little boy. He sat back down in his chair.

I stood facing him with my hands on my hips. "Do not touch me, do you understand? And Pierce, this never happened and will never happen again. Do not come by my office unless it's work related. Do you understand?"

"Not really, but whatever you say, Jane. Eh, what is about to happen?" he asked in a whisper.

"I'm serious, Pierce, this never ever happened."

"Okay, sure. No matter what happens, it never really happened. I get it and Jane, I can live with that," he said.

I knew he would say whatever he thought I needed to hear if only I would touch him. I put my hand out, and he handed me the condom. I ambled around the desk and turned his chair so that it faced me and away from the front of the desk. At that moment, I felt as if I had split in two. Rational Jane remained tied and bound inside my head. The other half of me—my body—took control.

I knelt down in front of Pierce, unceremoniously unzipping his tan pants. Pulling his already hard shaft out, I immediately unrolled the condom onto his penis. I tried to think of his cock as a separate entity, not attached to an owner. His rigid phallus jerked at my first touch and he moaned. I knew it wouldn't take long. I used both hands to stroke up and down on his shaft. In no more than twenty strokes he rewarded me with a large load of cum in the condom. Carefully removing it, I tied the top end into a knot.

I didn't look at him or say another word. I took the condom and did my best to hide it in my hand. Then I unlocked the door and closed it behind me. Leaning back against the door to gather myself, I became aware of the multitude of office sounds and voices.

As I walked down the hallway, for the first time in my life I had no idea who I was anymore. My body flamed with molten desire, craving to be fucked and whipped hard. My fractured mind pulled farther away from my old self.

I took the stairs back to my floor and locked myself in my office. Placing the condom in my purse I sat down at my desk; then I lowered my head onto my arms and cried. I cried for the girl I used to be and for the woman I had begun to become. I cried because I knew the path I had chosen would forever change me. I cried because I no longer knew what tomorrow would bring and how long I'd survive after that.

As my confusion and anger grew I opened the laptop and hit play on the webcam, angling it so he would see only my pussy. I harshly masturbated my clit until I came, screaming out, not caring who could hear me. I fought to catch my breath and get control of myself, slamming the laptop shut as the tears flowed harder down my cheeks.

In a panic, I paced my office until I got myself together. Then I wiped my face and chanced a walk down the hall to the bathroom. I made it there without crossing paths with anyone, sat down in the stall and peed. I cleansed myself of all my wetness and even considered taking out the plug. Although he hadn't ordered me to wear it all day, I decided not to chance it.

Just the effort of walking back to my office had my juices flowing again. I had four more hours to go and couldn't imagine how I'd make it through. I decided minimal movement would be best. I took my time taking care of my much neglected filing at my desk. Blessedly no one came by my office for the rest of the day.

By the time I made it back to the apartment, even my clothes seemed possessed. I felt strange and sordid, sullied in some way. I anxiously turned the shower to hot with the intention of washing some of the filth away. I removed the tulip, aware of the chaffing around my ass. Stepping into the shower, I allowed the water to cover my head and block out everything but my own thoughts.

I never made the call to Parker about going to the movies. Instead, I climbed into bed and checked my email. I realized I needed to email Luke the videos I had made. I didn't know what to write to him. I had expected an email back but felt extremely disappointed when I didn't receive so much as a short note.

To: LukeBandDphotos@controlme.com
From: PlainJane368@yahoo.com
Subject: Today
Attachment: Jane4u.avi & Jane2.avi

Luke,

I didn't complete Option #3, as an interruption threw me off. First video explains it all. I completed Option #2 to avoid #1. The second video shows my state after #2.

No email for me? I'm turning my life inside out for you and you can't scrape a bit of time to answer my email. That must be saying something. As I'm sure you can tell I'm not in a good space. I'm already in bed and don't plan to get out until I have to get ready for what normal people would call a lunch with Mother tomorrow. For me it's more like penance and self punishment.

Anyway, I have nothing more to say.

—Jane

I knew I would feel better if I went for a run, but instead I just lay there waiting for oblivion to take over.

The ring tone on my cellphone sounded. I snapped it up off the nightstand and opened it.

"Jane?" Luke said.

"Yes, it's me," I said, sitting up in bed, excitement erupting in me. "You called!" I remembered that I sounded like a little girl whose father had come home from a long trip.

"Of course I called after seeing the second video. Oh babe, are you all right? I never thought you would choose option two but I'm so damn proud of you. You continue to amaze me, Jane."

"I don't feel the least bit amazing," I said, lying there staring at the ceiling, fantasizing about his smile and feeling the happiness that came with hearing his voice.

"Oh, but you will when I get home. Spatula is off the list but you still owe me."

"What? What the hell are you talking about? I have a condom full of sperm for you!"

"I'm sensing a lot of attitude and here I was hoping to console you," he said. His voice sounded tiny on the cell, not the way it would sound when he was in the same room with me.

"Console me? You sure have a funny way of showing it."

"I was just letting you know that the second orgasm you gave yourself was taking matters into your own hands and, as you must realize already, your body is mine, Jane. All of it, all the time. So you owe me for your not-so-little release."

"Well, then, I owe you twice," I said, scooting back down and rolling on my side. Sarcasm never achieves what I hope it will but is almost impossible for me to resist.

"And why is that? Jane?" he asked.

"I masturbated before work yesterday at the idea of what I would do today."

"Jane," he said, this time with annoyance in his voice.

"Jane, rule number one states: Your body is mine. You no longer have control over your own pleasure. I will use your body as I see fit for your pleasure and mine."

"Oh," I said, sticking a finger in my mouth as if I didn't know that already.

"Yes, Jane. So now you owe me twice when I get home. I will take into consideration all the honesty you have shown me while I've been away. You could've started the video over but you didn't. That means a lot to me and hasn't gone unnoticed."

"I miss you, Luke."

"Oh babe, I miss you, too. You wouldn't believe how much. I'll show you when I get home. My flight gets in at nine a.m. and that should put me at our place by ten. Wait for me in bed, love."

"Okay, I will. I can't wait."

"One more thing. I don't want you talking to other men. I don't like you running 'into' Scott."

"Scott's nobody to me, Luke."

"Regardless, please avoid him if you see him again."

"If that's what you want. Okay."

"I have to go now but I'll be seeing you soon."

"I love you, Luke," I said.

"I love you too, babe. Sweet dreams. Oh, and have a good lunch with your mother tomorrow. Have to go."

"Bye."

His phone call changed everything for me. Before his call I'd felt so depressed and ashamed and downright depraved, but after hearing his voice my perspective shifted. He loved me and that made all the difference. I got out of bed, fixed myself dinner and watched a movie on TV. By the time my head hit the pillow again the anxiety and fear for my sanity was gone. I felt apprehensive regarding lunch with my mother but I figured that if I could jerk off Pierce and survive it, I could handle anything she threw at me.

CHAPTER ELEVEN

For lunch with my mother I wore a new outfit—beige shorts and a multi-hued green shirt. I looked in the mirror before heading out and smiled. Although dreading the time I would spend with her, I felt more powerful than I had in a long time.

I already knew what my mother would wear. A wool skirt hemmed right above the knees—probably brown, a colorful long-sleeved blouse that Jackson Pollack would be proud of and low beige heels. She wouldn't take the weather into consideration. I never understood how my mother's genes combined with my father's resulted in me. My mother was short and stocky with legs that ended in cankles. She had her hair done once a week just like her mother and kept it sprayed in place. I wore little or no makeup; she wouldn't leave the house without her "face." I never quite understood why my mother seemed more like my friends' grandparents than their parents.

"That's a smart outfit," she said as she approached. "You look younger, Jane, I like it."

"What do you want, Mother?" I said, pivoting to face her.

"Jane, why would you say something like that to me?" She threw up her hands in exasperation.

"Well, let's just say you aren't one for compliments."

"People change," she said, raising her eyebrows as if offering just one possibility.

"Have you met someone? Did you actually go out to the

community center?" I asked, suspicious as ever of her motives.

"Well no. Can't I just be happy to be lunching with my daughter?" she said as we followed the host to our table.

"Okay," I said. I sat down by the window, still waiting for her to reveal the real reason for her atypical behavior. The snake you know is far safer than the spider you don't.

"So, have you moved?" she asked.

"Sort of," I said. I took the black napkin off the table and placed it on my lap. "After we have lunch I'm going to swing back by my apartment and pack some more things."

"Oh, I was hoping to see your new place." She lined her silverware straight on two sides and moved her water glass closer.

"We aren't all settled in yet." I couldn't imagine my mother in our place. I couldn't visualize it at all.

"I see. So when do I get to meet him?" She drummed her fingers on the table.

"He's out of town until tomorrow but I'll ask him soon," I said to placate her.

"Good." Her fingers mercifully stilled.

I finally realized her little act had to do with wanting to meet Luke. If she behaved, she thought her chances of my introducing him to her would increase. My mother was anything if not crafty. She never seemed to go about anything straight on. Lying was second nature to her—one of the reasons I abhorred it.

"You'll never guess who I heard from last week," she said.

"Who?" I pretended interest.

"Jim," she said nonchalantly.

"Dad called and you're only telling me now?" I hadn't heard from my father for years. The only reason he would stomach calling my mother would be to get in touch with me. "That's bullshit, Mother. What did he say?"

"Jane, don't curse at me or I'll leave you sitting in this restaurant even before our food has been served." She moved her chair back, threatening to get up.

"Okay, okay, please sit down, Mother," I said. "I will control myself."

"I didn't hear an apology in that." She grabbed her purse off the table.

"I'm sorry for cursing, Mother. Please tell me." Although I pleaded with her, I really wanted to reach across and grab her by the lapels.

"He wanted to get in touch with you, but …."

A litany of curse words ran through my head. I took a deep breath before speaking. "But what?" I clasped my hands in my lap, trying to calm myself.

"I told him you were busy and I didn't want to bother you," she said, tilting her head, as if that were a perfectly reasonable response.

I stood up and walked outside the restaurant. I knew my mother could see me but I didn't care. "Fuck, shit, fuck, shit," I said out loud to myself. "If only I could slap her. That would feel so good." I took a couple of deep breaths and slowly walked back in, heading back to our table.

"Please tell me you got his current number," I said through clenched teeth. I sat down and placed my hands on the table in front of us.

She reached into her purse and handed me a piece of paper.

Why couldn't she have just given me his number? So like her to add stress where none was necessary.

"Thank you," I said, just barely managing to get it out. "What did he say?"

"He asked about you and how you're doing. I didn't say much and kept the conversation short."

"Did he say where he's living now? What he's doing for work?"

"Jane, I said I kept the conversation short. I gave you his number. Call him if you must but you should know he will just let you down again as he has done repeatedly in the past to both of us."

"Mother, you pushed him out. I don't know why you insist on blaming him."

"You have a warped sense of your childhood, dear. Things were never easy with your father. He would—"

"You know what? I don't want to hear the list again, okay? Let's change the subject."

I still clutched his number in my hand as the conversation became a blur. I hated that she reminded me of all the disappointment he had caused. I hated that I still wanted something from him that I never got. My mother wanted me to believe that people change. Could he have changed? Did I even want to risk it?

I shook my head at all the pauses as my mother gossiped about the people who lived in her condo building, not really hearing her. I wondered why he had come back around again and how long he planned to stay in touch.

&

After lunch I spent three hours sorting through the stuff in my apartment. I separated all my things into three piles as I contemplated calling my father. One pile held the stuff I would bring over to our new place, the second pile contained the things I would get rid of and the last pile was composed of stuff to go into storage. I left the kitchen alone, deciding not to pack it up.

By the time I had returned to our place and made several trips up and down the stairs, I experienced pure exhaustion. I had no interest in running on the treadmill or going to the beach. I stripped by the door and headed straight to the bedroom.

I unpacked the boxes and scattered my artwork around

the place. On the wall next to the table I hung my favorite photograph of an Indian boy. I thought Luke would approve.

After I finished organizing my things, I opened the laptop and checked my email.

> To: PlainJane368@yahoo.com
> From: LukeBandDphotos@controlme.com
> Subject: Re: Today
> Jane,
>
> I had hoped to have a chance to email you yesterday but the day was hectic, with last minute appointments. I hope the phone call last night helped. I'm getting ready to head out to the airport in a few. Can't wait to hear all about your week when I get there. Be ready for me, Jane.
>
> Love you,
> Luke

What did that mean? Be ready for him. I probably should have been worried about what he had in store for me but the excitement of seeing him again took precedence.

CHAPTER TWELVE

That night I barely slept. I was too preoccupied by thoughts of everything that had happened. While questioning the sanity of my life with Luke, I also realized I could never go back. Luke touched me, reached me in a way no one else had. The excitement and trepidation had me buzzing. When I finally got out of bed at 5 a.m., I decided the only remedy was a good run. Despite the lack of sleep I still needed to burn up excess energy. Instead of a run I opted for the treadmill and a series of sprints to quell the anxiety over my anticipation of Luke's arrival home.

Afterwards I took my time grooming for him. I shaved my legs, underarms, pussy lips, and bikini line. I plucked my eyebrows, showered and even did a Fleet just in case. I finished with time to spare. In the mirror I looked into the eyes of a woman I was getting to know better every day but wasn't absolutely sure I liked.

I decided to do some writing. I began chronicling my experiences with Luke starting with our first meeting. The process of recollection left me confused again about the true Luke, not to mention the true "me." Luke had many facets and I wondered if I could love them all. Was the person I had briefly grown to know truly him or just my vision of him?

I lost track of time when I wrote. Writing would become my solace. I sat there, on the bed, until I heard the door open some hours later.

I hit save and slammed the top of the laptop shut. At the last moment I remembered to turn the ringer on Luke's

phone back on. Then I ran to the other door to greet him.

"What a sight for sore eyes," Luke said, rewarding me with a huge smile.

"You can't even imagine how glad I am to see you," I said. I took his garment bag. "You must be exhausted."

"I slept some on the plane so I'm good. You have a reward and punishment due you, my love, but tomorrow's soon enough for all that."

"Will we ever have a normal hello, Luke?"

"Oh, probably not," he said, laughing. "Enough with the talking for now. I'm going to take a quick shower and meet you in bed. I need to show you how much I missed you. I've been thinking about tasting you again all week. Really, Jane, you need to think about leaving that job of yours and traveling with me. I don't like us to be apart."

He carried his suitcase into the bedroom and I hung his garment bag in the closet. Turning to me, he lifted me into a big hug. I wrapped my legs around his waist and we kissed deeply. It felt wonderful to have him home.

When he came strolling back into the room with his hair still wet from the shower—the towel wrapped around his waist revealing his taut stomach muscles—desire spun through me like never before. No man had ever ignited that kind of passion within me. Never had I met anyone so at home in his exquisite flesh. He took my hand in his and kissed my palm. "Too long," he said.

His lips encompassed mine, breathing them in, licking, suckling, and prodding them with his tongue. For the first time we met in bed as equals. He didn't tie me down or restrain me in any way. He moved his mouth slowly and softly down my neck, breathing me in. My arms were free to caress him. I buried my hands in his sandy brown hair and pulled his mouth to my breast.

"Oh," I cried out as he ran his tongue along my protruding nipple. "Yes, too long."

☙

We made love like a normal couple that night and the experience distracted me from thoughts of what might befall me the next day. We shared stories about our weeks but avoided talking about the circumstances of his departure on the previous Monday. I felt safe and our apartment morphed back into a home. Without Luke there, the place had felt like it belonged to someone else. With Luke home it again became our sanctuary, our refuge from the rest of world.

"I like what you've done with the place," Luke said, when we finally emerged from the bed in search of food. "Makes it feel homey and lived in. I especially like the sepia painting of the young boy, although I think we should move him into the bedroom."

"Whatever you'd like," I said, stepping forward to snuggle into his arms.

☙

I managed to forget about what I had done on Friday with Pierce until I woke up Monday morning. The knot in the pit of my stomach had me feeling nauseous and anxious at the same time. What Luke had in store for me was shoved to the back burner. For once I hoped he would order me to take the day off. I didn't want to face Pierce, my boss, or anyone else for that matter. Both Allison and my boss expected to have lunch with me today.

Please, please, I thought, *don't ask me to wear a new outfit to work.*

In an attempt to regain control, I attacked my treadmill, running hard and fast. I had hoped to burn out the stress, but once I was stretched and showered, I realized that the stress wasn't so easily excised. I guessed I'd have to walk through the fire. Luke still slept as I slipped out of the apartment for work in my typical business suit and shoes, hair up in a twist.

When I got into my car, I yelped. A package lay on the passenger seat. First I thought of Pierce but then knew that was nonsense. He didn't know where I lived. I took a deep breath and moved the package to my lap. Inside was my new Tulip butt plug, the small bottle of olive oil, a Fleet, a black strip of silk and a note. Butterflies jumped around in my stomach as I stared at the message.

> Be ready for me at 5:00 p.m. sharp outside of your office building.
> —Luke

"Shit," I said. I put all the items, including the note, into my bag.

I managed to make it to my office without crossing paths with Pierce. I didn't notice any strange or odd looks so I felt reassured that he hadn't told anyone about my deed.

I was fully absorbed with wicked thoughts of Luke's gift that alluded to what would befall me after work. I'd have to leave early. I'd have to get to the bathroom and hope it was empty to do the fleet. *Maybe I could ask Pierce to borrow his bathroom,* I thought and laughed out loud. Later on I would regret that nonchalance. One shouldn't get cocky before the jury is in.

I was quickly swept up in a hectic current of work that didn't subside until Allison showed up for lunch. I begged off, and we rescheduled for Thursday. Unfortunately that left me in the office for Pierce's arrival.

"We need to talk," he said as he pulled my office door shut and locked it.

"I thought I was clear," I said. "There is nothing to talk about." I crossed my arms in front of me. I tried to look calm but inside I was having a breakdown.

"I disagree," he said. Pierce pulled up a chair from against the wall and placed it backwards in front of my desk.

He sat leaning against the back with his arms folded across the top. "You never once showed interest in me and yet you show up at my office and jerk me off and walk off with my sperm. I was dazed at the moment but am no longer."

The condom filled with his cum still lay somewhere in my purse. I imagined dumping the contents of my purse out in front of him and handing him back his sperm. I suppressed the nervous laughter but not the smile.

"What do you find so funny, Jane?" he said, leaning farther forward in his chair.

"Nothing," I said. I placed my hands on my lap and leaned forward toward him.

"Friday was a fluke." *A Luke, fluke,* I thought and almost starting laughing again. "It won't happen again and as far as I'm concerned, it never happened in the first place. You said you understood."

"Well I don't understand. Why don't we go out on a date like normal people, Jane, and take it from there."

"You don't get it …. I have no interest in you."

"This is about that Luke guy? Then what the fuck?"

"I don't mean to be crude but did you not enjoy yourself?"

"Well, yeah, I guess," he said, shrugging.

"Then let's leave it at—"

A knock on the door startled us both. Pierce unlocked and opened it to reveal Brian standing in the hallway.

"Oh sorry, am I interrupting?" Brian said.

"Not at all," I quickly said. "Pierce was just leaving."

"Great," Brian said.

"We'll talk later," Pierce said as he left my office.

"He didn't look pleased," Brian said.

"Oh that's just him," I said. "What can I do for you?"

"I was checking on lunch." He turned around the chair in front of my desk and sat down.

Dealing with Brian was only slightly less nerve-racking

than dealing with Pierce. I didn't want to piss him off—he held the keys to my job security—but at the same time I wasn't interested in leading him on either.

"Is this a business lunch or personal?"

"Whichever you prefer," he said.

"I appreciate the offer, Brian, but I have a boyfriend." I squirmed. "It was the outfit, right?"

He laughed. "No, not really. I had wanted to ask you for some time … but I guess the outfit added urgency to it. And I was right, wasn't I? That's why Pierce was here, too, I imagine." He looked me over as if he could still see my outfit from Friday.

I took a deep breath and said, "I'm not sure what to say other than I'm flattered and I hope you aren't offended by my declining." I stood in a way that said, *It is time for you to go now.*

"Not at all. Had I known you were involved, I wouldn't have asked." He stood in response to my gesture.

I got the impression it had taken a lot of courage for him to ask in the first place and yet he seemed relieved. We just stood there for a minute looking at each other. I finally said, "Are there work related things you wanted to talk about?"

"Those can wait," Brian said. He walked back over to the door and said, "Jane, if you ever need anything …."

"Thank you," I said.

I had such an odd feeling as he left my office. It was as if a normal life could have been mine had I only been paying attention. It's not as if I had a crush on my boss or had ever really fantasized about him in that way, but at that moment I realized that had I not attended the party with Scott, had I never met Luke, I might have taken a completely different path and … that path might have just walked out of my office.

"Ugh," I said out loud.

At four o'clock I decided to do a scouting trip to the women's bathroom. There was no way I could use it to insert

the Fleet and crouch down on the floor for two full minutes while it worked. While there was plenty of room in the handicapped stall, there was too much space between the stall door and the floor, leaving me exposed for all to see. Anyone who came in would be able to see me hunkering down on the cold tiled floor. I thought to myself, *not pretty.*

As I saw it, I had three options. I could use the bathroom in Brian's office but I couldn't fathom a good enough excuse. I could run home, get ready, and hurry back. Again, I would need a creative excuse to leave and it would be hard to explain coming back after that. The third option brought me back to the dreaded Pierce. On his floor, right across from his office, stood a private bathroom. Like an executive washroom, it was reserved for those working on that floor. There had to be another solution, but I couldn't think of any. I thought of using the Fleet in my office but worried I wouldn't make it to the bathroom in time.

I couldn't think of anything to say to Pierce. My creative self had abandoned me just when I desperately needed her to come up with some plausible excuse to use *that* bathroom. Time was running out and I didn't want to give Luke any reason to administer a more severe discipline than he already had in mind. I decided to wing it.

I turned off my computer and straightened the paperwork on my desk. I fetched my bag and turned out the lights as I headed out of my office. The clock in the hallway read 4:45 p.m., which only gave me fifteen minutes to complete all my tasks. I rode the elevator upstairs and headed straight into Pierce's office.

"I need a favor," I said straight out.

"Interesting," he said, crossing his arms in front of him and leaning back in his chair.

"I need to use the bathroom across the hall," I said.

"Jane, you get stranger by the day, you know that?" Pierce said. He sat up in his chair. "I don't think any of the executives police the hall."

"Can I say I was up here talking to you," I said, "should I cross paths with anyone?"

"You can say anything you'd like but I think lunch is in order so you can explain what the hell is going on."

"Deal," I said, although I didn't mean it. Time was draining away quickly and I needed to get going.

"Tomorrow," he said. "Tomorrow."

"Fine," I said.

I ran across the hall and pulled everything out of my bag. I made quick work of the Fleet but then I couldn't seem to relax enough to insert the butt plug. After what seemed like ten attempts, I finally pushed gently but firmly, guiding the Tulip to its resting place between my buttocks. I closed my eyes. The feeling was warm, sensuous, and erotic.

I threw everything into my bag—including the used Fleet enema—and hurried to the elevator. I could've hit myself upside the head, because no one saw me going into or out of the bathroom and now I was stuck dealing with Pierce over nothing.

I stopped, took another deep breath and realized that after all the craziness I stood right outside the office doors with two minutes to spare. Remembering the silk material at the last minute, I placed it over my eyes and tied it behind my head. I only had a second to think of what would happen if someone saw me standing in front of my office building with the blindfold on.

"Just in the nick of time," Luke whispered in my ear. "I thought I would have the pleasure of more punishment but you managed to make it happen just in time." He held me under my forearm and led me at a quick pace I found awkward to follow. "These clothes are all wrong," he said when he slowed down to a stop.

I heard a car door open. Helping me in proved unwieldy. I felt the butt plug push deeper inside of me, which heightened the excitation of being blindfolded. Luke fastened

my seatbelt and got in on the other side. I wondered if this signaled the beginning of my reward or my punishment. As the excitement swirled through me, I decided I didn't care.

"I brought you an outfit to change into," Luke said as we pulled away from the curb.

"Where are we going?"

"If I wanted you to know that, why would I bother with a blindfold? I'm assuming you took care of the other matters," he said, not waiting for a response. "We will stop briefly for you to change, and there is another surprise for you. Any trouble from Pierce today?"

"Yes, he stopped by my office but I was sort of saved by my boss, who came by just a few minutes later. Although that was uncomfortable as well."

"You are the popular one these days."

"Well the hand job and the new outfit helped," I said. I laughed, trying to rid myself of the image. "I did a stupid thing today."

"Really?" he said. "How's that?"

"I couldn't use the regular bathroom and so I asked to use the restroom across the hall from Pierce. Turns out no one saw me going in or coming out but now Pierce wants me to have lunch with him."

"When?"

"Tomorrow."

"Don't imagine you'll be up for going to work tomorrow," he said as he cranked the car and shifted into first gear.

I was relieved not to have to face Pierce but scared by what would keep me from going to work. "Should I be worried?"

"That all depends on whether you trust me to take you where you need to go. You know you need this, Jane. You need me and you definitely need what I'm going to give you."

My heart rate jumped and I became increasingly aware

of the plug in my ass. Somehow my body had begun to confuse the signals of fear and sexuality. Along with genuine dread of what might happen that night, I also felt sexually stimulated.

The car came to a stop and Luke helped me out of the passenger seat. We walked up two steps and as soon as we entered through the door I knew I had been there before. I could smell the leather, latex and other fragrances. I felt embarrassed to be there blindfolded. If only Christian wasn't working ….

"Hello," I heard him saying to Luke, "How can I help you?"

"Please fit Jane with a corset. That one," he said. "We will need the large Tulip butt plug as well."

Luke walked away, leaving me alone with Christian.

"Hi Jane," he whispered.

I had hoped he wouldn't recognize me. I don't know why I felt so embarrassed in front of him. The store belonged to him, after all. "Please take off your blouse and your bra," he said.

I did as I was told and felt a chill run up my spine. My nipples stood erect as the shame flooded through me.

"Lift your arms, please," Christian said.

He wrapped the corset around my body and struggled to hook it in the back.

"Maybe it's too small?" I said.

"No, Jane, that is the point," he said as finished hooking the clasps down to my waist.

I could feel my breasts being pushed together and up. My waist felt constricted and much smaller as I ran my hands down my sides. Luke's aroma—no other smell like it, with a subtle hint of earthy sandalwood—alerted me to his presence. I couldn't hear his instructions to Christian, but I felt my skirt being unzipped and my panties removed. Christian's administrations made me so turned on I could feel the

wetness on my thighs. He had me step into a skirt. As he straightened my blouse he brushed over my nipples, causing them to harden under the strain of the corset. He must have moved in closer, because I could hear him inhaling the essence from my neck and hair. A thrill ran through my body.

My shoes were removed and replaced with much higher heels. I wished I could see what I looked like.

The next part, so stimulating and humiliating at the same time, left me breathless.

Christian led me deeper into the store and past what felt like a curtain. "Bend over at the waist please," he said.

"Easier said than done," I said. The corset complicated things. I had to draw myself up to my full height before I could bend over. I finally managed it.

"Please spread your legs for me," he said. He lifted my skirt over my bottom and gently pulled out the butt plug already in place. As I stood there exposed, I longed for a tongue to taste me. My body, which should have been uncomfortable and tight, was in full rebellion. I wanted to feel the warmth of his breath on me.

I felt his fingers coat my anus with lubricant. I moaned my pleasure as he stuck two fingers in and began stretching my hole. I wanted to rub my clit as he worked his fingers in my ass but did not have permission. I knew part of what I would experience that night would include punishment for previous infractions. What Christian was doing was certainly not part of that punishment, and I certainly didn't complain.

I felt the cold tip of the larger plug spreading my anus. "Oh, oh," I moaned.

As the depth and width began to stretch me even farther, I screamed. "Wait, wait that hurts."

"Shhhh," he whispered into my ear. "Relax."

I tried to do as he advised but the intensity of the pain came to a sharp point just before the widest part penetrated me. "Oh fuck, oh fuck," I said. I knew that if someone would

just flick my clit once I would cum. That plug filled me in a way the other had not. My legs trembled and my heart raced; I felt faint.

Christian pulled me upright and I felt a contraction in my gut. "Opf," I muttered.

"Jane, listen to me," Christian whispered. "Try to stay loose and relaxed and your body will accommodate it quicker. You look beautiful, by the way, and very fuckable." He ran his hand up under my skirt and caressed my ass. I felt so turned on and yet so dirty. I liked his touching and caressing me with Luke circling quietly around the edges. I was shifting further and farther away from my former image of myself. A twisted beast had been awakened in me—a barbarian whose clit ruled her rational mind.

"Thank you," I whispered seductively, inviting him closer. If I could've seen him, I would've kissed his face.

"Perfect," I heard Luke say as we walked back into the store. "How does it feel?"

"Big," I said.

"Good." I heard the cash register drawer open and close. Then Luke thanked Christian for his assistance.

"Anytime," Christian replied and I knew he meant it.

Luke led me to the car. I wondered if the blouse sufficiently covered the corset. I flushed, certain that I must look like a hooker or call girl.

As we headed to our next destination, Luke reached over and forced my thighs farther apart. He touched my wetness and massaged my clit with his right hand while adeptly steering the car with his left and taking time to shift when needed. He was driving me wild.

"Ohhhh," I said. So close to cumming, I hoped he would stop so I wouldn't betray myself.

"So you liked having another man handle you?" he said. "I will have to keep that in mind."

"Oh Luke, ohhhhhhhh."

"Yes, babe, I'd love to hear you cum. Cum for me," he said as he increased the speed of his fingers, circling gently, lightly teasing until I lost control.

"Oh yes, oh yeah, ohhhhhhhh!" I yelled and came.

"You look so sexy, Jane. Know that I will devour you tonight. First we must eat. You will need your strength."

ʘ

Luke led me through a door and I instantly smelled garlic and melted cheese. He exchanged words with the host and we were led to a table at the back of the restaurant—or so I guessed. I imagined people staring at me. Between my outfit and the blindfold, I was surely garnering too much attention. I should have felt embarrassed or at the very least self-conscious, but instead I felt safe with Luke. On his arm I had glided without fear through the throng. I adored being treated as special.

He helped me into my chair and sat on the same side of the table with me.

Luke did all the ordering. We started out with a glass of cold white wine. Although I wanted to see his eyes, the wine relaxed me enough to allow me to enjoy the experience. He fed me bread with garlic butter and another glass of wine.

"Jane," he said in a stern voice. He gripped my upper thigh and I realized I had let my legs close. "Two more lashes for you tonight."

"I'm sorry," I said.

"You may be later," he said and then bit the side of my neck. Moving his fingers between my legs, he flicked and pulled on my labia. It took all the strength I could muster to stifle the cries of pleasure that threatened to come out. I had no idea how close the other tables were or who could see us. I leaned my head back and enjoyed his manipulations. My arousal was climbing higher and higher, bringing me once again to the edge of orgasm, when suddenly the waiter

interrupted us with an announcement that dinner was served. The hot blast of embarrassment suffused my skin. I wanted to slide under the table to the floor.

While I recovered my equilibrium, Luke fed me my meal. I had never enjoyed so much attention. He fed me water and wine to wash down the eggplant parmesan. He dabbed my mouth with my napkin and cared for me in a way my mother never had. He whispered loving phrases as I ate and drank. We laughed and shared affectionate kisses. I experienced a raft of conflicting emotions—chagrin at my inexperience, euphoria at being cared for so thoughtfully … All these lows and highs were combined with arousal, which confused me the most. The turmoil reminded me of my dad.

"I forgot to tell you that my father got in touch with my mother hoping to get in touch with me," I blurted out. "I have his new number but I haven't called yet." It felt weird to share intimate details without being able to see Luke's face.

"Will you call? I'd like to meet him."

"My mother wants to meet you but—"

"But what, Jane?"

"She's a bitch … for lack of a better term." I played with the napkin on my lap and tried to imagine my mother with Luke.

"Are you worried for me?" he said, laughing. "Oh, you would be surprised at how well I can put someone in their place. They even end up thanking me for it. I think meeting your parents will give me more insight into you."

"Will I meet your parents?" I asked.

"They're deceased."

"Brothers or sisters?"

"No," Luke said.

Goosebumps rose along my arms. It bothered me that he had no ties.

"Will I meet your friends?"

"I'm mostly a loner, Jane. Many of my acquaintances are

work related. I only need one close friend at a time and you're it."

"Will you give me the chance to know you better?"

"Of course, my love. That takes time and we have plenty of that … or will, as soon as you quit your job." I could hear the smile in his voice. He had an uncanny ability to change the subject. "Let's take dessert to go, shall we? Cannoli?"

"Sounds perfect," I said.

"One more thing before we leave the restaurant," he said.

Angst clouded my mind. I knew I would soon be paying my penalty, but surely not in the restaurant.

I followed Luke's lead back toward the front of the front. All the sounds changed as we entered the kitchen. I heard the clinking of plates and the sizzling of food on the grill and in the pans. People hustled past us as we made our way through.

"Where are you taking me?" I said.

"Quiet," Luke said, sternly. "Not a word."

As soon as I met his new expectations emotionally and physically, he would push me even further past my comfort zone. Fear put me on high alert, and tears brimmed in my eyes. I knew in that moment that I'd never truly be able to catch up. I would forever be treading water with this man. I had thought the incident with Pierce would be the limit, but that night I realized that there would be no limits. Luke would continue to push and cajole me ever deeper. All these thoughts traveled through my mind as I continued to allow Luke to lead me further into depravity.

When we came to a halt, I could still hear the kitchen sounds muffled in the distance. Another set of feet shuffled into the room. My first instinct was to pull away out of fear, but I knew I had to bring those reactions under control. *Would he allow another man to fuck me?* I thought. I started to shake, quietly fighting the tears that threatened to betray me. The caring, comforting Luke had left and in his place was the dark Luke I had also come to know. The energy shift was

as striking as a cold front moving in after a sunny day.

"Put your arms out in front of you," he demanded.

Obediently, I held my arms out and felt them being tied together. My panic edged forward, causing involuntary recoil. Luke grabbed me even tighter, manhandling me. Then he led me straight ahead again. The edge of a table hit me at hip level, and my upper body was cast forward over the top. My toes barely touched the ground, causing my calves to cramp.

"Spread your legs," Luke said, kicking my feet apart. At that moment I knew for sure we had company. Someone else fastened me to the other end of the table. I turned my face to the side, feeling the cold surface. My body shook out of fear and lust.

I disgusted myself.

"I can see you need a little reminding to keep those thighs open for me and a bigger reminder that your clit belongs to me now. Your pleasure is completely under my control. Are you ready, Jane?"

"Yes please," I said, taking a deep breath to steady my mind.

I don't know what he used on me but it was the most painful device yet. It made a hissing noise as it went through the air. Determined not to cry in front of an audience, I tried to hold my breath in an effort to cork the flow. After a couple of strokes, I no longer thought of breathing or not breathing. The lashes sent such intense pain through me that it tangled my mind. My nipples engorged against the flat table and I felt my flower flush with wetness.

In the beginning I could hear feet moving around the table but after about ten hits with the whip I could hear nothing, smell nothing. I felt as if I'd left my body. My mind floated somewhere else, into oblivion. I returned to consciousness when Luke whispered in my ear. A rush of awareness inundated my senses; I could feel the energy and presences in the room.

"You were amazing, Jane. You took thirty-two hits of the whip and they all enjoyed the show. I will show you my appreciation when we get home." The sweet, caring Luke had returned, soothing the pain and fear of just minutes before.

Someone untied me and Luke lifted me to my feet. He fixed my skirt as a thunderous applause erupted around us. I was mortified as the tears I had successfully kept at bay began to flow, and I was grateful to have the blindfold capturing them. I no longer recognized the life I had chosen.

Luke led me out to the car and placed a pillow on the seat before helping me to sit down. This time he had striped not just my ass and thighs but the part of my back that lay exposed outside of the corset. The car ride home left me squirming for a comfortable position. I couldn't sit straight up so I positioned myself on my right hip, leaning against the door. I bit my lower lip, crying silently, and the tears did not cease as he opened the door.

Once inside the apartment, he gently removed all my clothing, including the corset and blindfold. Then he bent me over and removed the anal plug. I felt used and abused and very tired. Lifting me in his arms, he brought me to our bed and ever so gently laid my aching body down for a long night of recovery.

"You will need to take the day off tomorrow," he told me.

I rolled onto my side, away from him. He smoothed my hair as the tears finally subsided. Regaining my composure, I went back to questioning my choices. Would I survive this crazy odyssey of pleasure and pain?

Luke gently applied healing cream into the welts on my back. His words of love and affection again obliterated all my fears and apprehensions. I basked in his energy. *This* was the Luke I longed for.

Cradled in his arms that night, I knew I traveled on a dangerous path. I also knew I wouldn't be able to give him up.

ೞ

In the middle of the night I awoke. I tested my body slowly and realized movement came much easier than I would have thought. Cautiously I picked up my laptop and went out into the living room.

I felt so incredibly mixed up and isolated, having no one to tell of my confusion. I wondered why I had put myself in this predicament. I knew then that I was addicted and couldn't possibly let go. What was it about Luke? I didn't understand why my body responded to him as it did. I was watching myself morph into another person from moment to moment as though I had no say in the matter.

I questioned whether I could ever have what I really wanted with Luke. I sat there and typed, listening to his loud breathing coming from the next room. He made me so happy and scared at the same time. Terrified of where it all might lead, I still couldn't stop myself, let alone him. And truthfully, although I needed it to stop, I didn't want it to. I was fighting a battle from within as to which side of my personality was going to emerge the winner and rule my life.

What bothered me most was that he didn't need me. Oh, he *wanted* me, which was evident in his body's response and his insatiable desire, but *need*? I knew myself to be an interchangeable part in the grand scheme of things. You would think that hard truth would be enough reason for me to get out. Enough reason to say goodbye. Enough reason to pack my things and go back to my apartment. However, as he —and I—were all too aware, I would be going nowhere. How could I go back to normal life after all I'd experienced? I'd become so accustomed to his demands and control over me and my pleasure, I could no longer date a "normal" man.

My father always told me that life came down to a series of choices. Some choices we made would be good, and we'd be happy with the outcome. Some choices would be dreadful (he liked that word) and the outcome beyond our worst fears.

But mostly, he said, if we were willing to take responsibility for our choices, we could live with the outcome either way.

Certainly some choices are made for us, especially when we are young. The choice to stay, however, I made for myself. No one held a gun to my head. Luke didn't pressure me to decide one way or the other. So why did I choose him, choose that life? I know I said in the beginning of my story that I felt painfully bored. Looking back, I can see how lame boredom is as an excuse, but I never knew to what extent until I began experimenting with Luke.

Admittedly, it sounded better than my being addicted to pain/pleasure or whatever it ultimately might be. Maybe the endorphin rush ruled my body then. All I know is that when he was away I would get panicky and insecure, like I needed my fix of attention or approval from him. Sometimes I felt like I should have slapped myself upside the head and screamed, *Wake the fuck up ... what are you doing to yourself?* But then he would call or come home or send a sweet email and I'd be healed all over again and good until the next fix.

My dad never said much about stupid choices that I can recall. He thought of life as one big adventure. I could never understand what he saw in my mother. Why would my freedom-loving, adventurous dad pick someone so unlike himself? So scared and controlling? I wondered if I had chosen the same path. Was I also picking someone just because he was completely different from me?

I closed the computer top because I didn't want to think about any of it anymore. I climbed back into bed and Luke immediately rolled over and spooned me into him. Despite the pain of my welts, I reveled in his warmth and strength. I listened to his breathing and within minutes fell back asleep.

CHAPTER THIRTEEN

"Morning babe," Luke said as he rolled over, wrapping his arm around my waist. "How are you feeling?" He propped himself up on his elbow and leaned in to kiss my breast.

I moved around a bit in bed and said, "My body's sore and tight. I need to call into work. Don't think I'll be running today, either."

"Today will be a busy day for me," he said as he suddenly climbed out of bed. "Since you have the day off, plan a get together for your friends and family for Friday. Make the arrangements ... order some food."

"Oh, well ... I certainly can't have my father and mother in the same place and I usually don't mix my mother with my friends—"

"Jane, love, just work it out. As I've said, I can handle your mother. Wait on your father if you must but otherwise let's get it out of the way, shall we?"

"Okay," I said, filled with trepidation. I lay there wondering how I would feel if they all disliked him. Would they sense the danger lurking under the surface?

"If I have time today I would love to get some shots of you. Your welts are healing quickly," he said as he ran his hand down my buttocks and thighs. "But I think they will still photograph well."

"Hmmmm," I said distracted by his touch.

He rolled me onto my side and swatted my ass.

"Hey," I said, yelping.

"Time's a-wastin'," he said as he left the room.

CR

I left messages for Parker and Sandy but put off calling my mother. I thought of inviting Allison but worried about mixing work with my personal life. I didn't think Allison would talk about Luke at the office but couldn't be sure.

I wrote for a while and then made Luke and me turkey sandwiches for lunch. Taking the chance of bothering him, I knocked on his studio door.

"Come in," he said.

"Lunch," I said, holding out the plate.

"Come here, love," he said. He took the plate from my hand and pulled me toward him. "Thank you. That was very thoughtful of you." He kissed me thoroughly, leaving me dizzy with lust. I enjoyed sitting on his lap and pushing his light brown straight hair out of his eyes.

"Did you make all your calls?" Luke said, looking at me from under his brow.

"I called Sandy and Parker but have put off calling my mother."

"Give me her number," he said as he picked up the phone beside him.

I dictated the number to him and could hear the phone ringing. Luke held me in his arms as he waited.

"Hello," he said.

"Who is this?" I heard her say in her usual aggravated tone.

"Jacqueline?" he said. His voice sounded pleasant and inviting.

"Yes?" she said as a question.

"This is Luke, Jane's lover and we would like to invite you over on Friday evening ... say around seven. I look forward to meeting you."

"Oh ... well, I will have to check my schedule, of course," she said. I stifled my laughter but still shook up and down. I rolled my eyes.

"I'm sure you will cancel whatever you may have scheduled. Go now and get a pen so I can give you the address."

The ease with which he handled my mother gave me a great sense of relief.

"Jane, you still need to call Allison and I want you to invite Pierce and your boss as well."

"Oh Luke, you have got to be kidding," I said in a whiney voice. I stopped short of stomping my foot.

"Not at all. I don't want Pierce or your boss, for that matter, bothering you. Having them over will make things clear to all ... unless, of course, you're ready to leave your job. In that case just call Allison."

I knew what he was doing, but I also knew I wasn't ready to give up my independence. Leaving my job meant that I had to give up my apartment and car and I wasn't ready for that.

Another thought occurred to me. "Maybe we should have this get-together at a restaurant," I said. "That way we don't have to worry about the food or cleaning up."

Luke laughed so hard I thought he would fall off the stool he was sitting on. "You are so transparent, Jane. I haven't yet decided whether or not I will allow you to wear clothes. We may have to do a trade for that privilege. We have a couple of days to talk it over."

"If I'm so transparent then you should know I'd never consider meeting with those people naked."

"*Those* people," he said, still laughing. "Of course it won't be up to you. Rule Number Seven states clearly that you will always be naked in this apartment. We have already made an exception for your running on the tread. You, as always, are free to leave at anytime but make no mistake: this is up to me, not you. Get out of here," he said, pushing me away from him toward the door. "I have work to do. Make those calls, Jane, and thanks again for the sandwich." He dismissed me like some hired help.

I left the room in a furious mood. Who the fuck did he think he was? Why was nothing simple with this man? He was capable of making me so happy one minute and then completely pissing me off the next. I didn't want to call Pierce or Brian. I grabbed the phone from the table next to the couch without thinking and dialed Allison's work number.

"Hi, this is Allison, how may I help you?"

"Hi, Ally, it's Jane," I said.

"Oh, hi Jane, I didn't think you were at work today."

"Oh, I'm not."

"Are you okay?"

"Yes, I'm fine, I just needed the time off. I'll be back tomorrow and by the way, I told Brian I was fighting a cold."

"Okay, so—"

"So I called to invite you over to our place—mine and Luke's—for a get-together Friday evening at seven. Rick can come, too."

"Rick works until at least seven, but I'd love to come. I'm looking forward to meeting your man. By the way, Pierce came by my office today to ask if I knew anything about your Luke."

"Really?" I said. I was sure that was a bad sign.

"Yes, really. Of course I told him I know nothing and he took off quickly."

"I hope he's not going around asking other people."

"I wouldn't worry about him. He just has a small crush on you is all. See you tomorrow at work?" she asked.

I heard the other line pick up. "Jane?" Luke said. His tone of voice clearly told me he was livid.

"Oh, sorry," I said. "I'll be right off." My heart pounded out of my chest. I knew I shouldn't have used his phone but my anger propelled me to get the calls over with and clearly I wasn't thinking straight. I knew it would make no difference to Luke.

"Come in here as soon as you're done," he said and hung up.

"I have to go," I said to Allison.

"Is everything okay?" she asked.

"Yeah," I said. "I have to go." I hung up the phone. Petrified, I didn't move right away. I couldn't handle another disciplining on top of the one I'd received last night.

Somehow I managed to propel my feet in the direction of the office and knock on the door.

"We're not having a good day, are we, Jane?" he said. He stood there next to the whips and paddles as a way of intimidating me and it worked.

"It was stupid of me. I wasn't thinking. I just called Allison. I didn't mean anything by it. I thought you meant to use the phone when you said make the calls."

"I'm not sure I've impressed upon you the importance of respecting my belongings. I thought I was very clear that phone is for work only."

"I promise it won't happen again, Luke."

"I think you know by now how things work between us, Jane. Please sit in the chair."

"Luke, please," I said.

"Say the words, Jane, or shut the fuck up and sit down. What's it going to be?"

I moved slowly over to the chair that was on the canvas backdrop and sat down. The chair was bare metal and cold. Its hard surface pushed into my welts, making me wince.

Luke knelt before me and tied my legs to the chair. He then walked behind me and tied my arms together and fastened the rope to the chair's back legs. I couldn't imagine what he planned to do to me. He had never struck me anywhere but on the back of my body. I panted, finding it hard to breathe. I was more scared then aroused but my nipples disagreed.

After tying me securely, Luke knelt down in front of me again and gently sucked on each of my nipples. He seduced them until they were completely erect. By then the fear had

subsided and the raw need to be filled and used had taken over.

He strutted over to the wall and took down a small paddle. It looked exactly like the paint stirring paddle he'd used before but was much smaller.

"Oh … uh … oh," I said as I realized his intentions. I had almost blurted out NO! But I was fully aware of the consequences of such a reaction. *Please no,* I begged silently.

"This is going to hurt those big nipples of yours," he said without any particular expression, which frightened me.

I wouldn't let myself cry, although the tears were already brimming in anticipation of the first jolt of pain.

"Uh … uh … uh …." Sounds of protest came out of me involuntarily as the pain of the first swat on my right nipple ripped through my body. I needed to scream, *Oh fuck, oh fuck, NOOOoooooo,* but managed not to utter a word. The pain was so acute that it knocked the breath out of me. I tried desperately to twist my upper body to keep my nipples away from his strikes but he grabbed my breast and pressed my nipple down.

He switched to the other side of me and I braced myself in expectation of the pain my left nipple would endure. "Ugggggh." The sound tore out of me as a wave of nausea roiled my stomach. He grasped my breast as he had on the other side.

"One more on each side," he said.

"Oh, oh, oh," I said. What I wanted to say was, *No, please, wait. You've made your point,* but then I realized that the pain had already subsided somewhat. I would survive. The need to cry had vanished and a lustful craving had taken its place. I wanted him to untie me and fuck me hard. I wanted him to throw me down on the ground and ram his hard cock into me without mercy. I wanted to be devoured and reborn. My mind twisted inside with strange thoughts and visions.

Reality called me back with a harder thwack to my poor swollen right nipple and the tears I had struggled to hold back broke loose. I didn't think I could stand the hit to the other side. I struggled to pull my arms loose but couldn't free them. I wanted to protect my left nipple with my hand but I was exposed and bound and helpless.

"Last one," he said. "You are amazing, my love … such tolerance."

I wanted to hit him, spew my anger all over him. I wanted to make him eat his compliments. I wanted him to ….

"Oooopf," I groaned. "Uh, uh, uh, uh." The pain made me dizzy, and without the ropes holding me tight, I would have fallen off the chair.

"You can't imagine how beautiful you look," he said.

I shook my head no as he lifted my head by my chin and looked down on me.

"Oh, but you do, my love, so beautiful."

Tears spilled over my cheeks as I continued to shake my head in protest at his assertion that somehow under these conditions I looked beautiful to him. He knelt down in front of me and pulled my buttocks forward. He tasted me for the first time since leaving for Japan.

"You may think you don't care for pain, but your body says otherwise. You are so wet, Jane, and you taste so good. Should I continue or untie you?"

"Yes, please," I said.

"Yes, indeed," he said and lowered his mouth to my wet cunt.

After giving me two powerful orgasms he picked up his camera and took pictures. I was so satiated I didn't care what he did. He untied me from the chair and turned me around, leaning my upper body forward.

"Push your legs out more, Jane, so I can see the marks on your thighs."

My salvation came when he finally laid me on the

ground and fucked me hard from behind. My nipples pushed against the floor reminding me of my punishment. He came into me with the force of a powerful animal having its way.

We lay on the floor recovering together, my head on his chest. He gently stroked my hair and held me close.

"I need to get back to work, love," he said. "And you still need to make some phone calls. Your phone."

"I don't want to move," I said and snuggled deeper into his arms.

"It shouldn't take me much longer and then we can grab a bite out if you'd like."

"Okay," I said. I dreaded the phone calls I still had to make. I walked out the door of the studio, stopped by the bathroom to clean up, and headed to our bedroom.

My cellphone sat in its charger. I rested on the edge of the bed and stared at it. I couldn't decide what to say. These weren't men with whom I socialized. I decided to blame it on Luke.

"Brian, please," I said, after his secretary picked up.

"Hello, this is Brian," he said.

"Hi Brian, its Jane."

"Hello, are you feeling any better?"

"Yes, thanks. I'm calling to invite you to a small get-together we are having on Friday night at seven. Luke, my boyfriend, would like to meet you. Allison will be there and I am inviting Pierce as well. What do you think?"

"Oh well, sure, I'll come," he said.

"Great," I said but wished he had declined. I gave him the address and hurriedly ended the call.

The next call I put off for another twenty minutes. I knew Pierce would ask too many questions. I wondered if he would talk about me at work. I ignored the possibility that Luke would require me to be naked. He must have already figured out that it would be a deal breaker for us. I guess I'd learn soon enough if Luke wanted to keep me around.

"Hello, this is Pierce."

"Hi Pierce, this is Jane," I said.

"I know who this is," he said. I forgot that he would be upset that I missed lunch with him today. His voice made it clear he was angry. "What do you want? Another favor?"

I took a deep breath and said, "I want to invite you to a get-together on Friday evening at seven that Luke and I are having at our place. He'd like to meet you."

"I don't get you, Jane," he said.

"Is that a yes or a no, Pierce?" I said. *Please say no,* I pleaded silently. *Please.*

"The chance to meet the infamous Luke? Of course I'll be there."

Fuck, shit, fuck, I thought. I gave him the address and hung up.

I still needed to make the food arrangements. Pizza was too casual and sushi too formal. I decided on Italian and considered asking Luke what restaurant we had just gone to then thought better of it. Never would I willingly face those people again. Being blindfolded and not actually seeing them didn't lessen my humiliation. I called a place nearby and placed an order for Friday.

❦

The rest of the week went by too quickly. Luke and I avoided talking about the party until Thursday night just before bed.

"So, have you come up with something to trade me for the privilege of wearing clothes tomorrow night?" Luke said as we spooned in bed after making love.

"No," I said. I knew the conversation had to happen but it pissed me off anyway. I pulled away from him and turned around to face him. "How about choosing to be generous? You must know that I'd never prance about naked in front of those people. And really, do you want my boss and Pierce to see me that way?"

"Before we continue this conversation, let's just be clear that it's not up to you who sees you naked. You chose to give up that right. AND if I wanted you to prance or fuck or dance in front of *those* people, the only choice you would have would be to comply or to leave. Are we clear?"

"Crystal," I said. I sat up in the bed and crossed my arms in front of me.

"Are you sassing me?" he said, smiling and pulling me over to him.

I pushed him away and said, "What do you want?"

"My preference would be to see you 'prance' around naked, as it is my favorite way to see you, but I can tell that might be a bit beyond you at the moment and I do mean *for now*. So we must come up with a barter. I have a couple of ideas but thought maybe you had something in mind."

"I don't, so why don't you just tell me," I said. I crossed my legs and prepared myself for the worst.

"Here are a couple of choices: One, I could take you back to the Italian restaurant and let my good friend Marcello whip you himself. He can be a bit harsh in his application and he has requested your presence after the little show we put on for him. Two, I could give you another Pierce assignment that won't be as easy to get through as the first one. Of course that would have to happen tomorrow at work, and that might make it more awkward to have him over tomorrow night. I'm sure you could handle it, though, as you'd have your clothes to protect you and of course me as well. Three, and my personal favorite: You could go to your boss's office and masturbate for him. Again, having him over after that might be a stretch—"

"Those aren't really choices. I mean I couldn't possibly pick number two or three and I have no interest in letting a stranger have an opportunity to beat me—"

"Well, then, I suggest you come up with something good on your own."

Desperate and not thinking clearly I blurted out, "How about you invite your friends over? I could be naked in the apartment for that get-together."

"Brilliant, Jane. I love that idea. It's not only a fair trade but one that completely excites me. It'll take some planning on my part but yes, we have a deal."

I regretted it the moment I suggested it. I knew it would be worse than I could possibly imagine. I got out of bed and paced up and down our bedroom a couple of times.

"Can I take that back?" I said. "I'm sure I could come up with something else you would like."

"Absolutely not, Jane," he said, leaning toward me and grabbing my arm. "It's the perfect barter. I should've thought of it myself. Come here, babe. We need to get to sleep. Tomorrow will be a long day."

I acquiesced and crawled into bed next to Luke. He was out in minutes, but I lay there distraught. I couldn't shut my mind down as I agonized over tomorrow's party and what else might transpire in the near future.

CHAPTER FOURTEEN

On Friday morning I used my run as pure therapy, trying to run all the tension away. Fortunately, the busy day at work went by quickly. I left thirty minutes early, hoping to shower and do some last minute cleaning up. When I got back to the apartment I undressed quickly by the door and found that Luke wasn't there. An outfit was laid out for me on our bed, a note atop the neatly folded clothes.

> Dearest Jane,
>
> I have a couple of errands to run but should be back in time to greet our guests. You may dress at 6:30 p.m. If I am not back right at 7:00, know I am on my way.
>
> Vito's Restaurant called and said they will be delivering at 6:30 p.m.
>
> I hope you are looking forward to this as much as I am.
>
> Loving you,
> Luke

I wasn't looking forward to it; I only hoped to survive. To me, it was on a par with going to the dentist or the gynecologist.

I did a quick check around the place, picking up the newspaper and dropping it into the magazine holder. I placed my work clothes in the dry cleaning bag. I set out all the plates, glasses and utensils and spread the tablecloth I'd

purchased for the party. When everything looked just right, I headed for the shower.

There was a knock on the door at 6:15 p.m. I had just finished my shower and my immediate thought was that Luke had set it up. I wouldn't have been a bit surprised to find out one of his errands included dropping an extra tip by the restaurant.

"One minute please," I said.

I had a choice to make. Should I answer the door wrapped in a towel? I wouldn't be technically dressed but I wouldn't be naked, either. I knew what I had to do but stood there by the door waiting.

The knock came again and a male voice said, "This stuff is heavy, could you please get the door?"

"Ugh," I said out loud. "Fine." I opened the door and the man/boy, who couldn't have been more than eighteen or twenty, almost dropped the stack of containers.

"Well, come in," I said. I held the door and followed him into the kitchen. "There is fine," I said, pointing to the counter to the right of the sink. "Hang on a sec while I grab my wallet."

"Oh, it's all paid for," he said, averting his eyes to just above my right shoulder.

"Well, a tip then," I said, heading back toward the bedroom.

"That was taken care of as well," he said. He didn't move at all. He just stood there, rooted to the spot.

I had two simultaneous impulses. One was to say, "Well then, goodbye and there's the door,"—not very nice, but I was pissed after all. The second could have only come from the alter ego that seemed to want to claim me. I was so angry at Luke I wanted to kneel in front of the boy/man and suck his cock until he came. Of course that would enrage Luke—the desired effect—but then I'd suffer as never before. Although my body had quickly adjusted to his propensity for causing

me pain/pleasure, the wrath that I would face for that crazy act kept me in check.

I headed toward the front door and opened it for him. He pivoted on his spot but didn't move closer.

"Do you always answer the door naked?" he asked, making eye contact for the first time.

Desire surged through me as his blue eyes penetrated mine. He wanted me. I looked down and saw just how much. I knew I needed to get him out of my apartment as soon as possible. "Most of the time, yes," I said.

"You have a beautiful body," he said. He fondled his erection through his pants.

His tall lanky body hadn't filled out to manhood. Messy brown hair framed his angular face.

"You need to leave. I still have a lot to do to get ready for the party."

"Can I come by some other time?" he said.

"The man who paid you …." I said.

"Yes."

"He's my boyfriend and isn't much into sharing." That's what I told him, although I wasn't sure it was true anymore.

"Oh, him? I thought maybe he was your father or older brother."

I laughed because Luke was only ten years older.

"What's so funny?" he asked.

"Nothing," I said, "but I can't wait to tell him you thought he was my father. The sass cometh." I laughed even harder at myself.

"Oh … well then I guess I better go," he said.

He headed for the door but my rejection didn't deter his cock.

"Later," he said.

"Later," I said back.

I closed the door and ran to the bedroom to dress. The outfit was a bit more risqué then I'd have chosen but the

brown patterned skirt with beige and blue leaves pinched in my waist and the bra under my blue blouse pushed up my breasts to give me a curvier figure. I liked it. I appreciated how much more extreme the outfit could've been. He could've made me wear what I wore to the restaurant. Clearly even he had boundaries. At least I hoped he did. I still felt extremely wary of what would take place that night—if the delivery boy was any indication. Convinced Luke had put him up to it all—including being early—what might follow put my stomach in knots.

I fluffed my hair in the mirror. Just a few minutes before seven, I sat down on the couch, noticing how odd it was to be sitting there fully dressed. I decided that writing might relieve the butterflies in my stomach. No sooner had I opened the computer when I heard a knock at the door. I shut the laptop and took a deep breath.

"I'm coming," I said. There stood my mother. I should have prepared myself for the fact that my mother was timely if nothing else. I silently cursed Luke for not being here to "handle" her.

"Hello, Mother," I said as I leaned in to kiss her on the cheek.

She brushed past me and said, "Well, let's take a look at the place. I can see I'm the first one here. She walked straight over to the bathroom and said, "Is this the only bathroom?"

"Yes, Mom," I said.

"It's a closet, not a bathroom. Why didn't you just move into your place, Jane? You have two bathrooms there."

"This is more convenient for work, and although the bathroom isn't ideal, it works for us."

"Tsk," she muttered.

"Would you like to see the kitchen?"

"I guess," she said.

When I'd finished giving her a tour of the place, she pointed to the second bedroom door. "What's in there?"

"Luke's office."

"I want to see it," she said. She didn't wait for me to respond. She made a beeline to the door, grasped the handle, and found it locked. "Why is the door locked?"

"He likes it that way," I said. I couldn't think of anything else to say.

"What does that mean, Jane?" She faced me, hands on her hips.

A blessed knock saved me from my mother giving me the third degree. She followed me as I opened the door to find Brian. I had hoped it would be Parker or Sandy.

"Hi Brian," I said as I welcomed him into the apartment. "Please meet my mother, Jacqueline. Mom, this is my boss, Brian."

"Jackie," she said, offering him her hand.

"A pleasure," Brian said as he held my mother's hand and kissed it.

I saw my opportunity to slip away and said, "Mind if I leave you two for a few minutes while I check on the food?"

"No problem," my mother said. She didn't even turn to look at me. All her focus was on Brian. Brian raised an eyebrow and smiled.

I mouthed, *Thank you* and walked away to the kitchen.

Fortunately Allison, Parker, and Sandy all showed up in the ensuing fifteen minutes and did a wonderful job of socializing with everyone.

Pierce's absence was a relief. I hoped he had changed his mind. As for Luke …. Where was he? My anger intensified as the minutes ticked past and he failed to materialize. At one point I was close to tears and excused myself to the bathroom.

At five minutes to eight both Luke and Pierce walked into the apartment together. That made me even more furious. Had they been out together? If so, what the hell had they been talking about?

Luke strode in and scooped me into his arms, hugging me to him. "Sorry, babe," he said in my ear. "I'll make it up to you."

"You better," I said, whispering back.

Once Luke was there the energy of the party completely shifted. In the midst of lively conversation, he kept everyone's glass full, including mine. Our guests ate Caesar salad, spinach lasagna, and chicken penne with broccoli while consuming several bottles of wine and champagne. I barely picked at my food.

Luke wielded remarkable power over the group. With him there I actually enjoyed the party. I looked on in awe and once in a while we'd lock eyes and he'd smile that all-knowing smile. It felt warm and endearing.

My mother fell in love with Brian that evening and, several times over the next couple of months—especially when I was most unsure of my life with Luke—she'd tell me how I'd missed out on happiness with Brian. She was convinced that he was the perfect man for the perfect wedding. More to the point, he was the perfect man for *her*, if she'd only been younger.

On that evening Luke won them all over, even my mother. When she told Luke she wanted to see his office, he thankfully declined. I think the locked office had her a bit disconcerted, but he made her laugh in a way I'd never seen. My mother drank her share of champagne and behaved herself for the most part.

When I walked her to the door she said, "I can see why you let Luke sweep you off your feet. You seem happy, Jane, and that's good." I knew that part of her affability was the liquor speaking but I appreciated it nonetheless.

"Thank you for coming," I said and actually meant it. "Are you okay to drive, Mom?"

"Yes, of course I am. I never let myself drink too much. Let me by, please."

"Drive safely," I said.

Pierce left next and said, "We're good, Jane. Luke explained it all to me and now I understand."

Pierce's *understanding* had me more worried than Pierce's confusion. I wondered what Luke had actually said to him.

Sandy left next. As she was leaving she said, "I would love for the four of us to go out. I'm sure Jason and Luke would hit it off famously."

"I'll ask Luke," I said. "It was so good to finally see you. I feel like it's been months but it's only been a couple of weeks."

"Life really has changed for you in a short while. That's obvious. I think it's a good change and I'm happy for you, Jane." She gave me a big hug and I accompanied her to the door.

"This was a lot of fun," Allison said. "Rick is going to kill me because I invited another person to the wedding."

Parker said, "If it's going to cause problems, Ally, I won't—"

"Not at all," Allison replied, laughing. "It was so great meeting you and I definitely want you there. He'll live with it, not to worry."

"Thanks Jane," Parker said, "This was great and I can see I've nothing to worry about. Sometimes we just get lucky. Hopefully I'll be next."

"They say weddings are a great place to meet someone," Allison said.

I hugged them both goodbye.

Brian was the last to leave. Luke and Brian were deep in conversation as I said goodbye to all of our other guests. I couldn't fathom what they'd have to talk about or what they could possibly have in common.

Luke walked Brian to the door and Brian said, "I clearly waited too long, but the best man won." He smiled and then said, "See you at work on Monday."

"Oh," I said. "Okay then, thanks for coming."

The night had put me in a tailspin. I should've been happy that everyone liked Luke so much, but for some reason I was even more concerned.

"Well, that turned out well, Jane," Luke said as he closed the door. "You did a great job. You have wonderful friends who really care about you, and your mother is a hoot. I even thought Pierce and Brian were an interesting pair."

I turned to face him, the wine giving me courage. "Why were you late? I had to make excuses for you. I remember that first day outside my office when you said, and I quote, 'I am never late.' " I began to undress, avoiding his eyes.

"Is that really what you want to talk about? I thought we would climb into bed and I could make it up to you."

"Were you out with Pierce? What did you say to him? Why, all of a sudden, does he 'understand'?"

"Jane, come here and let me take you in my arms. We can talk about all of this tomorrow." He reached for my hand. "Did you tell the restaurant to deliver the food early?" I would not be deterred.

Luke laughed but then tilted his head. "If you aren't interested in cooperating, I could tie you down and have my way with you."

"Answer my questions and then you'll see just how cooperative I can be."

"I told you. *Tomorrow*, Jane. You're pushing it. Please come to me, as I truly want to make my tardiness up to you."

Unwilling to let the matter rest, I crossed my arms in front of me.

"Have it your way," he said. "Don't think I'll enjoy it any less. To the contrary, I will enjoy it even more."

"No," I said, stepping back as he approached.

He just laughed and easily scooped my slight body up into his arms. I kicked like a little kid wanting to be put down.

"So you want it rough, do you?" he said, laughing again. He hauled me to the bed, dropping me in the center.

I scurried to the side and tried to stand. In the meantime he retrieved leather straps from the nightstand, pushed me back down on the bed, and flipped me over. I kicked him in

the stomach but he foisted his body forcefully over mine. I wiggled to get out from under him but he held me fast. He flipped around so his head lay at my feet. After fastening the strap to my right ankle he managed to attach it to the corner of the bed. He did the same with my left leg. Tethered to the length of the bed instead of the width, I was spread out as much as possible.

His leg was near my mouth so I bit into it with all the force I could muster.

"Oh, Jane, you're going to pay for that."

"Fuck you," I said.

"And for that as well. My advice is to cooperate and shut the fuck up because I have an entire weekend to keep you tied up and show you the error of your ways. Unless …. Just say the word. Is that what you want?"

"I want you to answer my questions! That's what I want."

"I answer questions when I'm good and ready. I apologized for being late and planned to make it up to you but you wouldn't let me. I never implied I'd be willing to account for my time. That's none of your business. I'm surprised, completely surprised, by this turn of events. I thought we threw a wonderful party. It was a good night and yet …. Too much wine, perhaps? At any rate, you've more than earned what you'll be receiving."

He walked around the bed and fastened my arms to the side corners.

I had stopped fighting the inevitable. Did I want him to punish me? Is that why I goaded him? I used to think I knew why I behaved in certain ways but at that point I struggled to understand myself. The party had turned out great, as he said, even though he showed up late. Why was I pushing him?

He didn't go to his office to get a whip or paddle. He didn't use his hand to spank me. He simply fucked me up the ass without lubrication until he came. I had never felt more

humiliated or violated. The game of pleasure and pain didn't exist that night. The sex didn't turn me on in the least, and I'm sure that was his intention. Even with all the discipline he had inflicted in the past, my pleasure was the ultimate reward. After the party there was none.

He abruptly released me and left me alone in the room. He didn't return to our bed that night.

 beginning

The next morning I found him sleeping on the couch. I removed my blouse and bra before I crawled back into bed. The sobs shredded me as the reality of my life besieged me.

He must have heard because he came in and spooned me to him. He held me as the weeping racked my body.

"I love you, Jane, and in time you'll come to learn my ways. I'm not one to be pushed."

I continued to cry. He stroked my head as he held me and after a while the tears subsided. I didn't say anything because I didn't know what to say. I felt confused, hurt, and angry—but also safe in his arms. My mind split over feeling safe and rescued by my persecutor.

I lay there, wondering if we could ever have a normal, healthy relationship. The core of me already knew the answer. I just wasn't ready to face it.

CHAPTER FIFTEEN

That night several things became clear. It was as if my tears had washed away my self-deception.

After the party I essentially had no one I could talk to about this crazy life I'd chosen. My mother and my friends had experienced the normal, happy, great guy who moved about with confidence and a winning smile. They didn't know that the artwork behind the couch was used to tie me up and whip me. They had no idea what lay behind the door to the second bedroom. They didn't realize I spent my time naked, that Luke's control over me was absolute even if I fought it.

"Are you ready for some breakfast?" he asked.

"I guess," I said.

We got up and walked into the kitchen. He had cleaned up the party from last night. It was as if it hadn't happened until he opened the refrigerator and I saw all the Italian food.

"Shall we reheat leftovers?" he asked.

For me, eating that food again would have been like reliving the party.

"We can toss the rest of it as far as I'm concerned," I said.

"It's not nearly as good as Marcello's Restaurant. Why didn't you order from there?"

"I thought the food was fine, but I cannot stomach eating it again. You're so funny sometimes, Luke. First of all, I didn't know the name of the restaurant you took me to because …."

"Right," he said, laughing.

"And, secondly, I'd never show my face there again willingly."

"They didn't see your face because you were blindfolded. Now who's being the funny one?"

"Regardless, I'd think they were all staring at me."

"We'll have to work on some of those inhibitions of yours, Jane."

"Inhibitions? How many people are okay being whipped in front of an audience? A small number, I would think."

"Perhaps. Perhaps not. People change. You'll see."

"So, breakfast?" I said, changing the subject.

"I'll whip something up," Luke said and laughed.

I still wanted my questions answered but I didn't dare poke the sleeping lion. We ate in silence, the distance palpable. I watched him as he read the paper. Being disconnected from the one I loved made my heart feel as if it were physically breaking. I felt depressed and lonely. I knew I should've gone running first thing, but now that my belly was full of eggs and toast, I had no interest.

"How about a bed day?" he asked.

"What's a bed day?"

"We spend all day in bed. We can read, make love, talk, watch a movie on the laptop, eat dinner, etc., all in bed. You could write if you wanted to."

"I'm not in a very good mood, so I'm not sure what kind of 'bed company' I'd make," I said. I leaned my face on my hand and looked up at him.

"I'm sure I can help with your mood. How about we shower, and after, I answer your questions from last night? What do you say? Come on." He put his hand under my chin and brought his mouth to mine. I fell into the kiss as his energy overtook me. He explored my mouth with his tongue and sucked on my lower lip. My treasonous body responded to him as if I was a fiddle for his playing.

He lifted me up and pulled me onto his lap. His cock was hard and I was wet. I slid down on top of him and he used his arms to lift me up and down. I avoided his eyes. I was aroused

but sad at the same time.

"Look at me," he said.

I didn't comply. He stopped moving my body and used his hand to lift my chin. "Baby, look at me, please."

This time I did as he asked. I saw the love there and allowed it to penetrate me. When we connected like that all thoughts of my ultimate doom vanished and euphoria took over. Again and again he could bring me back to him.

❦

After the shower, as I climbed into bed, I pondered how to best approach him. I had learned to make my words count. "Question time," I said.

"You know how to kill a perfectly good mood," Luke said but smiled.

"You said you'd answer all my questions. Better to get them over with quickly than drag them out. It'll be like ripping a band-aid off a wound," I said.

"I guess your mood's improved, Sassy Girl," he said, hugging me close to his chest.

"Why were you late?" I hurtled forward with abandon.

"I had errands to do and they ran long. That's all I'm going to say. I don't ask you to account for your day and I demand the same respect. Next?"

I pushed away from him. "If I had showed up almost an hour late for a party here …. I can't even imagine the consequences, so don't give me that crap."

"That crap?" he said. He pushed me down onto my back and straddled my waist. He held my arms down around the top of my head.

"Hey, let me up!" I said. I was completely pinned to the bed by his strength.

"Not until we are done with these silly questions. Continue, please," he said, smiling down at me. He leaned in and kissed my nose.

"Don't patronize me." I struggled to get out from under

him but his sinewy body and strong arms kept me in place. "You think holding me down is going to keep me from asking the questions I need answers to?"

"Remains to be seen, does it not?"

"Again, why were you late? Under those circumstances, I would have to account for my time. I'd also receive a good paddling, I imagine."

"Are you saying you want to paddle me? This big man? Now that's funny." He laughed so hard it rocked us both on the bed.

"That's a funny image, hmmm. Maybe something for me to write about," I said. He moved one hand to hold both of mine and tickled my right side with his free hand.

"Hey, that's not fair," I said, laughing.

"I never said things between us would be fair. Did I?"

"No, but hey …. Wait, wait," I said between laughing. "How am I supposed to ask my questions?"

"That's the point," he said.

He stopped his tickling and began drawing circles around my right nipple. My breathing increased, revealing my craving.

"LUKE," I yelled. "Seriously!"

"Okay, but get it over with already. You're taking such a long time." He shook me again with his laugher.

"Were you out with Pierce?" I said, quickly.

"No, of course not. But to answer your next question and to get back to my exploration of your bodily reflex responses, I did have an opportunity to speak with him before coming up to our place. I told him I put you up to the task you performed. He seemed to buy it. I also asked if he was willing to be used in the future and guess what he said."

"Yes," I said. "But that won't really be necessary, right?"

"We shall see. Next?"

"The delivery of the food."

"Oh, did you like the delivery boy? I picked him out for

you. They were going to send some old guy. I thought you'd have more fun with the boy."

"Di— Did you change the time the food would be delivered?"

"Of course," he said. He smiled as if he was proud of himself.

"And his coming onto me?"

"I think your nudity was the culprit in that."

"How did you know I opened the door naked?"

"I was waiting downstairs to give him an extra tip."

"You're too much."

"Much better than too little I would think."

I laughed out loud. "Can I get up now?"

"Definitely not," he said. "Is the interrogation over? Because I have other plans for us."

"One more question that's been bothering me for a long time," I said.

"Let's get it over with quickly," he said, running his hand down my stomach and stopping just above my mound.

I squirmed, finding it hard to focus. "Luke, come on!"

"Ask me already, Jane, really!" He chuckled.

"Why did you tell me to get you a pack of cigarettes at the party when you don't smoke?"

The bed shook uproariously as the laughter exploded out of him. "Why do you think?" he said. "You're a smart girl."

"Oh," I said. I understood. He had just wanted to make the challenge of going downstairs even more difficult.

"Please tell me you're done with the interrogation."

"Just one more thing," I said, trying to suppress my giggles.

"Out with it."

"The delivery guy thought you were my dad," I said.

"Well, then, little girl," he said, adjusting us and rolling me over his lap. "This bad girl needs her spanking."

On Sunday I took my last pill and freaked. I would get my period in a couple of days and yet I had to be naked in the apartment. The fact that I hadn't considered that challenge earlier just showed how detached I had become from reality. Surely Luke would understand. I used tampons, but as every woman knows, they are not foolproof.

"I took my last pill today," I said.

"And?" he said.

"Well, I'll get my period in a couple of days and want to be able to wear underwear during that time."

"No. Keep a towel with you. That's what the others did."

His comment took my breath away. "The others?"

"We've been through this, Jane. There have been others before you. You already knew this. Yes, the others used a towel. Put one on couch, one on the bed and one for the chairs if we sit at the table. You'll get used to it like everything else. One woman just kept a towel with her and moved it around. You'll figure it out." I had been dismissed. He went back to reading the paper.

"How many others?" I asked. Angst constricted my throat trapping my breath.

"Jane, please, let's not do this again. We have a wonderful day ahead of us. We had an amazing day yesterday. Let's leave the past in the past."

With Luke I suffered jealousy for the first time in my life. My closest brush with jealousy up until then had happened after a boyfriend and I had called it quits. There was this woman from work who would get drunk and hit on him while we were still dating. After we broke up he slept with her. It pissed me off. He wasn't cheating on me but it still made me mad. I wasn't sure if that qualified as jealousy or righteous indignation. With Luke I felt jealousy at the very thought that there had been women before me and worse, that there could be women after me.

Why was I insecure about his love … about his loyalty? He'd been constant from the start, but I still questioned if our

love was special to him and even more importantly, whether or not I could easily be replaced. His reassurances didn't seem to help.

Luke put the paper down and turned to face me. It was as if he could hear my thoughts. "Baby, you're my one and only. As long as you choose to stay, you'll have my undying loyalty. I love you and have no interest in others."

"Okay," I said but wanted to say so much more. I wanted to know all about his past girlfriends. I needed to know if he had taken pictures of all of them and how they were different from me, but it would just piss him off if I asked.

He broke my train of thought by saying, "I have to go away again, love."

"When?" My shoulders dropped and I tried not to pout.

"Tuesday," he said.

"For how long this time?" I knew there was bite in my question but I couldn't control myself.

"Possibly a week. I don't want to be away from you that long so it may be shorter. I'm only flying to Seattle, so the turnaround time won't be as long."

"Oh."

"Of course you are welcome to come along. I'll be busy but will have time for you at night. Don't you have vacation time you can take off from work?"

"Yes, but we're required to give four weeks' notice prior to taking off longer than a day."

"You can always quit that job of yours and try your hand at writing a book. You have taken to writing, it seems. I watch you get lost in your own world when you're on the computer. Think it over, love."

"How would it work? I mean, I need my paycheck to pay for my condo and car. I get health insurance, life insurance and a 401K from my job."

"This is how it would work. You would get rid of your apartment. Sell it, and we will invest the money. Your car is a

lease right? You can turn it in early and I'll pay the penalty, if there is one. As we will be together most of the time, I can't see why we'd need more than one car."

"Oh ...." I didn't know what to say.

Being raised by a single mom had made me long for the day when a man would sweep me off my feet and free me from having to work. I had dreamed of writing the next great American novel. I imagined I should be jumping for joy but inside I felt petrified. How much autonomy would I have left? I wondered if I'd lose all control over my life.

"Jane?" he said. "Are you okay?"

I thought about what my mother said regarding the small bathroom. He said he had a lot of money but our apartment was small. I found it cozy and perfect for us, but if he had loads of money, why had he chosen that particular apartment?

"I don't know how to say this and I mean no offense but—"

"Just say it," he said.

"Well, our apartment is fairly small and has no elevator and really, I'm not complaining at all, but if you have so much money ...."

"That's not what I thought you were going to say," he said, laughing. "I picked this place because it was close to your work and immediately available. That's all. I figured we'd move when you finally decided to leave your job. Maybe move closer to the beach, because you love to run there, or move across the country. If I didn't love what I do, I could retire now. So there's no need for you to worry about insurance or anything else."

"It's a lot to think about," I said. I felt an instant shift in his mood.

"You can think about it while I'm away again. Keep in mind that I will tolerate us being apart less and less."

"What does that mean?"

"Exactly what I said. I want us to spend our lives together. My life involves a lot of travel and I want to share that part of it with you. There are many temptations out there when I'm traveling, and I've never strayed, but I only have so much tolerance for being alone."

"That feels like a threat to me," I said, standing up from the table and beginning to pace.

"Take it as you will, Jane. I'm a man with needs and I only have so much patience. I'll never do anything without telling you first and I'm telling you nothing will happen on this trip, but eventually we'll have to come to some arrangement if you plan to keep working at your job."

"Arrangement?" I said. I moved back toward the table. I wanted to cry and hit him at the same time but did neither. I just stood there in front of him with my arms hanging at my sides. I felt raw and exposed, as if my heart was splayed open for him. He was like a crow picking away at it.

"We'd see other people while I'm gone. You'd have the same prerogative as I, although I've been known to get jealous. It can be ugly." He paused. "At any rate, Jane, my preference is for you to give notice at your job as soon as possible."

☙

Luke left on Tuesday and, thankfully, we parted on good terms. However, while he was in Seattle, I discovered more than I had bargained for.

CHAPTER SIXTEEN

On the Thursday after Luke left I got home from work and heard his phone ring for the first time. I hadn't bothered turning off the ringer because the calls had been infrequent. By the time I went to bed, though, there had been a couple more, so I turned it off. During the night I was awakened several times by the phone in the second bedroom and realized they were coming hourly. By three o'clock in the morning I had convinced myself the caller had to be an exgirlfriend because no business associate would keep calling every hour throughout the night.

My stomach churned and I got very little sleep. At five in the morning I sent an email to Luke.

> To: LukeBandDphotos@controlme.com
> From: PlainJane368@yahoo.com
> Subject: The Phone
>
> Hi Luke,
>   The phone has been ringing every hour since I arrived home from work last night. I turned the ringer off on the phone in the living room but the one in your office keeps ringing, and I can hear it through the wall. I got very little sleep last night and am pretty grumpy.
>   Did you piss off an old girlfriend? Should I be worried for my safety? I know you hate my jealousy but it's running rampant right now.

Is there something you can do about the phone? I mean I know you're on the other side of the country but if there's a way for you to turn off the ringer remotely, please do so.

You can't get home soon enough, Luke. I hate us being apart.

I'll have a surprise for you when you get back.

I would love to get a call from you just to hear your voice.

Missing you so,
Jane

The calls continued until I left for work. When I returned home on Friday, only twenty minutes passed before the phone rang again. I checked my email but found nothing from Luke. I realized I didn't have his number. Or did I? I looked around the bedroom for the card he had given me with his email address. I dialed the number on the card from my cellphone. When the phone started ringing in his office, I felt defeated.

Staring at the card, I wondered if controlme.com was a website. I opened my laptop again and typed in www.controlme.com. As the first page populated, my own image stared back at me. There could be no mistake. I clicked on the picture of me tied to the chair following my nipple torment and subsequent orgasms. The click took me to another page of pictures. Had he taken so many of me already? There I was, tied to the bed, tied to the artwork behind the couch. There were pictures he had taken in the studio and even of me sleeping. I had to admit, as pissed off as I felt, that the pictures were good. But I couldn't imagine why people would actually buy these when they could already view them on the site. I wondered if anyone had framed photographs of me on their wall. Trepidation seized me at the thought.

I went back to the home page, where I found photos of at least twenty-five different women. Many were in school-girl outfits, exposing themselves under their skirts. One woman I recognized from the photograph in Luke's office. I clicked on her picture and found hundreds of photographs—several of them part of a series. Her first pictures were similar to mine, but as I scrolled down the webpage, they became more and more extreme. In one photo she had what looked like needles, thick ones, piercing each nipple. Frightened, I shut the laptop. I wondered if that was what he intended for me.

As with a bad car accident on the side of the road, I couldn't look away. I had to see the website again. I opened up the computer and resumed my hunt. Farther down on the same woman's page, she was shown tied face down on a table, spread-eagled. Six men, all erect, surrounded the table. I could have sworn one of them was Luke but couldn't be sure. His scar wasn't visible, and he was looking at the woman, not the camera.

My breathing became labored, but not from arousal. Two conflicting emotions tore at me. The first was raging jealousy. Although I had little experience with it I was sure now that it flowed through my veins like lava. The second was fear. Not your everyday fear, but abject terror. Was this the path I had embarked on? Was there still time to leave now while I could still, if only slightly, recognize myself? How could I be jealous and petrified at the same time? It made no sense whatsoever. Did I want to be her? I couldn't, could I?

I tried to rationalize the photos away. They had to be staged. Surely the men hadn't all fucked her. They had just been posing for the camera. Of course the link saying, "To see more of the series, please click here" challenged my efforts to mitigate the situation. I hit the link and it brought me to an email address. Luke's.

The realist in me said, "Jane, *your* photos weren't staged."

"SHUT UP," I screamed at myself.

As exhausted as I felt, I put on my running clothes and tied my sneakers. I checked my email once more as the phone rang again in Luke's studio. Taking a bottle of water, I flounced to my car.

Once on the beach I could finally breathe. I was able to find composure again as I ran. I knew I needed much more information than Luke had given me. It hadn't occurred to me to be enraged at him for posting my pictures without my express permission. What enraged me were the twenty-four *other* women on his site.

I was just a temporary means to a business end, money in Luke's pocket. I stopped running about halfway down the beach when a panic attack of mass proportions overtook me. I had given notice earlier that day at work and now my life with Luke was crumbling down around me. I dropped to my knees in the sand and cried. I knew I was making a scene but I couldn't stop myself.

When had I become the person who cries all the time? Constant weeping was another foreign phenomenon taking over my life.

As fate would have it or the annoying god above, Scott approached me with a look of utter concern.

"I'm fine," I said, pushing myself up to a standing position.

"Are you sure?" he asked, taking my arm to hold me steady.

"Perfectly," I managed.

"If you want to talk, you know where I am," he said, his green eyes piercing my teary ones.

"Talking was never our strong suit, Scott," I tried to joke as I wiped the tears off my cheek.

"Is it that guy from the house? Do you want to go back to my place?"

Such I guy, I thought. "No," I said. "Just a case of PMS

and a twisted ankle. I'll be fine." I limped off the sand onto the boardwalk for dramatic effect. As I went through the motions of stretching out my foot, I waved goodbye to Scott.

I ran back the way I had come, ending my run early.

Back at our apartment I undressed, stretched, and heard the damn phone ring again. I had fantasies of breaking the office door down and smashing it. The calls represented all the women on his website.

After my shower I sat on the bed staring at the computer. I wanted to check my email but knew if I opened the computer I would go back to his website and continue to torture myself with the women and photographs. It wasn't until about an hour later, when the phone rang again, that I opened the laptop and checked my email.

To: PlainJane368@yahoo.com
From: LukeBandDphotos@controlme.com
Subject: Re: The Phone

Baby,

Sorry about the phone calls. I've taken care of it but just in case you can go into the office and turn the ringer off. The key is just above the door on the frame. I'll make sure to do that in the future when I'm out of town.

Jealousy, as I've said, is okay in moderation. When it takes over, it's very unattractive and not at all sexy.

I miss you, too … and feel you need to be disciplined for leaving me on my own again. Expect it when I get home.

Looking forward to your surprise. I hope it's what I think it is. If so, expect a huge celebration.

You can't imagine how I'm missing that naked body of yours.

I will be home Sunday around lunchtime.
As always, be ready for me.

Love,
Luke

I couldn't believe he had left a key to the office door right above it. I went into the living room and sat on the couch. I looked over at the door, stared at it. *Had the key been there all along? Was this some sort of test?* All my answers were waiting in the office. I knew I could spend hours exploring the studio and all the files. Tomorrow would be soon enough.

I reached up on tiptoe and felt for the key. Sure enough the key worked. I turned the handle and walked through the sacred doorway straight to the phone. I turned off the ringer and quickly left. If I'd been smart, I'd have locked the door behind me, but I couldn't make myself do it.

I went back to the bedroom and crashed for the night.

When I awoke the next morning I remembered having a dream. I had gone searching through Luke's office but when I tried to leave, I found myself locked in and unable to get out. I knew my psyche was trying to warn me about something but I couldn't make any sense of it.

Taking only the time to brush my teeth and pee, I set my sights on his office. I had a plan of attack. I entered the office and closed the door behind me—it seemed weird to leave it open. I began my search at the wall on the right, rifling through the cabinets above the counter and sink, but only finding photo supplies. I assumed I would discover the same under the counter and went to the first of two file cabinets, surprised to find them unlocked. I sat on the floor and opened the bottom drawer.

I found exactly what I had been expecting—alphabetical files with women's names on them. They held negatives in

plastic protective sheets, photos, notes, and sometimes more.

I pulled several files at once, placed them on my lap, and went through them methodically, making sure to keep the contents in order. As I worked my way up I found one folder with a black and red garter in it. None of the photos or negatives showed the garter. I wondered what that meant.

Somehow it was easier to tolerate the pictures in the hundreds of files than on the website. I wonder if he rotated the images or if the ones currently displayed were the most recent.

I took out several files from the top drawer of the second cabinet and as I sat back down on the floor they slipped from my hands.

"Fuck, shit, fuck!" I screamed. I knew I was screwed. I paced back and forth, with the mess lying on the floor beside me. "That was pretty fuckin' stupid, Jane. Fuck, fuck, fuck," I said as I glanced down over and over again.

I quickly retrieved my computer from the bedroom and went back into the office, forgetting about the door. Sitting on the floor, I spent the next hour searching controlme.com to match the names and pictures. Of the five files I had dropped, I confidently matched three. In front of me lay a Jessica and a Betty. That left me with a fifty-fifty chance of replacing the remaining two correctly. Maybe because of reading Archie comics when I was a kid, I put the blonde in the Betty file and the brunette with the obviously enhanced breasts in Jessica.

I knew my mistake could come back to haunt me. All my searching hadn't revealed anything new. I had been looking for something more personal than just photographs. The garter discovery seemed the closest. I went back to that file and took note of her name. Page.

Could he have been married before? I had never asked him.

In a box on the floor at the far end of the room, I found a variety of restraints. Some looked worn and old and others, hardly used.

I rose to my feet, about to give up, when I remembered the cabinets under the counter. I started on the one closest to the door, finding nothing of interest, just more developing supplies. In the last cabinet near the far wall was a large black box. I pulled it onto my lap and opened the lid, revealing a photo album. I knew instinctively that the album was the treasure I had been seeking.

I sat for a minute with my heart racing. *Did I really want to confirm my suspicions? Hadn't that been the whole purpose of rummaging through his office in the first place?* I opened the album and saw pictures of Page first. The pages contained photos you would expect in any couple's album—pictures you could show your friends and family. In the first grouping, taken at a picnic, Luke appeared younger by about five years. Another series were of her laughing on different amusement rides. I paused, afraid of seeing them being married. Finally, skipping a bunch of pages, I flipped to the middle of the book. Janice—the woman in the photo on the wall across from me—surfaced in the next series of pictures.

I eventually made my way through the entire album, which held photos of six women in all. Each section exhibited normal relationship pictures, some with Luke, some without. The empty pages at the end of the book held impressions of photos. I wondered why the pictures had been taken out.

Over the next few days the photos in the album ate at me. I couldn't explain my justification for making a big deal out of nothing. *Why should I care, right?* After all, he had lived to the age of forty-five before meeting me and had never claimed to be celibate. What bothered me was the intimacy and normalcy I had seen in the photo album.

Where was the normalcy in our relationship?

I put everything back where I'd found it and even got a cloth from the kitchen to wipe down the file cabinet drawers and the other cabinets. Placing the album carefully back in the black box under the counter, I left the office.

I remained in a funk for the rest of Saturday. I didn't go on my long run and stayed in bed most of the time. Writing a bit about how I felt and questioning what I was doing to myself didn't help shift my mood.

When had I become like my mother—a liar and a snoop? What had happened to the girl who valued honesty above all else?

I wrote down all the changes I had experienced. I listed the pros and cons of calling my father and debated why I kept putting it off. Part of me wanted badly to see him, but my emotional state was so fragile and my heart so vulnerable at present that it seemed unwise. Fear of letting him in just to have him leave again also kept me from making the call. I ate a bagel only when hunger wouldn't allow me to rest. I knew I needed to snap out of it, for Luke would be back tomorrow.

On Sunday morning I decided my new goal in life was to get pictures of me into his photo album. Somehow creating a new focus for myself helped me to cope with everything I'd discovered. I contemplated telling Luke about my exploration of the website and hoped and prayed he'd never find out about my excursion into his office.

I needed to combat the increasing anxiety that filled me, but running was out because of the danger of another chance meeting with Scott. I used the treadmill instead. I expended the rest of my excess energy in cleaning our small apartment. It felt good to make it spotless for his return.

I decided to hold off telling Luke that I had checked out the website because I didn't know how he would react. I wanted him to be happy about me giving notice at work and being able to travel with him. I wanted our reunion to be wonderful.

CHAPTER SEVENTEEN

Luke breezed into the apartment, dropping his garment bag and suitcase at the door. He held a huge bouquet of Gerber Daisies and Gladiolas. I jumped up from the couch, closing the laptop as I stood, and met him half way. He lifted me into his arms, kissing me full on the mouth, breathing me in.

"Please tell me your surprise is what I think it is," he said as he presented me with the flowers.

"It is," I said, wrapping my arms even tighter around his neck.

"Then it's official. Two more weeks and then you're totally mine. You can't even begin to imagine the fun we'll have. I have many new ideas for pictures of you. I have plans for those flowers but first have you eaten because I'm starved." He spoke faster with more animation than I had yet experienced.

I laughed because I felt such joy in seeing him so happy. My gut wrenched momentarily over the things I had done while he'd been traveling but I managed to push them away. There would be time to torture myself over my indiscretions later.

"I love you so much," I said. "I'm so damn happy you're home *you* can't even imagine."

"Oh, but I can imagine. When you've found the woman you want to spend your life with, being away is very hard. Hard on both of us."

"Is that me?" I said.

He lifted me up like a bride and carried me to the bedroom. He put me down on my feet and slapped my ass. "Get dressed quickly, and you can do it in here. I need to devour you but Maslow's Hierarchy of Needs dictates I must eat first."

He went into his office and my heart skipped a couple of beats. I prayed he wouldn't notice anything out of place. After dressing quickly, I met him in the living room. He had a camera in his hands and my heart soared. Forgetting my crimes and misdemeanors, I danced about on the spot.

He took my hand in his and spun me around and around. I laughed as I almost lost my balance.

"Let's go," he said. "Grab the flowers."

ભ

At a grocery store we bought wine, cheese, grapes and bread. He drove east to the beach and pulled into a driveway of a house right on the shore.

"Whose place is this?" I asked as I climbed out of the car. The house had a 1970's architectural design. The rather large one-story structure had palm-frond fencing surrounding the back.

"A friend's," he said.

"Oh."

We walked around to the back, which faced the ocean. A large raised deck was built around a small pool and hot tub. Settling on a table and chairs at the far end that faced the beach, we unpacked our groceries and Luke uncorked the wine.

"You're prepared," I said.

"Always," he said and smiled. "You've made me extremely happy, Jane. We have much to talk about and much to celebrate."

I smiled and tossed a couple of grapes into my mouth. "Cups?" I asked.

"Be right back," he said. He walked into the house and returned with two wine glasses and a couple of napkins. He poured us both glasses of Chardonnay.

"You look beautiful in this light," he said. He lifted his camera off the table and took a picture of my profile.

One picture with my clothes on, I thought, smiling and rejoicing until he said, "Undress for me, love." Fully engaged in opening the cheeses and tearing off a hunk of bread, he missed my reaction.

"Huh?" I said. The house was mostly protected from the wind by sea grape bushes, but people could still see in if they looked. I had thought this would be a date, as in the photo album. There would be pictures of me and Luke with our clothes on.

He quickly pushed the table forward between us and seized my arm. His strength continued to amaze me, because he had yanked me onto his lap in a matter of seconds. He spanked my ass very hard with an open hand.

"Were you questioning me, Jane? Because—"

"Oh … no … of course not," I said, quickly moving to stand up. I disrobed responsively. I covered the bottom of the chair with my shorts and sat down.

"Are you sure you want this, Jane?"

"Yes, please," I said, but tears filled my eyes. "Do you love me, Luke?"

"Very much so, Jane. BUT I have my ways and it would serve us both if you learned them well."

"I know. I'm sorry. I'm trying, really. Truly I am. I'm so happy to have you back home. When you're away it's like a vital part of me is missing. It's just, well, everything is going so fast. You ask a lot of me, Luke. Sometimes I think we're going in one direction and the next second it all changes. It's hard to keep up." I wiped the tears off my cheeks and looked at him.

"You'll be freed from all that worry once you truly turn

your body over to me. You'll never have to worry about what direction you're going in because that is my job. You'll know I'm there to direct and protect you. Once you truly understand I only want your happiness and to fulfill your true desires you'll relax into us. We are an US, you know. You and me. We are family now."

He held out his hand and I walked over to him. He scooped me into his lap and held me as I cried. I cried for the life I had turned my back on for the unknown. I cried for the woman I was becoming and didn't really know. I cried because I felt desperate to belong. I wanted a place where I fit in, a place of safety. I questioned whether he could provide that for me.

"I'm scared, Luke," I said as the tears slowed their course down my cheeks.

"Baby, I know you are. That's a normal reaction. A lot is changing in your life and I'm here to help you through all of it. Trust in my strength and we'll get through it together. I know this is right."

"I still have so many questions. The ones you don't want to answer. You want me to trust you completely, give myself over to you but you don't trust me enough to give me my answers."

"We are at a standstill of sorts. You need me to become more open for you to give yourself to me and I need for you to give yourself to me before I can fully open up to you. And that's not something that would happen all at once. I'm a very private person and slow to share myself."

He placed me on my feet and stood himself.

"This is not how I planned it but," he fell to one knee, "will you marry me?"

So taken by surprise, I screamed, "Yes!" before I had a chance to even think about it. "Yes, Luke, oh yes! I will marry you."

"We can shop for a ring tomorrow if you'd like. Let's

commemorate this moment with some pictures of you." He swung the camera strap over his shoulder and took the flowers off the table. Clasping my hand in his, he led me naked to the beach.

People walked by, and some stopped to watch what was happening. He had me lie on the sand near the water. After fanning my hair out around me, he placed a Gerber Daisy behind my ear. Soon a daisy covered each areola and another, my mound. He lifted my arms over my head and positioned my legs into sevens. My upper body leaned to the right while my lower body leaned to the left.

He shot pictures from many different angles, adjusting my position and switching flowers.

As I lay there I found myself in another world. I stopped worrying about the onlookers and found a similar space I found when writing.

Gradually the way Luke posed me became more and more risqué, and he abandoned the flowers for complete nudity. He asked a young man watching us to join me. He stood about 5' 8," and his curly blond hair made him very attractive. He was lean and his tanned muscles rippled throughout his body. Without much prodding, he stripped off his trunks and lay beside me.

Luke continued to pose us, move us around, move the flowers in the sand. After what seemed like hundreds of shots he said, "It's time for a new location."

As we walked back toward the house Luke whispered in my ear, "Trust me, Jane, and remember, your body's mine … nothing to think about."

A chill ran over me and my skin broke out in goose bumps. *Go along*, I thought. *He wants to marry you.*

Luke moved us over by the pool, away from the opening in the bushes.

"Lie down on the lounge chair, arms above your head," he told me.

"Okay," I said.

Luke removed his belt from his shorts and wrapped it around my wrists. He fixed the belt to the top of the lounge.

I lay still, looking up at Luke and our new young friend. My nipples were rigid and ripples of soft wind caressed my exposed skin. I was turned on and fueled by anticipation. I had chosen to put my life in someone else's hands and although it frightened me, I felt a profound freedom.

Luke spoke to our stranger, who lowered himself at the far end of the lounge. Luke spread my legs wide and then came to kneel next to me. I turned to look at him and he stared into my eyes. He shook his head at the guy and looked back at me.

I felt warm breath and then a tongue on my thigh. The stranger kissed and nibbled his way up until his tongue lavished my clit. Luke and I kept eye contact the whole time. I knew this was for him. I knew that he got real gratification in controlling my body and my satiation.

Our boy/man did his best, but his style didn't cause my desire to grow. Luke looked at me questioningly and I shook my head. He immediately understood.

"Stop," he said. "She doesn't care for your technique. This has been fun but it's time for you to go."

"But …." the young man said, rising to his feet. His erection stood prominently in front of him.

Luke made a slight movement, the implied threat clear. My male model hurriedly snatched his clothes, threw on his trunks and left.

"You are amazing," Luke said to me as he removed his belt. "Sorry our friend wasn't as skilled as we would have liked. How about we go for a swim?"

Luke disrobed and we walked together into the shallow end of the pool. We sat down on the top step and looked at each other.

He kissed me deeply, our eyes open. "Do you want a big

wedding?" he asked. "Because I prefer it to be small and accomplished as quickly as possible."

"Yes, please," I said.

He laughed and lifted me easily onto his lap. "I'll make all the arrangements. We can have it here on the beach. We can talk about who to invite later."

"Can I ask you a question?"

"Sure," he said with a huge smile.

"Have you been married before?"

"No, love, I haven't," he said.

"Good," I said. My heart soared. I no longer cared about the website; I no longer cared if I got into his silly photo album. We would have our own album, not one filled with other women.

"Face me," he said.

I straddled his legs and his hard thick cock penetrated me.

"I love how wet you are for me, always. Your body not only wants me but needs me, babe." His eyes caressed my soul as his cock slid in and out of me.

If I could've stopped time I would have lived in that moment forever. I'd never felt such happiness and contentment. I rejoiced at being filled by another person fully, spiritually, and emotionally. The bliss flowed through me and out into the universe. I wanted to scream my joy to everyone. I wanted to wax poetic and glory in the freedom of my captivity.

Luke kissed me with the expertise he had acquired with his other women and I ceased to care about them. Each woman had brought him closer to me and they all lived in the past. *I am solely his future, me,* I thought.

"We will have a wonderful life together," he said, reading my thoughts.

He lowered his head, breaking our eye contact, to draw my nipple into his hungry mouth. His pulling and sucking

offered exquisite pressure and pleasure. Taking a fistful of my chestnut hair, he tilted my head to one side and ravished my neck, biting and kissing his way from just under my ear to my collarbone. My groans of lust and gratification filled the warm air as he applied his lips and tongue to my other protruding nipple. His suction caused me to cry out while he continued to move his rock hard phallus against the walls of my pussy. His roar began softly and, just before he filled me with his cum, his cock expanded and I moaned my pleasure along with him.

After we both recovered, we swam awhile in the pool. Neither of us spoke. We remained connected without words. I could hear the waves from the ocean coming in for the day as Luke held me in the pool. I lay back in his arms as he swirled me around.

I remembered something my father had told me during one of his reappearances. He said that for a relationship to remain healthy, each person needs to stay separate but connected. I couldn't put much stock in his relationship advice—he seemed to struggle with it for himself—but I did wonder. Could Luke and I stay separate but connected? I didn't think so. At that moment I wanted to merge myself into him, letting go of my separate self.

"Let's get out," Luke said. "I want to show you the house." He pulled two towels from a trunk by the pool and used the first to dry me off. After drying himself off, he took my hand.

We walked naked through the French doors and into the house. On the right sat a space for a dinner table with a low light hanging from the ceiling. Deeper in, to the right, was a kitchen that could have fit at least three of our kitchens from the apartment. I admired the black speckled granite countertops and the stainless steel appliances. Certain my mother would approve of this house, I laughed a bit.

To the left was a sitting area currently occupied by a

yellow flowered couch. We walked through three empty bedrooms, each larger than what we currently shared. I wondered why the house stood mostly empty. The location couldn't be more ideal for any beach lover.

"What do you think of it?" he asked.

"What's not to like? It gets great light … it's on the beach … it has a big bathroom …."

"We could shower and bathe together," he said.

"What do you mean? Now?" I spun around in the bathroom, which had to be five times the size of our current one. "I could get lost in here," I said, laughing.

"I thought you might like it." He smiled as he watched me looking around.

"So is this place yours?" I said, turning to face him.

"Could be, if you tell me you could see us living here."

"Really? I mean, this place must cost a fortune. It's right on the beach and not far from where I usually run and it's beautiful and big and oh my god, you must be kidding right?"

"Not at all. For all those reasons I thought this place would be perfect for us."

"The kitchen is way bigger than we need," I said, thinking how we could both fit into the huge almond tub. "Actually, the whole place is larger than we need, but I love it."

"You could use the third bedroom as your office. Set up a place to write and make it your own."

"My head is spinning, Luke."

"It's a lot to take in. I know. We wouldn't get this place right away."

"I see," I said. I couldn't imagine that he made all his money from the website I had seen. I was baffled by the luxury of what he was offering. It wasn't the house, really, but the freedom from work and bills and the ability to pursue my dream of writing.

"I need the extra space," Luke said, "and I'd like to

consolidate my things. I still have art supplies at the house and some furniture. The second bedroom could serve as office space and a studio. There are other places we can check out, though. We don't need to decide right now. This one isn't on the market yet, but I've been promised first consideration."

"Luke, I love it and you should know I'd live with you anywhere. This place is perfect."

"Then consider it done," he said. He hugged me to him, lifting me off of the ground. I wrapped my legs around his waist and kissed him all over his face. He laughed and laughed as he spun me around. "This is going to be great, Jane. *We're* going to be great."

I lowered my legs and stepped back. "I'd like to give you something if you'll let me," I said. I blushed from head to toe.

"What, my love?" he said. "What makes you blush so adorably?"

I leaned forward and went up on my toes to whisper in his ear. "Please allow me to pleasure you." Just the thought turned me on and I became less inhibited. "I want your cock in my mouth," I said, looking directly into his eyes.

"My way," he said. "My cock hasn't yet been past those beautifully full lips of yours and it's definitely the time; the perfect way to commemorate the occasion."

Luke walked outside and came back with his belt. His rigid cock signaled his interest. He put a cushion from the couch on the tile floor. "Kneel," he said.

He belted my wrists together behind me, walked back outside and returned with the camera. After taking a few shots of me, he pulled a side table next to us and rested the camera there.

He stepped toward me and I opened my mouth for him. This version of giving Luke pleasure contrasted greatly with my very vanilla vision of a blowjob. Instead I worked hard to use my tongue and suck as he controlled his very thick and hard cock. He leaned forward, pushing his entire shaft into my mouth and down my throat. I couldn't breathe until he

pulled back out. I tried to stay relaxed so I wouldn't gag but the in and out of his pushing against my throat made it impossible. Tears poured down my cheeks as I struggled to catch my breath between thrusts. Each time I gagged, he would pull out just enough for a breath and then proceed to fuck my mouth.

He picked up the camera and photographed his cock going in and out. "Beautiful," he said.

He rewarded my efforts by shooting his load of cum deep down my throat, and I managed to swallow all of it. As he pulled out, he wiped his cock down the corner of my mouth.

"Don't move," he said as he shot several more frames of me on my knees with my arms bound behind me. "It's time for me to take care of the business our young friend couldn't handle."

He helped me to my feet and guided me back outside, where he seated me in the chair near the beach. My arms were still fastened behind my back. Luke moved my hips forward, straining my shoulders.

"You're so wet, Janey. You thought you didn't care for my idea of a blowjob? But look at you, love, your body knows what you need, just as I do. I'm exactly what you need. Hmmm," he said as he lowered his head and devoured me.

When I came I screamed with abandon, not caring if the beachgoers could hear my shouts of pleasure and release. I collapsed against the back of the chair with my eyes closed, relishing the warmth of the sun on my face and the coolness of the breeze in my hair.

I heard the whiz of Luke's digital camera and remembered the website. I had to tell him I'd found it. I even wanted to tell him about my exploration of the office but I knew he would not forgive me. He probably wouldn't want to marry me anymore, and I couldn't risk that.

"Luke, I need to tell you something," I said as I opened my eyes.

He stood in front of me, just watching. He had such a look of love on his face that I was crushed by guilt.

"Are you okay?" he said. He unbuckled the belt and released my arms.

"I went on your website," I blurted out. I stretched my arms out in front of me to lessen the tightness but also to provide distraction.

"And what did you think? The shots of you came out well, didn't they? I'm excited to see how the photos we took today will turn out. You can help me decide which ones we will upload if you'd like."

"Wow, that's not what I was expecting," I said.

"What were you expecting?" he said. He looked puzzled.

"I thought you would be mad at me for going on the site without asking you."

"I see," he said. He walked to the opening in the bushes and stood gazing out at the ocean.

My hearted pounded in my chest as I waited for him to acknowledge me again.

"I gave you my card with the website on it, so I don't have an issue with you exploring it. What bothers me is that you would do it thinking I wouldn't want you to. This type of relationship requires a huge amount of trust and I'm not sure you're up to it."

"Luke, I'm sorry, you're right. I am up for it. I want this, all of it. It was when the phone kept ringing and I wanted to reach you. Please don't be upset with me." I hated begging but I didn't want him to give up on me. My heart hurt because I wanted to come clean about the office but could not. I wanted to start our marriage out right. The guilt weighed heavily.

"I need to be able to trust you and you me or this will not work."

"You can … I do. I promise to discuss anything that comes up in the future."

"Why do I feel there's more? Is there something else you need to tell me?"

I swallowed like there was a lump in my throat. "No, nothing," I said.

"Are you sure? Because this would be the time to start with a clean slate."

"That was it, Luke."

"Okay," he said. He stood looking out at the ocean for a while longer and turned back to me. "We have a lot of planning to do, and I have phone calls to make. Let's get dressed and head home."

CHAPTER EIGHTEEN

My first task at work on Monday had me locating my replacement as the personnel coordinator. I walked down the hall around the cubicles to Allison's office.

"Want my job?" I said, barging through her door.

"Your job? You're kidding, right?"

"It's a yes or no question," I said, smiling at her.

"You're serious," she said. She stared at me with her eyebrows raised. "You're leaving?"

"I gave notice on Friday and need to hire someone to take over. Interested?"

"I'm interested in knowing what the hell is going on. Then I'll think about the job." She pushed her hair behind her right ear and looked directly at me.

"I'm getting married."

"WHAT?"

"Well, that's not why I gave notice. The proposal came after that or because of that or well … who cares? I'm getting married!" I said. I laughed and stared back at her.

"When?"

"Would you believe me if I told you I'm getting married before you?"

"Do you know what you're doing? I mean I'm happy if you're happy, but Jane, you haven't known him that long."

"That's true, but how long should it take?"

"I don't know. I really don't know." Allison stood up, leaned down and placed her hands on top of the desk. Looking me squarely in the eye, she said, "You seem happy.

Just tell me you're sure and I'll be there …. Tell me when and where."

"I'm sure, and thank you," I said. I went around the desk and gave her a big hug. I knew she would be the easiest of the bunch to tell. "And the job, do you want it?"

"I have to think about it and talk it over with Rick. I like my job okay and would love the extra money but I'm not sure about the added stress. My job's a piece of cake. Can I let you know tomorrow?"

"First thing if you can because if it's not you, I need to dig out the files."

"I'll come by your office tomorrow to let you know, and thanks for thinking of me." She sat down at her desk and as I headed for the door, I heard her say, "Wow, she's getting married."

ℭℛ

I called Sandy on my lunch break.

"I have some news," I said.

"Give me a sec," she said. I could hear rustling and a door shutting. "Back, so tell me."

"Well I've given notice at my job—"

"Wow, what will you do instead?"

"I'm going to try my hand at writing a novel."

"And Luke's okay with this?"

"It was his idea. He's wanted me to quit my job."

"Oh, I see. Well you must be excited. I don't know what I would do with all that time on my hands but I'm sure you'll be able to handle it."

"There's more—"

"More … well spit it out."

"Stop talking and I will," I said, chuckling.

"Me stop talking? That'll never happen. I'll try holding my breath." Sandy laughed and I could hear her taking in a huge intake of air. She spit the air out and giggled.

"I'm getting married," I said.

"Get the fuck out of town. Really?"

I laughed hysterically at her response. "Yes, really."

"Wow, Jane, when you do it, you do it fast. I thought Luke was just great. I'm very excited for you."

"You're not going to tell me to slow down and be careful and all that?"

"I think you have Parker for that," she said.

"Right," I said, giggling.

"Have you told her yet?"

"No. We were supposed to meet for dinner tomorrow but she left me a message that we need to reschedule. I'll try to reach her later."

"Well, give her my love. I have to get back to the grind. I'm so happy for you. Jason will be thrilled, too. Oh, and ask Luke about all of us getting together."

"Will do."

∞

I thought about calling my mother. I weighed calling my father but I couldn't have them both at the wedding, and I owed it to my mother to include her. Would Luke agree to call Mom? I knew I was being a chicken shit but I didn't want to have to explain to her that her idea of a huge wedding would never happen. And so that day I called neither.

I bought a wedding magazine on the way home from work. I was finally buying one for my own actual wedding with excitement and confidence. "No bag needed!" I told the saleswoman. I wanted to flash it around as I walked back to my car. I hoped my dream dress lay between the covers of the magazine.

I undressed by the door and sensed the emptiness of Luke's absence. I happily plopped down on the couch and flipped through the pages and pages of wedding dresses. I couldn't decide what kind of gown interested me. Would the

wedding be by the pool or on the beach? I liked the idea of a simple ivory dress with a slight train trailing behind me as I walked barefoot on the sand.

Toward the middle of the thick magazine I found a dress with a halter top that wrapped around the neck of the model. It had no bustle and flowed nicely to the ground. I folded the corners of pages to mark the few others that interested me. I could not wait to show Luke.

Luke had said we'd go ring shopping that day so I soon became annoyed by his continued absence and my growing hunger.

I was still browsing the magazine when the door finally opened.

"Hey, babe," Luke said as he strolled into our place.

"Hi," I said and stood.

We walked toward each other and embraced. He lifted me off my feet and placed me back down. Smacking my butt, he said, "So is Allison going to take your job?"

"She's letting me know tomorrow. It's a considerable jump in income so I imagine she'll say yes. She's used to not having to do too much at her current job so she's not too keen on the added stress."

"I see."

"I'm starving," I said, moving back to the couch. I picked up the magazine and turned the pages until I found the dress that I liked best. "What do you think?"

"As we will be having the wedding at our new house … no dress will be necessary."

"Very funny, Luke," I said. "What do you think of it? Not your taste? There's another …."

He seized the magazine from my hands and tossed it down on the coffee table. I looked down where it had landed. He lifted my chin so I looked up to him. "No dress, Jane. Your body's mine. It's the symbol of what you're pledging to me."

"My mother won't come, my friends won't come. Luke, no, I have to draw the line somewhere." I flumped down on the couch and crossed my arms. "I want a dress."

"Then what you want is to marry someone else. You clearly don't want me and what I'm offering. I guess I'll go return the ring." He pulled a black box out of his pocket. "I was going to present it to you over dinner, but now …."

"Wait," I said. "I don't know."

"Your body's either mine or it's not. Apparently it's not. So we're done here, Jane. Sorry you wasted my time."

"LUKE, wait," I said as I stood and began to pace.

Panic-stricken, I didn't know what to do. I wanted him, I wanted Luke, but did I really want what he offered me? He had bestowed such freedom upon me and yet exerted such control. I couldn't fathom who I'd become if I continued to let him push my boundaries. He'd push and push. Would there ever be an end to it? How far could I or would I go? I thought all of this as I stood there, forcing back the tears. I willed myself to walk away but I couldn't. When someone has intertwined their energy with yours, walking away is akin to having your guts ripped out, your soul torn in two. I couldn't will myself to leave any more than I could will myself to stop breathing.

The tears finally mutinied and spilled down my cheeks as I walked up to him. "You haven't wasted your time," I said.

"Good. I hate being wrong about a person," he said. He lifted me off the ground and I wrapped my legs around his waist. He hugged me to him, his sandy brown hair tickling my cheek. "You actually scared me, Jane, and I don't scare easily," he said into my ear.

Somehow that disclosure made me sure I'd made the right decision. I had no idea how I'd survive a wedding naked but in my mind I made as if it was in the far off future and not right around the corner. I decided not to think about it again that night.

"So what would you like for dinner," he said as he sat

down on the couch with me on his lap.

"The ring," I said.

He laughed. "I don't think that will be very filling."

"Oh, I'll manage," I said. "I'm not quite as hungry as I was before."

"Well then," he said, shifting me onto the couch and getting down on one knee.

"Jane Jesse James ... will you marry me?" He held out the box and opened it.

"That's Jane Jessica Stiles. Pretty darn close, though."

"Ahem. Jane Jessica Stiles, babe, my love, will you spend the rest of your days with me?" He took the ring out of the box and held my left hand.

"Yes, Luke," I said. I threw my arms around his neck before he had a chance to put the ring on my finger.

He hugged me and set me back down on the couch. He slipped the ring onto my finger and it fit perfectly. "I have friends in the business and they sell one of a kind jewelry. The minute I saw it I knew you'd love it."

"What a gorgeous ring. Are those purple stones on the sides? I've never seen anything like it. It's beautiful."

"The center stone is one and a half carat. I wanted it to be something you could wear every day."

"You continue to amaze me. I hate the really big diamond rings and somehow—"

"I know you, love," he said, taking my face in his hands and gently kissing my lips. He pulled away and said, "So, Soon To Be Mrs. Luke Hall, what would you like for dinner?"

CR

It wasn't until Thursday of that week that I finally met up with Parker. She was dressed impeccably as always, and I thought, not for the first time, that she'd missed her calling as a runway model. I wondered if her lack of success in love had more to do with the sheer intimidation of her beauty and

poise or her no-nonsense nature.

We hugged each other and took our seats at the café.

After we settled in, I blurted out, "We're getting married."

"Wow. Okay. Let me digest this," she said. She looked out at the walkers along the boardwalk while we sat at a table outside the restaurant awaiting our food.

"I want to be happy for you, but have you really thought this through? I mean, what do you know about him? How long has it been? A few weeks, right?"

"Almost a month and a half. Forty-two days, to be exact. Why do I know this? I shouldn't, right?" I laughed at myself. I wondered if all women kept track of that sort of thing. I failed to mention his absence for two weeks of it.

"That's a very, very short amount of time to get to know someone," Parker said.

Our food arrived and we ate without speaking. I couldn't fathom how I would prepare her for the fact that I'd be naked. *How do you explain that to someone?* I had no idea how to tell her about my new lifestyle. I hadn't told Sandy, either, or Allison. I still thought that Parker would be the one who would refuse to come. I did harbor some hope that everyone had their private kinks and could relate on some level. Hell, I didn't want to do it, so why should other people want to take part in it?

I must want to do it or I wouldn't have agreed, would I? At least I tried to convince myself of that. I knew it would make Luke happy and proud and maybe for that reason alone I'd be strong enough to go through with it. It seemed far easier to imagine myself doing something in the future and down the road—especially a challenge such as this one—than actually doing it.

"There's more," I said as we finished eating. My heart pounded out of my chest and I tried to calm my breathing.

"More? More than what? More than getting married?"

"Yes. More to tell you and you are not going to like this any better than me getting married in the first place."

"Terrific. Let me have it," Parker said, leaning back in her chair and crossing her arms.

"I will be naked at the wedding," I said. I experienced intense relief in saying it out loud to someone.

"Oh, so Luke's a nudist?" Parker said, matter-of-factly.

"Not exactly. I'll be naked, he'll be dressed."

"What the hell?" she said, uncrossing her legs and leaning forward. "You've got to be kidding. And you're okay with this?"

"Well, it's not my first choice but yes, I'm okay with it."

"Jane, what about your mother? What about your other relatives?"

"The wedding will be small and I imagine my mother won't come."

"You haven't told her?"

"I haven't even told her I'm getting married."

"Look, I like Luke and all but that, but come on, Jane, do you know what the hell you're doing? This sounds crazy to me. And controlling. Do you want someone controlling you like that?"

I didn't know what to say. *Did I want someone controlling me like that?* My mind said, "No fucking way." But my body said, "Yes, please!"

I needed Parker to be there. I needed to convince her that this was what I wanted.

"I want everything Luke is offering me. Please tell me you'll be there."

"Of course I will. Who else will give the Justice of the Peace the reason the wedding shouldn't happen?" she said, laughing.

"You wouldn't," I said, laughing with her but scared she meant it. "Oh, and one more thing—"

"I'm not sure I can take much more."

"Very funny," I said. "I've given notice at work."

"Yeah, I know. Allison told me. We've been in touch since your party."

"Oh cool. Um, let me tell her about the nudity, 'kay? I'll do it tomorrow. That way you can talk to each other about it and decide just how crazy I am."

"Sounds like a good plan," Parker said and chuckled.

଼

Allison did take the job, as I suspected she would. Training was a breeze and even fun. Nice to enjoy the last two weeks of work knowing it would all come to an end shortly.

On Friday I told Allison about my lack of attire for the wedding. Parker had beaten me to it but I couldn't be mad because it actually took some of the stress out of telling Allison. I laughed.

"What's so funny?" Allison said.

"I was thinking I should have Parker call my mother and Sandy to tell them about my nakedness."

Allison laughed with me and said, "Oh, she would be good for that."

଼

When I got home that Friday with just a week of work left, Luke greeted me at the door.

"It's all been arranged," he said.

I began unbuttoning my shirt and said, "Are we talking about the wedding?"

"The wedding, the house, movers ... all of it," he said, taking my blouse from me.

"Wow," I said. "You're fast."

"We need to deal with your apartment. Do you want me to send my guys over to pack the rest of it up or—"

"It's mostly just the kitchen stuff and cleaning supplies

under the sinks in the bathrooms. Oh and the furniture. I forgot about the furniture. What am I going to do with that stuff?" I handed Luke the rest of my clothes and we walked into the living room together.

"Like I said, I can have my guys take care of it. Is there anything personal you still want from there?"

"I don't think so, but I've had that furniture for years. I got some of that stuff back in my college days."

"If anything is important to you we can bring it over to the new place. If not, we'll buy whatever we still need or want to fill the house. Do you have a desk you want to keep? We can put it in your new writing room."

"Oh, I guess not," I said. A part of me wrestled with letting go of all my old possessions; it was one more step away from my former self. I wasn't really attached to any of my things, but I knew giving them away would make it even more difficult to turn back.

"When is all of this happening?" I said. I stared down at my hands, not looking directly at him.

"Baby," he said, lifting my face. "Look at me, love. I know you're scared. It's a lot of change. Tell me what you need."

"It's just that it's hard to let go of everything in my other life and I'm doing it all at once ... or, well, it feels that way."

"We can keep your condo and rent it out if you'd prefer. We can even leave the furniture there."

Just having the option made me realize I didn't need it. All I needed was Luke. All I wanted was our life together.

"Thank you for offering but I think you're right. It's time to sell it and move on with our life."

"Excellent," he said. "I'll take care of everything except calling the people you want at the wedding. You can do that."

❧

The last week of work flew by, leaving me to sit in the

apartment writing on my laptop. The movers came and went as I sat naked on the couch pounding away on the computer. I had stopped caring who saw me naked. It did help that the laptop covered my lower half. Luke came in and out while running errands. I made it over to the beach most days to get my runs in and never encountered Scott again.

Time was growing short and I still hadn't called my mother or told Sandy about my nakedness. I knew Luke and I would be moving into the beach house soon and that the wedding would take place a week after that. A part of me had resigned myself to my new life but another, larger part remained in denial about dealing with the old one.

"You haven't mentioned your mother," Luke said as we lay in bed together. "You still haven't called her, have you?"

"No, and I haven't told Sandy about my attire—or lack thereof, I should say." I ran my hand back and forth over his chest.

"Jane," he said.

"Hmmmm?" I said.

"What are you waiting for?"

"I'm just too happy right now to let my mother rain on my parade. With Sandy it's just laziness."

"Go get me the phone," Luke said, "and know that you owe me for this." He pushed me to the edge of the bed and I climbed out.

"The cell?"

"No, mine from the office."

I walked into the office. Boxes were scattered everywhere. The photo album I had surreptitiously leafed through lay out on the counter. I wondered why it wasn't in its box. I picked up the phone and grabbed the photo album as well.

"What's this?" I said as I strode back into the bedroom holding out the black bound book.

"What does it look like?"

211

"It looks like a photo album, obviously. It was sitting out on the counter. Are these pictures of your models?"

"Please put it back in the office, Jane." The tone in his voice changed and I knew I was treading dangerously.

"What about trust and not keeping secrets? Is that just on my end?"

"Look at it then if you must but then put it back. I don't want to talk about it after you're done."

I didn't need to turn the pages because every picture remained engraved in my memory. I went through the motions of seeing the pictures for the first time. I asked him each girl's name, even though I already knew them from matching them up with the files. When he said, "Janice," the tone of his voice became dark and ominous. Janice already worried me the most because only her picture hung in his office.

"Tell me about Janice," I said. I knew I was pushing where I should've left well enough alone but even though we were getting married, jealousy still lurked beneath the surface.

"I have no interest in talking about old girlfriends, Jane. They're in the past, and you're my future. That's all you need to know."

"You have Janice hanging on the wall of your office. There are more pictures of her than anyone else on your website AND she's in your photo album. I think it's more than reasonable for me to be curious about her."

"BUT Jane, I have no interest in talking about her. She is dead to me."

"Dead to you? That's such a load of bullshit. You do not hang a picture of someone who's dead to you. What gives?"

"Nothing gives. Just leave it alone. She's gone and in the past. She's nothing for you to worry about. Now give me the damn phone and let's call your mother."

I wanted to ask about the empty pages in the back of the book but I acquiesced because what else could I do? I couldn't

make him talk to me. Plus, he offered to deal with my mother, which made me unbelievably grateful. I walked the photo album back to the office and climbed back into bed with him.

"Here," I said, handing him the phone.

"Jane, before I call your mom I want to say this: I am marrying you. I've chosen to make a life with you. Don't waste your time on my past. I don't. I will not hang Janice's photo in our new house—just pictures of you and us." Something shifted and the energy change in the room became palpable. He said, "Do not bring up Janice again." His tone chilled and bewildered me.

I wanted to know about this person who'd had such a noticeable impact on him. I had to learn the truth about what had happened between them. I wondered if I could find her somehow and hear her story. I had to assume because of all the pictures that she had been with Luke the longest. I also knew what that meant: she had gone the farthest. Her boundaries and lines of demarcation had been pushed the deepest. I hated her. I hated how her name impacted Luke. I wanted to smash her picture hanging on the office wall.

Luke brought my attention back as he placed the phone on speaker and I could hear it ringing.

"Hello? Who's calling at this time of night?" my mother said in her usual annoyed voice.

"Hi, Jacqueline, it's Luke."

"Oh Luke, why didn't you say so?" Her voice immediately changed. She had switched to her sweet persona.

"Jane and I have some news to tell you. She's been a bad girl and has put off this call so I decided that we should call you together. Say hi, Jane."

"Hi, Mother," I said.

"Hi, Jane. What is this about?"

Luke answered for me. "Jane and I are getting married in a couple of weeks and we want to make sure you'll be there."

"Married? Where is this happening? What about all the

planning? That doesn't leave a lot of time."

"Jack, there's nothing for you to worry about. I've taken care of all the details." I cringed when he called her Jack. That's the name my father used to have for her. Luke continued, "Janey and I are moving in less than a week to a house on the beach and that's where the wedding will take place."

"Who will be there because I won't come if—"

"Jane's father will not be present for the wedding so you have nothing to worry about. Can we count on you attending?"

"Of course I'll be there. Jane?"

"Yes, Mother," I said.

"Have you found a dress yet because I know of a place—"

"There's no need for a dress," Luke broke in. "Janey will be naked at the wedding. She was sure you wouldn't come and that's why she's put off this call. I, on the other hand, know you'll decide to be supportive of your daughter's choices and come regardless of her lack of attire."

A long pause ensued and I realized I was holding my breath. I couldn't be sure which way I wanted it to go. If she didn't come, then one fewer person—the person who would be most shocked to see me married naked—would be elsewhere. On the other hand, even with all the fighting my mother and I did, I had always pictured her being a part of my big day.

I knew she was sitting there on the couch in her condo deciding which way she wanted to go. She could make a big stink and not come to the wedding or she could buy into Luke's attempt to manipulate her.

After what seemed like a decade she said, "Why does Jane have to be naked for the wedding?"

"Because I want it that way and she has agreed. You can choose to come and be a support for Jane or not. Either way, it's up to you."

Luke played her like a violin. He gave her the power to choose but denied her the power to influence the outcome. I began to find the process amusing. It felt more like a chess match than my life in the balance. I waited to hear my mother's next move.

"What if it's chilly out or her friends don't like it?" she said.

"I get to worry about all the details. All you have to do is show up and be the kind, supportive mother you already are."

Could he blow any more smoke up her skirt? Jeez. The load of crap was getting thick in there.

She aimed her next move at me. "Jane?"

"Yes, Mother," I said.

"Are you okay with this? The Jane I know doesn't care for being naked and would never consider it around a group of people. What happened to the wedding you have been planning for years?"

"Yes, Mom, I'm okay with it. If you can't handle it, then I understand."

"And give you a chance to invite your father? I don't think so. I will be there but don't expect me to be thrilled to see you go down the aisle in nothing other than what God gave you."

"Jacqueline, I knew you wouldn't let us down. Janey will call you with all the details in a few days."

"How you handle my mother is truly brilliant," I said to Luke after he disconnected the call.

"I can already tell I'll have to talk with her on the wedding day or she might try to make it miserable for you. Trust that I won't let that happen."

"I do," I said.

"Your turn. Call Sandy and get it over with."

I sat there on the bed listening to the phone ring. I hoped she wouldn't answer so I could procrastinate a while longer. The prospect of telling Sandy loomed almost as large as

telling my mother, because she knew me so well in college. She knew the issues I had with my body. She understood how I struggled to be comfortable with men seeing me naked in the light. She would be the only one there to truly know how far I'd come. Not that she would see it that way. She would see how far I had moved away from myself, from the person I had previously been. She was the keeper of the old me.

"Jason here, who's calling?"

"Hi Jason, its Jane."

"Oh, Jane, hold on a sec and I'll get Sandy. Congrats by the way. I'm very excited to hear you're writing a book. I'd love to hear about it. Here's Sandy."

I heard the shuffling of the phone and then she said, "What's up, girl?"

"I need to tell you something about the wedding. You might want to sit down."

"Sit down? Just spit it out. What is it?"

"First off," I said. I thought of it in the moment and decided my course of action. "I would love for you to be my maid of honor." I looked over at Luke and he gifted me a big smile.

"Yay, of course yes. That will be fun. Tell me what you need me to do. Will I need to help with your train or find you a garter or—"

"That brings me to the second thing," I said, cutting her off.

"Okay," she said.

"I won't be needing a garter—or a dress, for that matter."

"Oh. So, what will you be wearing?"

"Nothing."

"Nothing? What does that mean, nothing? Is this a joke?"

"No joke. I'll be naked at my wedding. I know you think it's strange but please just say you'll be there."

"Jane, I don't get this. This isn't you. You always wanted

an ivory dress for your wedding, right? I mean, I'm having trouble taking this in. Hang on a sec."

I heard muffled voices and knew she was covering the receiver. I did the same and told Luke, "This isn't going well."

"Give her a chance to accept it. She'll probably tell you that she needs to think about it. It's understandable."

"Jane?" she said.

"I'm here," I said.

"Can I call you tomorrow or the next day? I need time."

"Okay." I couldn't think of anything else to say. I hung up the phone. "Well, that didn't go well. Pretty much as expected."

"It'll be fine. Jason will talk some sense into her," Luke said.

I sat on the bed, my shoulders down, feeling defeated. I needed Sandy to be there.

Luke scooped me up into his arms and cradled me to him. "Trust me, love. It's all going to work out."

ᘉ

The days flew by and before I knew it only a day separated me from matrimony. Luke and I didn't discuss the wedding. He said he had it all taken care of and I trusted that he did. I spent my days exercising and writing. The movers transitioned us from our apartment to the new house within one day. Luke worked on his new office/studio space and I set up my new writing room. I enjoyed the freedom and joy of the days leading up to the wedding. Luke found no reason to discipline me and our lovemaking sessions became more normal rather than exotic encounters from the strange world of bondage and discipline.

"Luke," I called out. "Come see my new writing room."

"I'm busy hanging up my favorite tools for your discipline," he said, chuckling from his studio office. "You should come in here and see."

"Luke!" I said. I knew I was whining.

"Is that bottom lip of yours sticking out?" he said as he entered my room. "I thought so." He came at me in two long strides, capturing my bottom lip with his teeth. "Yum," he mumbled as he sucked my lip into his mouth.

"Hey," I said, giggling. I pushed him off of me. "Look around, please, and tell me what you think."

"I think we need to christen your new desk right away."

"Come on, Luke, I'm serious," I said as he closed the distance between us and lifted me onto the desk.

"So am I," he said, his intention already evident in his jeans.

"I can see that now," I said, looking down.

He leaned into me, still fully clothed, and ruled my mouth with his tongue. He pushed his hard cock in between my legs, letting me know what would be taking me shortly.

"I should discipline you for distracting me from my unpacking," he said as he stood up to remove his button fly jeans.

I hopped off the desk and leaned over it, presenting my ass for him.

"Don't think I won't take advantage of that position." He pinned me to the desk, spreading my arms out in front of me. "Such a naughty girl you are," he said, spreading my legs and using his other hand to ease his cock into me from behind.

I felt stretched wide and pulled forward. I turned to look at him and he regained his pursuit of my mouth. Each penetrating stroke of his erection pushed me hard against the edge of the desk.

He broke off his kiss and let go of my arms. "Jane, stroke your clit for me so we can cum together."

I snaked my right hand underneath me and slowly circled my pussy, covering my clitoris with my wetness. My carnality grew from the point of my arousal and trailed out past my nipples, which Luke now held clamped between his

fingers. He rubbed them back and forth, causing pleasure to shoot out and encompass my whole body. Luke's invasion penetrated me so deeply and fully that I could feel him hit against my uterus.

"Oh fuck me hard, fuck me hard … that feels so good," I said as he continued to slam into me.

"Your ass looks so good and your pussy is so wet for me. Your big swollen nipples are so hard. Tell me when you're getting close," he said as he bit my neck.

I could feel his panting against my shoulder and his sweat against my back. "I'm already close," I called out, gripping the left side of the desk with my free hand.

"Okay, babe, it's time! Cum with me," he roared out as he slammed against me harder than before, forcing my hips against the edge of the desk.

I frantically rubbed my pussy, cumming with him as we both collapsed.

I laughed, "Goddamn, where did that come from?" I wondered how many more pieces of furniture we would be christening.

He laughed with me as we both tried to catch our breath and slow our racing hearts. He pushed himself off me, swatted my ass and said, "You are fucking amazing. I love you so much, Soon To Be Mrs. Hall." He pulled me to my feet and wrapped me in his arms. "I would love to crawl in bed with you and take a nap but I really want my office set up before tomorrow."

"Maybe we can try the kitchen next time," I said as he pulled on his jeans. I swatted his butt as he left my writing room.

He leaned back in the doorway and said, "That's a great idea! There are a lot of spatulas in there."

"Luke!" I pouted, but this time he headed back to his office.

The deliveries began by ten. Men were out on the beach setting up a tent for tomorrow and other men covered the pool with a wooden dance floor. I still hadn't heard from Sandy. Parker had agreed to be my backup maid of honor. She felt sure Sandy would come through but I had my doubts.

I had such mixed feelings about our upcoming nuptials. I couldn't wait to be Mrs. Luke Hall but I could wait forever to walk down the aisle in front of my mother and friends. I could barely breathe for the whole day leading up to the wedding.

I sat and watched the workers transform the back of the house. I couldn't focus enough to write down my thoughts and feelings. If only I knew whether Sandy would show up and support me through it .... Finally I gave in and picked up the phone.

"Hi Jason," I said when I heard his voice on the other end of the line.

"She's not here," he said.

"Oh ...." I said.

"We will be there, Jane," Jason said, to my utter relief.

"She hasn't called and—"

"Yeah, I know. She's being a bit stubborn but she'll be there. We'll be there to support you. We don't get your choices but as I've told Sandy repeatedly, we don't need to. We just need to support you in the choices that you make because we love you."

"Jason, if you were here I'd give you a big hug. Thank you so much. It's such a relief to know you'll both be here."

"Wouldn't miss it, Jane. How often does one get invited to a wedding where a beautiful woman marches down the aisle naked? This is a once in a lifetime opportunity." He laughed. "No way I'm missing it."

CHAPTER NINETEEN

On the day of the wedding, I awoke in a panic. In my last dream there were hundreds of people in attendance and I had to walk past all of them. I breathed a sigh of relief that it was only a dream.

After my morning ritual, I settled myself on the couch by the window. When I looked out back I saw a gazebo on the beach and men arranging chairs behind it. One man came around back with an additional set of chairs on a hand cart.

"Luke!" I said, yelling toward the back of the house. My dream was manifesting before my eyes.

He stuck his head out of his office and said, "Give me a sec."

I never considered that anyone other than the people I had invited would attend the wedding. *Fuck, shit, fuck*, I thought.

"What is it?" he said, waltzing up behind me.

I knelt on the couch, gazing out the back window. "How many?" I said without looking at him.

"We're expecting fifty guests."

"Fifty? Fifty! Motherfucker!"

"Janey," he said, touching my shoulder.

"Don't," I said, moving away from him. "Did it ever occur to you to tell me you had invited an additional forty-four people to our wedding? What happened to the small wedding we were going to have? Fuck, Luke." My hands had clenched into fists.

"Jane, honey, you never asked. Come on, babe, it's going

to be fine. Come here," he said, pulling me toward him.

"No Luke. NO! This is supposed to be the happiest day of my life and you decide it would be a good idea to hide the fact that—"

"Wait a minute, Jane, I've hidden nothing. All you had to do was ask besides you still owe me for being clothed at the little get-together at our apartment."

"So you thought our wedding was a good time for that to come due? You should have told me. I didn't know there was anything to ask you. You led me to believe …."

"I did nothing of the kind. You left the wedding for me to plan and plan it I did. You made no specific requests. These are all the people I want you to meet anyway and some you already know."

"Does it not register in your brain that I might not want to meet ALL your business associates and friends naked as the day is long?"

"You need to check the way you're talking to me, Jane, because I will not tolerate your disrespect. You would meet them that way eventually when they came by the house."

"You can't be equating meeting them one by one over time with meeting them en masse on my wedding day. You must be the most insensitive man I've ever met."

I had hopped down off the couch and was moving away from Luke when he clutched my arm. "Wait, Jane," he said. "I don't want us to get married when we're fighting."

"You might have thought about that sooner than right the fuck now, don't you think?"

"Jane, you're pushing it with me."

"Well, Luke," I said, "you've pushed it with me. It was one thing to be naked in front of my people and or even a small gathering of your friends but a whole other thing to be greeting all of your associates naked and exposed. I don't know what I was thinking but I've made a huge mistake. You don't know me at all. Who the hell was I kidding?"

I wrenched my arm out of his hand and ran to my room, slamming the door. I threw myself onto the overstuffed chair in the corner of my writing space and wept. I hated my life in that moment. I hated every choice I had made up until that second. I condemned my stupidity and wanted to run away.

Where does one run when they've just relinquished their possessions? My car was gone, my apartment, everything I owned, gone.

Time passed amid endless babble and debate with myself about my lack of judgment. I started when a sudden knock at the door commanded my attention.

"Fuck off," I said.

"Jane, it's me," Parker said.

"Oh … come in," I said. I wiped the tears off of my cheeks the best I could and changed my position on the chair so my arms covered most of my body.

"Luke called."

"Apparently," I said.

"He explained it all to me. Tell me what you want to do and I'll make it happen."

"You're not here to talk me into going through with it?"

"Is that what you want me to do, because I'll do that, if that's what you need? If you want me to call it off, I'll do that, too."

"I'm just so damn mad at him right now, I can't see straight."

"I can understand that. Is it true you left the planning of the wedding to him and didn't ask any questions about it or make any requests?"

"Yes but—"

"Seems like you're starting married life with a great need to learn better communication."

"Are you saying you think I should go through with it?"

"Do you love him?"

"Yes, I do."

"Is this something you can get past? Because Jane, today's the day. Luke doesn't strike me as the kind of man who will reschedule, if you know what I mean. So it's all or nothing. Tell me what you want."

I could always count on Parker to tell it like is. She had my back, whichever way I wanted to go.

"How do I get past this?" I said.

"You forgive him. That's all there is to it. Go talk to him so we can get you cleaned up and ready for your big day. Luke planned a spa day for us and we're due in thirty minutes."

I walked to Luke's office and as soon as he saw me he took me in his arms and said, "I'm sorry, Janey." He pushed my hair behind my left ear and continued, "I really wasn't trying to surprise you. I should have realized. I've just been so focused on making this day perfect for us that I was probably being a bit myopic. Can you forgive me so we can get back on track to having the most wonderful day of our lives?"

"You owe me," I said. I tried to stay mad but a smile tilted the corners of my mouth upward.

"Oh, and I will pay you back in spades, love. I have a lifetime to make it up to you." He lowered his mouth over mine and I accepted the path I had embarked upon.

"I'm glad you called Parker," I said.

"So am I," he said and I knew he meant it.

CR

The time at the spa with Parker relaxed me in the exact way that I needed. Luke had taken care of everything. We received full body massages, facials, manicures and pedicures. I felt buffed and shined for the wedding.

By the time we got back to the house the caterers had arrived and the kitchen was a hotbed of activity. Staff worked to set up a bar by the pool and a long buffet table. I could see birds of paradise in vases leading to the gazebo on the beach and gold tablecloths dancing in the wind atop the tables surrounding the pool.

I removed my clothes by the door without much thought. Luke must have warned the staff because no one took much notice of me.

"Do you always do that?" Parker said to me.

"Yes, always by the door. I get dressed in the bathroom just before going out. I honestly don't think about it anymore. It's normal for me. Of course, having all these people running about isn't."

Luke walked over to us with a huge smile. "It's almost that time," he said.

I walked straight into his arms and he held me close.

"How was the spa?" he asked.

"Just fabulous," Parker said. "Anytime you want to send me along, just say so."

"I'll keep that in mind," Luke said, chuckling. "In all seriousness, Parker, I'm indebted to you. Thank you for being the kind of friend Jane needs and deserves."

Parker blushed, which I'd never seen before. "Two amigos, that's us," she said. "Jane and I have stuck together for a long time now. I'm very excited to see her happy. I expect you to keep her that way."

"Consider it done," Luke said. He turned to me and said, "It's time to get you ready."

"Oh, I thought I was ready, stark naked and at your service."

Both Luke and Parker cracked up and I chuckled along with them.

I looked back outside and said, "If they're setting up the chairs and tables by the pool, what's the tent for?"

"Backup, but I have a couple of ideas for later," Luke said.

"Uh oh, should I be worried?" I said, smiling.

"Very," he said. "Now off with you." He pushed me toward our bedroom at the front of the house. "Parker, you go, too. I'm sure she can use your help."

Parker and I walked down the hall to the bedroom. A chair had been placed in the middle of the room. I sat in front of the large mirror on top of the chest of drawers, suddenly all too aware of being utterly naked.

"Hi, I'm Karla and I'm here to get you ready," she said. "I'm going to do your hair first."

Dressed in sweat pants and a tank top, Karla had an all-business demeanor that made her seem older than her plain, unlined face indicated.

Parker sat on the bed and watched Karla part my hair in the center and French braid either side on the top. The rest of it flowed down my back. She connected the two braids behind my head and I imagined I looked like a hippie chick from the '60s. She wove tiny yellow flowers throughout the braids. I felt like a teenager, not a thirty-five-year-old woman.

"Okay, please stand up," Karla told me. "And can you help for a minute?" she asked Parker.

"Sure," Parker said.

Karla handed her a tube of lotion that had a gold hue to it, and they both began spreading it over my entire body.

"Bend over please," Karla said to me.

I bent over and she proceeded to put the lotion on my folds and in the space between my butt cheeks.

"Who the hell will be seeing there?" I said out loud.

Parker cracked up laughing and said, "At least she didn't ask me to put it there."

I giggled along with her.

Once completely covered from head to toe I looked at my reflection in the mirror. My body looked rather stunning. I had a golden glow. The lotion produced a much subtler effect than gold paint, imbuing my skin with a metallic sheen. The gold on my face made my green eyes sparkle with striking clarity.

"You look sensational, awesome," Parker said with a grin.

"Once you're completely dry we can continue. Keep your arms up," Karla said as she left the room.

I turned to Parker and said, "I can't begin to thank you. You've been the most amazing friend. I'd be so honored for you to stand with me when I get married. I'm sorry I didn't ask you first but—"

"You and Sandy go further back and I know she always says you will be in her wedding. I'm not the least bit upset. I'm truly happy that I've been able to be here for you. I know you'd do the same for me."

"I absolutely will. Thank you. I'd hug you if I could." I gave a little shrug. My arms ached from holding them out.

Karla came back into the room carrying a box. "You can put your arms down now," she said.

I relaxed my shoulders and walked back over to the chair. Placing the box on the dresser, Karla opened the lid and took out a set of what looked like starched satin cuffs from the ends of a white tuxedo shirt. She affixed one to each wrist and ankle.

Next she retrieved two gold chains. She wrapped one around my waist and clasped it right below my belly button. A charm dangled from it that simply said MINE. She put a similar strand around my neck. This one was a bit thicker and had a charm with diamonds that read LUKE. She placed matching dangling diamond earrings in my ears and turned me toward the mirror.

She applied a subtle line of brown eyeliner under my eyes to bring out their green color and a darker shade of gold lipstick.

A nymph stared back at me from the mirror. I had put on a few pounds since quitting my job and spending all my time at home with Luke, so I appeared more voluptuous and curvy. The overall effect of nakedness plus the cuffs and jewelry was arresting.

"I can't believe I'm going to say this to you, but Jane, you

look amazing. The idea of you walking down the aisle naked still makes no sense to me but you have nothing to be ashamed of. You'll be the most beautiful bride."

"Thank you for that, Parker," I said.

"Time for you to leave," Karla said to Parker.

"Oh, okay. Jane, I'll wait for you in your office," she said as she left us alone.

Karla placed a towel on the chair and had me sit down. She spread my legs and made sure all areas, including my mound, was covered with the gold sheen.

"There's one more thing," she said. I heard hesitation in her voice.

"What?" I said. My stomach started to churn.

"I need you to bend over again," she said. Her demeanor had changed.

"What is it?" I said, getting quite impatient with the process.

She opened the box again and pulled out a butt plug.

"Oh, is that all. It's the small one at that. Give it to me. You can go. I'll take care of it."

"I'm supposed to make sure—"

"OUT!" I said, pointing to the door.

"Okay," she said. She packed up her brushes and other supplies.

"Thanks, by the way. You did a great job."

"Right, okay," she said and scooted out the door.

"You ready for me?" Parker said from across the hall.

"Give me a few," I said.

I closed the door and looked back in the box. The olive oil was there waiting for me. I went into the bathroom and put my leg up on the tub. After a few tries I managed to get the plug inside. I looked into the full length mirror on the back of the bathroom door and made sure no one could tell that I had the butt plug in me.

I walked out and went into my writing room.